BREAKING BONES

MARIANI CRIME FAMILY SERIES BOOK TWO

By

AMANDA WASHINGTON

Lindy – Thank you for your support!

ISBN: 978-1530054688

Published in the United States

ACKNOWLEDGMENTS

Special thanks to my husband, Meltarrus, our boys, and all my friends and family who supported, encouraged, beta read, and just plain ole' kept me sane during the writing of this book. You know who you are and how invaluable you are to me.

Huge thanks to my invaluable editors, Ellen Tarver, Kim Gates, Roslyn McFarland, and Karen Flanery.

I'm greatly indebted to the talented creative team who developed my cover. Cover design: Jackson and Tracey Jackson.

Dedicated to:

all the people who practice random acts of kindness, like showing up on the doorstep of a struggling friend with a basket full of love. Thank you for all you do.

CHAPTER ONE

Bones

MY POPS ONCE told me that a real man provides for his family, no matter what the circumstances. It's ironic since the old man disappeared when I was ten, leaving my mom to raise me and my brothers alone.

I've spent years wondering what happened to him. Did he wake up one morning and decide he'd had enough of the responsibilities of being a man? Or did he piss off the wrong people and end up taking a dirt nap in one of the luxurious Las Vegas landfills? Regardless, he left for work one day and never bothered to show his face again.

Ma did her best in his absence, evolving overnight from a sheltered housewife into an exhausted housekeeper, pulling double shifts to ensure her family's minimum-wage survival. She worked hard, but she could only do so much. So when I saw an opportunity to help her out, I jumped on it.

It all started while I waited outside my school for Ma to pick me up. The disapproving Principal Jones leaned against the bike rack beside me, occasionally breaking into another lecture about the importance of keeping my hands to myself. But the kids at my school were loud-mouthed punks, and my fists were the only weapon I could afford.

While we waited, a slick black-and-chrome Jaguar rolled to a stop in front of us. The front doors opened and two men dressed in suits and shiny black shoes emerged. The passenger was broad-shouldered with no neck and more muscles than any suit could contain. He approached with his head on a swivel, one hand in his pocket, and a threatening scowl. The driver was older and walked slower. He had a potbelly and a lit cigarette was hanging from his lips. He took a drag of the smoke and gave me a calculated smile. I had the feeling I was being sized up. He flicked the butt of his cigarette away and gave a slight nod to Mr. Jones. Expecting my principal to go ballistic about the man smoking on school property, I turned. Mr. Jones was walking back toward the school, leaving me alone with the two suits.

"You Gino Leone's boy?" the older man asked, still watching me. He had a scar on his cheek and the bridge of his nose zigzagged like it had been broken a time or two.

The mention of my pops gave me pause. When Ma had reported his disappearance, she told me and my brothers the cops would be by to ask us questions. It had been months and they hadn't bothered. The men in front of me didn't look like any cops I'd ever seen, but I wasn't going to risk it. If they knew something about Pops, I wanted to hear what they had to say. I nodded. Then, because my inner voice of self-preservation told me to be a little more respectful, I added a hasty, "Yes sir. How do you know my father?"

Instead of answering, the old man stepped closer and patted me on the shoulder. I was big for a ten-year-old, but his hand was enormous. It slid down to my bicep and wrapped around my arm. Shocked, I watched his giant mitt probe my muscles. A few of his knuckles were bent funny, like they'd been broken or popped out of place too many times, which seemed odd paired with his nice suit.

"We can work with this," the old man said. "It'll take some training, but you got heart, kid, and that's what matters. You did a good thing today," he said, pulling my attention back to his face. Something lingered behind his eyes. Pride? Amusement? I couldn't tell.

A good thing? I searched for sarcasm in his tone, but he seemed genuinely pleased with me, which didn't make sense since I had been suspended for breaking a kid's arm. Hell, I wasn't pleased with myself. Mr. Jones said Mom would most likely get stuck with the kid's hospital bill. She'd probably ground me for life. Then she'd have to pick up a third job. Just thinking about her having to work more because of my temper made me sick.

The old man grinned, splitting his face in two and making him look like a frog. "Not just a good thing. A great thing. A smart thing." He leaned closer to me and added, "You opened doors for your future today, kid. Doors that pay well." He eyed my too-small T-shirt, my faded jeans, and my worn sneakers. "You look like you could use a little extra cash."

I knew exactly what I looked like, but his words still stung. I scowled at him, and he held up his hands and shook his head.

"Just an observation. No offense meant. Look, you did me a favor today, so I'm trying to return the gesture. That's how it works with the family. You scratch our backs, we scratch yours. Now, you interested in some work or not?"

I glanced back at the school and then scanned the street. Mr. Jones hadn't returned, there was no sign of my mom, and the entire conversation was confusing me. Before I could answer his question, I needed details. "I did you a favor?" I asked.

"You helped my nephew."

I blinked. *Nephew?*

"The boy being harassed by that little ingrate you attacked."

My mind raced, trying to think of who he could be talking about. My fight today had been to fulfill my own personal vendetta. Some new kid, a jackass richie-rich, had been pissing all over the school, trying to mark his territory. Yesterday he'd been in the lunch line behind me, close enough to see my free-lunch status on the check-in computer and had been talking crap about it ever since. I'd been waiting for an opportunity to teach him a lesson, and saw it today when he was stuffing a kid into a locker after recess. I hadn't even seen who was being bullied, just saw the richie-rich with his back turned and pounced. I thought back to the layout of the lockers, trying to figure out who the poor sap shoved into his locker could have been. "D'Angelo Mariani," I whispered.

"His friends and family call him Angel," the old man said. "Mariani."

Even had I never heard the name before, the reverent way he uttered it spoke of power and authority. But all Vegas natives knew who the Marianis were.

"What do you want me to do?" I asked.

He cracked a smile and turned toward his associate. "Gets right down to business. Just like his old man."

"How do you know my father?" I asked again.

Emotion flickered across the old guy's face, but before I could place it, it was gone. He nodded. "Don't worry about it, kid." When I didn't respond, he added, "Good man. Stand-up guy."

The way he didn't use tense wasn't lost on me. Nobody seemed to know whether or not Pops was alive or dead, and if this guy knew, he wasn't telling. Pops had warned me to stay away from the families though. I knew he'd tell me to run… to get the hell away from the Marianis.

But if Pops wanted a say in my life, he should have come home.

The old man pulled out a billfold and made a big show of thumbing through the wad of cash clipped together. Hundreds, fifties, and twenties floated through his fingers like they were Monopoly money of no real consequence, but it was more cash than I'd ever seen. He tugged several bills loose and offered them to me. It had to be at least four hundred dollars. My mind raced, imagining what I could do with it. I had to force my gaze back to his face, and remind myself I still didn't know what the job entailed.

"My nephew needs a friend. A guy on the inside who can look out for him. He's a smart kid, but his blood will make him some enemies. You do this for me, and I'll make sure your family will be taken care of. Protected. *Capisce?*"

My attention drifted back to the cash. I was young, but I wasn't stupid. There were no Good Samaritans in Vegas. Everyone sought the big payout, nobody gave away anything for free. And this offer was way too good to be true.

"You want me to be his friend and protect him? That's it?" And he was willing to pay me hundreds for it? There had to be some sort of catch.

"Yeah. You'll get training. Like I said, you got heart, but we'll teach you the skills you need. Other opportunities might arise—chances for you to earn more—but Angel will always be your primary responsibility. What do you say, kid?" He added a few more twenties to the stack, sweetening the deal. "You ready to step up and become a man? Ready to help your mom out?"

The mention of Ma made me pause. Whoever this man was, he was too personal… too familiar. It felt strange, worrisome.

He chuckled. "I'm asking you to be my nephew's friend and bodyguard, Franco Leone. You better believe I know everything about you."

And what did I know about him? Not a damn thing. Angel, though—Angel was a quiet kid. Respectful. A little geeky. I could hang out with him and watch his back.

Before I could agree the old man said, "Leave everything to me. Don't worry about what Mr. Jones said, you make sure your ass is in school tomorrow and every day after. Your mom will never see a hospital bill for what you did to that kid. I'll handle it."

It *was* too good to be true. "You can really do all that?" I asked.

"'All that'?" He laughed, and his associate joined in. They carried on for an uncomfortable minute while I wondered what was so funny. Finally, the old guy wiped a tear from his eye and said, "Kid, you have no idea what I'm capable of."

Something in his tone made the hair on the back of my neck stand up, but his offer was too good to pass up. He offered me the money again, and this time I took it.

"I'll be his friend. I'll protect him," I promised.

Mom's beat-up old sedan turned the corner and came barreling toward us. No doubt she was pissed at the interruption in her work day my suspension caused. I stashed the cash in my pocket and stood straighter, dreading the guilt trip I was about to receive. The old man squeezed my shoulder in a gesture that bordered on painful, getting my attention. When I looked up at him, his smile had disappeared.

"He's putting a lot of faith in you. Do not disappoint him, Franco," he said.

Before I could ask who this mysterious 'he' was, the old man's smile was back and directed toward the Celica, which screeched to a stop behind his Jaguar.

"Make sure she gets those brakes looked at," the old man said to me. "Ron's Brake and Tire on Decatur will help you out. Tell 'em Carlo sent you. You take care of your mom now. We owe her that much at least." Before I could ask him why he owed

Ma anything, he shuffled me toward the car as my mom was getting out, extending his hand to Mom. "Mrs. Leone, hello, so nice to meet you. You've got a great boy here. You should be proud."

Mom's brows knit together in confusion as she looked from the man to me.

"Now don't you worry about this little misunderstanding one bit. A bully was picking on my great nephew and Franco here stepped in and defended him. It was admirable, and I'm fixin' to go in there and talk to the principal right now. I'll set him straight about what happened and you have my word Franco's suspension will be lifted. You'll be getting an apology call from the principal tonight."

Ma's expression softened. "You helped a kid?" she asked me.

I decided right then that protecting Angel Mariani would start with making him sound less like a sissy. If I was going to be his best friend, he needed to be someone I could respect. "He got jumped. It wasn't a fair fight."

The old man released my shoulder to pat me on the back and I knew I'd said the right thing. He headed toward the school and I climbed into Ma's car and put on my seatbelt.

"You really helped a kid?" she asked again.

Well if that didn't make me feel like the scum of the earth. Was it so difficult to believe I'd done something nice? "Ma—"

"Don't look at me like that, Franco. This is the third suspension since your father… disappeared. You can't blame me for being surprised."

No, I couldn't. Especially since I couldn't have cared less about D'Angelo Mariani when I'd done it. "Yeah." I patted the cash in my pocket. "Seemed like the right thing to do."

I watched the old man disappear behind the school doors, realizing I hadn't gotten a phone number from him. Somehow I knew it didn't matter, though. He seemed like the type of guy who'd be in touch with me.

It's been thirteen years since I accepted the cash from Angel's great uncle, Carlo Mariani, sealing my position as Angel's best friend and bodyguard. My "opportunities" did increase and Carlo has kept his word, protecting my family and growing my bank account. It's been a good run, but Angel just flipped my world upside down with his plans to leave the family.

He'd invited me to leave the city with him before taking his girlfriend, Markie, out onto the balcony to talk.

My phone rang. As I reached in my pocket, Nonna—Angel's grandmother who had everyone call her by the Italian title for "grandma"—looked up from the magazine she was reading and said, "That'll be Carlo. Give that old coot my regards."

I glanced at the display. Sure enough, Carlo was calling. I hurried for the door, answering as I walked.

"Carlo?" Markie's sister, Ariana, asked. She was sitting beside Nonna, watching Angel and Markie out on the balcony.

"Family business," Nonna replied. "Bones'll take care of it."

Nonna apparently had more faith in my abilities than I did. I stepped into the hallway and spoke to my *capo,* my boss.

"What the hell's going on?" he asked.

I glanced down the hallway, making sure I was alone before replying. "I don't know, but it sounds like the boss is setting Angel free."

"What about you?" Carlo asked.

Angel's great uncle usually had all the information long before I did. "Angel asked me to go with him."

"No. Neither of you is going anywhere. You fix this, Franco. You need to talk Angel into staying."

And how the hell was I supposed to do that? Angel had already made up his mind. "He's in love, Carlo," I replied. It sounded lame even to my own ears, but it was the truth. Angel would do anything for Markie, even abandon his family.

"Well, that's inconvenient. I'll see what I can do."

The line disconnected.

For the first time in his life, Angel was happy. Of course his family would try to take that away from him. Dreading the meaning behind Carlo's threat, I slipped back into the apartment and waited for my friend to return and tell me what the hell I was going to do with the rest of my life.

CHAPTER TWO

Ariana

THREE A.M., THE third week of December, and I was awake and doing a full evaluation of my life. Despite the hiccups over the past year (douchebag ex-boyfriend who conned me out of my money and my inability to catch a freaking break in my career), I'd been surviving on my own. So what if I couldn't always pay all my bills, and I'd made a couple of bad decisions, at least I had a plan and I was working toward it. Until my sister popped back into my life on Halloween and changed everything

Now she was lying beside me, fast asleep. She'd had brain surgery a little over a month ago, and was still recovering. A layer of blonde fuzz covered her head, almost hiding the scar that went from her front hairline to behind her ear. She was the strongest, bravest person I knew, and thanks to the help of her boyfriend and his powerful and scary family, she'd even kicked cancer's ass. Markie's position with Angel's family put her at greater risk than cancer ever had, earning us a bed in Angel's two-bedroom condo while his best friend and roommate, Bones, slept on the couch. It was a temporary arrangement, and as soon as the doctors released Markie to travel, Angel, Bones, Markie, and Angel's grandmother would get the hell out of dodge. They'd invited me to come with them, and I was thinking about it while I should be sleeping.

Honestly, I could think of nothing worse than suffocating in Markie's happily-ever-after as her doting boyfriend whisked her off to their agreed-upon destination where they'd most likely marry and start popping out perfect little babies.

But at least I wouldn't be alone in my envious suffering. Bones would be there too. He and I had gotten close over the past month and a half, and although I wasn't certain how he felt about me, Angel's muscle-bound bestie made my heart flutter every time he glanced in my direction. I could leave Vegas with them and explore the possibilities that lay down a road shared with him, or stay behind alone, forever chasing after my elusive big break, likely to become a lonely old washed-up never-was.

Decisions, decisions.

I gave up on sleep at about five and stumbled for the coffee machine. Bones was already awake and pouring himself a cup. He offered it to me and pulled down another mug.

"Thanks," I mumbled, trying not to be too obvious as my gaze raked over his muscular arms and drifted over the tank top barely hiding his well-defined chest. My entire body heated up, and it had nothing to do with the coffee cup in my hands.

"I'm taking you to work today," Bones said, pulling my attention back to his face and my mind out of his pants, reminding me what a bossy control freak he could be.

Lucky for him, I was too exhausted to argue. "Whatever." Bones wasn't the boss of me, and he had a lot going on. If I really wanted to, I could sneak out and catch the bus before he even knew I was gone. I'd done it yesterday and, judging by the scowl on his face, he still hadn't forgiven me.

Why had I done it? I don't know. Maybe because I felt suffocated and helpless in my own damn life. Maybe I wanted to feel like I could do one thing on my own, even if that one thing was as simple and stupid as getting to work without a babysitter. Or maybe I was immature and acting out. What the hell did they expect from me? I'd been happily living on my own before they invaded my life and started bossing me around. Making a mental note to analyze my motivation further when I was more awake, I reached for the sugar.

Bones beat me to it, clapping down the lid as he watched me. We were inches apart—so close I could feel his body heat—and he gave me a cocky half-smile that made my brain short circuit. "I'm taking you to work today," he repeated.

The challenge in his voice had an interesting effect on me. I couldn't decide whether to cower in a corner, come out swinging, or wrap my legs around him and rake my fingers through his military-short dark hair as I kissed him into submission. I would have been all over that last option had the sexy bastard not friend-zoned me early on, but there was no way in hell I was cowering in the corner. Swinging was my only option. I held his gaze and stepped into him. I hadn't put on a bra yet, so only the thin fabric of my night shirt and his tank top separated me from his delicious wall of muscle. He raised his eyebrows in surprise as I reached around him and plucked the sugar container from his grasp. His eyes darkened, betraying the fact he wasn't as immune to my advances as he pretended to be.

My lips were inches from his when I repeated my earlier answer. "Whatever."

His crooked smile faltered and he stepped away. He always backed down first. I didn't like to play games, but Bones was forcing my hand. Knowing I'd affected him, I smiled and sweetened my coffee.

"You got time to hit the gym?" he asked. He'd moved over by the fridge, putting the entire kitchen between us, the chicken.

"Yeah, yeah. Give me five."

I crept back into the bedroom and threw on my workout clothes between sips of caffeine. By the time I reemerged Bones stood by the door, still wearing his tank top, but had swapped his pajama pants for athletic shorts and sneakers. I downed the rest of my coffee and we headed out. Neither of us had the gift of small talk, so the elevator ride was blissfully silent and charged with sexual tension. Regardless, he didn't even twitch when I "accidentally" brushed against him on my way out of the car.

The condo building had an incredible gym, made up of three separate spaces. One room held weights and cardio equipment, one held an indoor lap pool and hot tub, and the last was stocked with punching bags, yoga mats, and Pilates balls. It seemed a bit much for an apartment building, but Angel's dad owned the place and he clearly had money to spare.

Bones and I stretched, and then warmed up with cardio and weights before he asked, "Feel like trying some boxing?"

By that time I'd woken up enough to return to my smartass self, so I settled into a fighting stance, thumbed my nose, and put up my dukes. "Sure. I think I can take you. Let's do this." Besides, I'd been trying for weeks to get my hands on Bones. If this was what it took, I was willing to get a few bruises.

He chuckled, shaking his head. "How about we try the bags first?"

He led me into the room and positioned me in front of the nearest bag. The scent of Bones—a delicious blend of shower gel, sweat, and metal—invaded my senses as he leveled my fists, adjusted my shoulders, and situated my upper body. My pulse skyrocketed and goose bumps sprouted across my skin. The rock-hard muscles of his chest tempted me to explore every dip and curve. Hoping he wouldn't notice my body's many reactions to his proximity, I said the first thing I could think of to distract us both. "This is the part where I fly like a bee, right?"

He chuckled again. "Float like a butterfly; sting like a bee."

I loved Bones's laugh. His deep, throaty chuckle caressed my senses, making me want more of it. More of him. I did not, however, want him to be laughing *at* me. Trying to play it cool, I refused to be embarrassed. "Psht. That's totally what I said. Shouldn't I be wearing gloves?"

He pulled my arms in closer to my chest and turned my fists. "We're not doing that kind of boxing. I'm gonna show you how to defend yourself if someone comes at you on the street. For the next time you decide to go off and do your own thing." He gave me a pointed look. "Chances are you won't be wearing gloves."

I shrugged. "I could be, though. Boxing gloves are in this year."

That earned me a smile. "Hit the bag, Ari."

I took a swing, made contact, and the bag moved maybe an inch. Fail.

"You dropped your shoulder," Bones admonished, readjusting my stance.

When? How? All I'd done was swing. "No I didn't."

He cocked his head. "Yes, you did. Here, step into it and swing like this. Move your arm, not your shoulder." He demonstrated the move and I tried not to gawk at the way his muscles flexed. "Your turn."

I did my best to mimic his swing. This time the bag moved a little further.

"Did you see that?" I asked. "I'm a badass. You can have my autograph though." And I planned to write it with my fingers… right across his chest.

"Keep it up," he said, stepping toward his own bag.

I threw half-hearted punches as I watched Bones dish out some serious punishment. As his bag swung to and fro, he seemed to anticipate every rotation, stepping around and countering its rebounds like a pro. It was an incredible sight, and it took everything I had in me to focus on my own bag enough to give it the occasional punch. I was probably drooling, but I didn't care. The man was so hot all he had to do was beat on an inanimate object to make me pant.

Desperate to match his thug status and prove I wasn't some wimpy loser, I stepped up my game, punching harder and harder. My bag swung wider and wider as odd battle cries tore from my throat, like I was channeling that butterfly guy. Screw that. I was gonna be the next Ronda Rousey. But before I could even say "cage match" my bag swung too hard and plowed into me. I panicked and flung my arms around it, locking it in a hug. It swayed. I swayed with it.

Bones glanced over at me and arched an eyebrow.

I patted the bag, hoping he'd mistake the red of my face for exertion. "We just made up. I kicked his ass, he apologized. We're cool now."

"So… you're dancing?"

Yep. I was still swaying with the bag. I released it and stepped away, eyeing the bag lest it come at me for another round. "How is this supposed to teach me to protect myself?"

"The more you hit the bag, the more comfortable you'll get with swinging punches. The key is not to hesitate. When you get a shot, you take it."

It sounded like he was repeating something he'd heard. "So, if someone attacks me, this will help me punch them?"

He took another swing at his bag. "Or kick them, or poke out their eye, or whatever. When it's about survival, you fight as dirty as you need to."

I considered his words while sizing up my bag and pretending it was an attacker. I hit it, kicked it, and kneed it in the crotch.

"That's better," Bones said.

"You been in a lot of fights?" I asked.

"As many as necessary."

"That wasn't an answer."

"Sure it was."

His crooked smile and elusive answers made me want to punch him. Then kiss him. Then maybe punch him again. Trying a different angle, I asked, "Do you like to fight?"

Bones's brow furrowed as he hit his bag a few more times. "I'm a bodyguard, Ari. It kinda goes with the job."

Another non-answer. "Yeah, okay. But say you weren't a bodyguard. Pretend you could be anything in the world. What would you want to be?"

Bones's gaze cut to something above my head before he looked away. I followed his glance to the dark glass bubble hiding a security camera. They were all over Vegas.

"I like being Angel's bodyguard," he said, pulling my attention back to him. "I have everything I need. Nothing else I could imagine doing."

His declaration made me both jealous and sad. Jealous because he seemed genuinely content with his life. He knew what he wanted to do, and he was doing it. But at the same time, it made me sad because I realized he had no life dreams or goals. Sure, I was a waitress, but I had hope of being something more. There was zero hope in Bones's eyes, and he seemed fine with that. I wanted to know why, but before I could launch my barrage of questions at him, he stepped away from his bag and nodded toward the door.

"We should head up, Ari. You gotta get ready for work."

I glanced at the clock on the wall and realized he was right. Following him to the door, I swallowed my questions. For now.

CHAPTER THREE

Bones

I TOOK ARIANA to work, but before she got out of the Hummer she made me promise to be careful.

I hadn't told her a damn thing about my job, but the girl didn't miss a thing. I really liked that about her, even though it often frustrated the hell out of me. "I'm always careful."

She beamed me a beautiful smile before wrapping me in a quick good-bye hug. I stiffened, both wanting her touch and wanting to avoid her all together.

"Thanks for the ride," she called out, like she didn't try to ditch me every chance she got.

I watched as she headed into the casino. Her short black uniform showed off her long, sexy legs and her slender waist. Her caramel-colored hair came just past her chin, teasing me with glimpses of her perfect neck. Heads turned as she walked by, but Ariana didn't seem to notice. The girl had no clue how hot she really was, which was another thing I liked about her.

As I pulled away from the curb, Carlo called me in for a meeting at his home office. No matter how good Angel's phone distorters were, most of the old-school wiseguys still didn't trust technology and insisted on in-person meetings. Carlo Mariani was as old-school as they came, only carrying around a cell phone because the boss insisted on being able to reach him at all times.

Carlo's house was a modest, split-level Southwestern stucco in a gated community. A guard greeted me by the garage entrance and took me past the same Jaguar that had pulled up to my middle school thirteen years ago. Carlo had to be loaded, but neither his home nor his car showed it. I wouldn't put it past him to keep his millions buried in booby-trapped jars in his backyard, waiting for the first disillusioned schmuck to think he was smart enough to steal from the underboss of the Mariani family. Thankfully, that would never be me.

The guard passed me on to the live-in housekeeper, Constanza. She was a little Hispanic woman in her early fifties, and Carlo had kept her around for as long as I'd known him. He'd never married, and I had a sneaking suspicion she did a lot more than cooking and cleaning around there.

"Bones, it is so nice to see you!" Constanza said, embracing me. She'd always been kind and welcoming, but a few years ago I'd helped her nephew out with a bully situation, and she treated me like family ever since. "Can I get you something? Water? I'm making some tamales. They'll be ready soon."

"Explains that intoxicating smell," I said, taking a deep whiff and smiling. "You know, if Carlo ever cuts you loose, I'll put a ring on your finger."

And if Carlo overheard me say that and thought I was serious, he'd put a bullet in my head. Constanza knew I was bluffing, though. She beamed me a bashful smile.

"You are too kind to an old woman, Bones," she replied, leading me toward Carlo's office. "Whenever you're ready to settle down, I do have a niece who'd be perfect for you, though. Beautiful girl. Smart, too. She's in nursing school right now."

Just like Ma, Constanza was determined to make sure I settled down with a nice girl. She had more nieces than anyone I knew, and this was the third one she'd brought up in the past six months. My question was always the same. "But can she cook like you?"

Constanza frowned. "Not yet, but maybe someday. But she's got a face like an angel."

"It'll never work, then." Besides, I already had one smart and beautiful girl complicating my life. I had no desire to add another one.

"Too bad," Constanza said, opening Carlo's office and motioning me in.

"Bones. Good to see you. Please, come in." Wearing the typical uniform—suit, tie, dress shoes—and standing in front of a bay window with a great view of his backyard, Carlo was the indisputable king of his castle. He crossed the room and shook my hand before gesturing to the chair in front of his desk. "Have a seat. Can Constanza bring you anything?"

I declined, but she promised to wrap me up a few tamales to go before leaving Carlo and me to our business. As always, I passed him an envelope of cash, a percentage of everything I'd collected on over the past few days. He slid the envelope into the breast pocket inside his suit jacket and leaned against his mahogany desk.

"What's going on with Matt Deter?" he asked.

Matt Deter, the current bane of my existence, was a low-life dealer who owed the family three thousand dollars for a shipment of dope he'd taken to the streets and never paid for. He also happened to be Ariana's ex-boyfriend. Last time they were together, he pumped her pretty little veins full of enough dirty dope to kill her, then pulled a disappearing act. That was Halloween, the night I met her. She'd recovered physically, but she never talked about Matt or the experience. I had every intention of finding the asshole and making him pay for what he'd done to her with his life.

"He's been layin' low, but I got eyes and ears watchin'. First squeak that rat makes, we'll be all over him," I reassured Carlo. "He's arrogant. He'll show his face sooner or later. Can't help himself."

"Good, good. As soon as he pops his head out of whatever hole he's hiding in, do him up good." He paused and leaned against his desk. "But shake him down and find out who he's getting his junk from first. We need to get that shit off the streets. It's bringing too much heat down on the market."

Although I was just an enforcer, I understood the drug trade to be a tricky business. The product had to be cheap enough to keep buyers loyal, but also of high enough quality to keep them alive. The family policed the market to make sure balance was kept, but during the war with the Pelinos we'd lost control. Someone had flooded the streets with dirty dope, causing enough deaths to make the politicians pay attention. Carlo's team had been hunting down the dealers and slowing distribution, but if we didn't get it cut off at the source soon, even the greased cops would have to get their noses in Carlo's business. Nobody wanted that.

"Yes sir. I'll make sure he squeals."

He nodded and crossed his arms. "In the meantime, I have another job for you. Renzo has a fence by the name of Jimmy Foster… you ever hear of him?"

Renzo was Angel's third cousin, but I was unfamiliar with the fence. "No sir."

"This guy Jimmy stiffed Renzo on a big deal. Probably thought the Pelinos were gonna come out on top of this war and wasn't worried about offending one of ours. I'm sending you with Renzo to set this *stronzo* straight."

Regardless of how big a bastard Jimmy Foster was, sending me with Renzo was a strange move for Carlo to make. Renzo was a made man—formally inducted into the family—who had his own team, and they were more than capable of handling some suicidal fence. But I'd learned long ago not to question the orders of my capo. "Understood."

"I'll have the new Tech send you the details when Renzo's ready to make his move." Carlo pulled a pack of cigarettes from his pocket, stuck one between his lips, and lit it. He took a drag and then said, "Now tell me about Angel. The kid's really going straight?"

Carlo knew everything about Angel the boss had tried to hide. He knew Angel was different. It wasn't that Angel was soft—because he wasn't—but he had a higher regard for life than what was acceptable for someone in our line of business. Even if Angel managed to physically survive leading the family, it'd tear him up inside.

"Looks like it. He's already got a job offer with some big-time tech company."

"So you know where he's going yet?"

"No. The job's remote. He can live anywhere in the U.S."

Carlo shook his head, looking disgusted. "I always figured he'd come around. That one day his blood would kick in and he'd change. Always thought Angel would be your capo. You know that's why I never brought you in, right? We were waiting. But with Angel out of the equation… well, we're opening the books later this month, and it's past time we brought you in."

Now? I'd waited years to be made, and now that Angel wanted me to leave with him they were finally ready to go through with it? Why? Information was Carlo's currency. He had to know I was planning to leave with Angel. Careful to keep my expression neutral, I nodded. Saying or doing anything else would most likely get my throat cut.

Carlo glanced at his watch before taking his seat. "I have to make a phone call. You know the way out." He gestured toward the door.

Suspecting that my lack of enthusiasm at his offer had upset him, I left. Constanza caught up to me on my way out the door, filling my hands with foil-wrapped fresh tamales. They smelled great, and I thanked her, even though I no longer had an appetite. The meeting with Carlo had made me realize how screwed I was. How screwed we all were. Angel's father had taken out the Pelino family's heir apparent, and if the Pelinos had any chance at saving face they'd need to whack Angel as retaliation. As a Mariani son, Angel would always have some level of family protection, but his father couldn't throw any more men at protecting the son who wanted out of the business. Then there was me. If I refused Carlo's offer, my protection would be completely stripped. We needed Markie's doctor to hurry and clear her so we could get the hell out of Vegas. In the meantime, I had to stay alive and keep myself from getting made.

My mind heavy with worry, I climbed into the Hummer as my phone buzzed with an incoming text. Angel sent me a list of groceries he needed me to pick up so he could cook dinner. Since Markie's surgery, the two of them only left the condo for doctor visits. Her doctor had told her to take it easy, and Angel was making damn sure she did. With family tensions what they were, it made my job easier since I only had to watch out for myself.

Somewhere between Carlo's house and the grocery store, I picked up a tail. A black, newer-model Toyota Camry hung three cars back but followed my every move. I changed lanes, the Camry changed lanes. I turned, it turned. I made a complete circle, and it was still behind me. Knowing I needed to find out who was after me, I changed lanes again and made a sharp turn down a wide alley. Parking the Hummer on the other side of a Dumpster, I killed the engine, grabbed the gun in my pocket, and waited. Time ticked by and the Camry didn't show. Wondering if the perceived tail had been some sort of bizarre coincidence, I got the hell out of there.

While in the grocery store, I ran into a club waitress named Trixie. After asking me about Angel and feigning sympathy for Markie's surgery, she said, "Whatever happened with that douche bag in the condom wrapper?"

My ears perked up. "Matt Deter?"

"Yeah. That jerk. You know, he pinched my ass and asked me if I wanted to unwrap him. As if. The loser was kicked out of our club last month for pushing drugs in the bathroom."

Trixie was a nice enough girl, but trying to get her to focus was a losing battle. "Have you seen him lately?" I asked.

"Not me personally, but one of the bouncers had to run him off the other night. He was dealing by our back door."

I thanked Trixie for the first lead I'd had on Matt since Halloween, and she promised to pass the word and have everyone call the second he resurfaced. Feeling hopeful, I made a couple of calls on the way back to the condo, but nobody else had seen the illusive Matt Deter.

CHAPTER FOUR

Ariana

I ENJOYED WORKING breakfast at the diner because it was our busiest shift, full of friendly old people who tipped well. But today was busier than normal because, in addition to my duties, I was training our new girl, Piper. Piper had short, dark hair with blue spiked tips which went great with her nose ring and thick, dark eyeliner. Most importantly, Piper was talkative and interesting, melting away the hours with each entertaining story.

"What's Los Angeles like?" I asked her as I filled up the coffee machine.

Piper shrugged. "Loud. Crazy. Lots of really great bars. And you haven't lived until you've been to a Dodgers game."

"And you're close to the ocean, Disneyland, and Hollywood. Ohmigod, I would kill to see Hollywood. Did you ever meet any big stars?" Vegas hadn't worked out like I'd planned, but Hollywood… I was certain Hollywood would be incredible. It was the place of stardom dreams after all.

"Didn't make it out to Hollywood much. Not really my scene." Piper wiped down a table and grabbed the water pitcher. "I did see J Lo coming out of a restaurant once, though."

"Jennifer Lopez?" I asked, feeling like a star-struck small-town girl, which I basically was.

"Yeah. No biggie. You've never seen anyone famous in here?" she asked.

"No. Never." Big stars probably stayed in the nicer hotels and had room service bring them their meals.

The coffeepot finished brewing. Piper filled a water pitcher and we floated around the restaurant, refilling drinks. Once we were done making the rounds, we broke for lunch. She headed outside to smoke and I made a beeline for my favorite seat in the casino, a stone wall beside a peaceful little pond. The spot was mostly hidden by a fake tree, allowing me privacy to eat or play on my phone. I'd only showed one other person my special spot, so I was shocked to see someone sitting there. Especially someone wearing a suit. Disappointed, I turned to leave.

The suit stood, catching my attention. "Hey baby."

The familiar voice brought on a wave of mixed emotions: first relief because he was alive, and then anger because the bastard should have called me to let me know he wasn't dead in a ditch somewhere.

"Matt," I breathed, unable to believe my eyes. He looked good—real good. He'd been my agent and my boyfriend, but when I'd needed him most, he abandoned me. And now he was here, in my spot, breathing the same recycled casino air as me. The question was... why? "What do you want?" I asked, taking a step back.

His frown told me it wasn't the reception he'd been expecting, which only pissed me off more. He'd almost killed me. What did he expect? For me to jump in his lap and lick his face like his faithful bitch? Not this chick. I'd trusted him, and Matt had royally screwed me over, shattered my heart, took my money, and left. Now he was back wearing a new tailored suit and shiny black oxfords. He'd cut his hair and shaved, like he was trying to pull off a respectable-man look. Too bad I knew the truth.

"Don't be like that, baby. I missed you."

I used to love it when he called me baby. Now it made me want to rip out his tongue. Unimpressed, I crossed my arms. "Cut the bullshit and tell me what you want."

He held up his hands in the universal gesture for surrender and took a hesitant step toward me.

"Stay back," I warned, afraid of what I'd do if he didn't. This would be a bad time to practice the punches Bones showed me. If I attacked Matt, casino security would be called and I'd probably lose my job. A little voice in the back of my mind kept whispering that it'd be worth it. My job wasn't all that spectacular anyway.

"So glad I found you, Ari. I have great news," Matt said. Apparently he intended to pretend like I didn't want to kick his face in. "I went to the apartment to find you, but you'd moved out. By the way, what did you do with my stuff?"

Everything Markie and I hadn't taken to Angel and Bones's condo was in a storage unit. Everything except Matt's crap. "I left it in the apartment."

"You abandoned my stuff?" he asked.

I snorted. "Technically, you did. Had I taken it with me, it would have been considered stealing. I should have sold it all to pay for the security deposit you owe me, though. Turns out the apartment was conveniently only in your name. I paid for everything, but I couldn't even change the locks. I couldn't give notice. All I could do was move out."

"We talked about that, Ari. Remember? Since the place was such a dump we decided it would be best if we kept your name off it."

Having no recollection whatsoever of that conversation, I stared at him, wondering again why I'd trusted him so much.

He kept talking. "That way, when you got your break… Oh yeah. That's why I'm here. I did it, Ari! I finally did it!" He lunged forward and grabbed my shoulders, shaking me as he laughed.

My exhausted brain couldn't follow him. He was too close, too personal, too overjoyed. Probably hitting the blow early. Wondering what I'd ever seen in him, I shrugged him off and stepped back. "Did what? What are you talking about? And where did you get that suit? Is that what you did with the last of my money?"

Smile faltering, he patted down his jacket. "This old thing? No, I had this in my closet. I have to look slick when I'm out representing you. I gotta look good to make *you* look good."

God, he sounded like a salesman.

"Which is what I've done, Ari. Are you even listening?"

No. Kinda. My subconscious kept picking up on key words and phrases, but none of them seemed to make sense. "Your closet? What closet? Did you go back to the apartment after you flipped me the bird and rode off into the sunset, wearing a giant condom wrapper?"

That condom wrapper Halloween costume had probably been the closest thing to a suit hanging in his closet when he'd lived with me. But even if there had been a suit, didn't he just ask what had happened to his stuff?

He had the decency to lower his head. "Yeah, that wasn't my best moment. I was messed up, you were messed up… But hey, I found a way to make it up to you. Oh God, Ari, I got you a gig!"

"A gig?" I asked. As my manager, Matt had been trying to get me on a stage—any stage—since I'd moved to Vegas a year ago and handed him an outrageous sum of money.

"Well, not a gig exactly, but I landed you an audition."

I'd suffered through enough of Matt's "auditions" to last me a lifetime. "Right. An audition. What's this one for? Pole dancing? Twerking in front of perverted old men?"

He looked genuinely offended, which was weird since those were both "auditions" he'd sent me to.

"I already told you, I'm not singing with my clothes off."

"No, this one's legit. A local nightclub is looking for singers and I talked the manager into giving you a try. This is it, Ari. Trust me."

And now he was asking the impossible. I didn't trust him. How could I? "Last time you told me to trust you, I almost died." I would have died had Angel and Bones not come looking for Matt. "You almost killed me."

He stepped forward again and reached for my hand, pleading. "It's not like that. You make it sound intentional."

I pulled away. "Don't touch me."

"You know I'd never hurt you on purpose. I took that shit too, remember? I had no idea you'd… You must have been allergic to something in it."

"You could have stuck around to make sure I was okay."

"I was messed up. We were having fun before your sister showed up and you got all pissy. I didn't want to get into some big fight with you, so I bailed."

And he stayed gone for almost a month and a half without checking to see if I was okay. Didn't even answer a single text or phone call. Before I could point this out, he continued.

"We've done all kinds of shit and it's never kicked your ass like that. Remember when we got high while hiking the Red

Rock trails? I've never seen you laugh so hard… thought you were gonna pee your pants. We had so much fun that trip. I wanted Halloween to be like that. Us laughing and having a good time like we used to. I miss that. Don't you?"

Memories of the Red Rock hike tickled the corners of my mind, but I refused to give in to them. Refused to let Matt in. "It's too late for that now, Matt. You shoulda called. I gotta get back to work."

I turned to go, but he grabbed my hand again. Paper slid against my skin. I looked down to see digits scrawled across it. "My new number."

His new number? He must have ditched the old one when he was sick of my texts and voicemails. Awesome. "I'm not gonna call you, Matt. That ship has sailed and sunk."

"It's for when you change your mind. You better hurry, though. I don't know how long my contact will wait. He's already got several auditions lined up, but I assured him you're the best."

"Oh, I'm the best," I said, my voice dripping with sarcasm. "That must be why you wouldn't stop calling me. You just couldn't stay away."

"Don't be like that, baby. This is for real. Can't you see I'm sorry and I'm trying to make it up to you?"

He sounded sincere, but could Matt really have gotten me a legitimate audition? I'd convinced myself he was nothing more than a conman. But what did I have left for him to con me out of? He'd taken it all. "If it's so real, why don't you just give me his number?"

"He's a professional, babe. Only agents can contact him."

As I chewed on that little piece of information, Matt turned and left me standing there. The bastard glanced back once, just to make sure I was watching him. Caught, I looked away, but felt my cheeks redden. I still didn't trust the slimeball, but I was desperate. Singing in a nightclub? I'd be all over that, but chances were it was just another lie. Angry with myself for even considering it, I stuffed his number in my pocket and headed back to work.

Piper was clocking in when I got there. She took one look at my face and asked what was wrong.

"Run-in with the ex."

"Tell me all about it," she said.

The restaurant was experiencing a bit of a lull, so we refilled sauces and napkins while I gave her the rundown on my failed relationship with Matt. When I finished my tale of woe, she said, "Sounds like a real d-bag. You stayed with him for a year?"

It was a reasonable question, but it made me admit, "It wasn't all bad. We had some good times too."

"Oh really?" Piper asked.

"I have a pretty screwed up past. I came to Vegas to get away from it all and start over, but it was harder than I thought it would be."

"Reality sucks," she said, nodding.

"Yeah, and Matt had everything I needed to escape it."

The sound of his laughter floated through my memories, accompanied by the smell of smoke and lines of powder. Truthfully, I missed the escape, but not enough to risk my life.

"All in the past, though. That little near-death experience helped me realize I didn't want to escape reality *that* much."

She smiled. "I'm glad you didn't tap out."

The hostess signaled us toward two families she was leading in.

"Because then you'd be missing out on all this glorious fun," Piper added.

Feeling better, I laughed and grabbed the water pitcher.

CHAPTER FIVE

Bones

I DIDN'T TRUST Ariana to wait for me after work, so I arrived early and met her by the door. When she came out, I could tell something was wrong. She had a piece of paper in her hands and her forehead wrinkled as she looked at it. When she saw me she stuffed it in her jacket pocket.

"Everything okay?" I asked, searching her face for clues as to what was on that paper.

She waved me off. "Yeah, fine. Just tired. Long shift and I didn't sleep so well last night."

"So I guess you wanna go straight home?"

"Depends. What are Mom and Dad up to? Baking cookies to solve world hunger? Adopting rescue kittens?"

"Cooking dinner, not baking cookies. Although there probably will be some sort of dessert involved."

She wrinkled her nose. "As long as it's not the kittens."

I laughed. She was so funny, bordering on inappropriate at times. I loved the way she always knew how to make me laugh. And judging by the smile she beamed at me, she enjoyed the experience too.

People were watching us, no doubt wondering what to think about me in my suit walking beside her in her waitressing uniform. Ariana seemed to notice the looks we were getting and decided to ramp it up. She closed the gap between us and slid her arm into the crook of my elbow, giving me a conspiratorial grin. "Wonder if they think I hired you or you hired me?"

I could never tell if Ariana was legitimately flirting with me, or just screwing with my head. Lately it seemed like she was looking for any excuse to touch me, though, and I'd be lying if I said I didn't enjoy the contact. Neither of us had been exactly open about our pasts, but she'd dropped enough hints to let me know she'd been through some pretty tough shit. I was thankful she hadn't lost her sarcastic sense of humor in the process.

As we walked out into the fading sunshine, she leaned over and stage whispered, "You should probably pay me up front for my services. Just so there's no confusion."

It was just loud enough for the young couple walking past us to hear. The woman's eyes widened as she led her partner away from us, whispering and casting glances at us over her shoulder.

I eyed Ariana, trying not to laugh.

"What?" She gave me her best innocent smile, blowing me away with the seamless transformation she went from sexy to sweet. Ariana had both looks mastered. "That was providing free entertainment to the tourists. I'll tell you what, tomorrow when you pick me up, wear sweats and drink from a paper bag, and we'll give them a real show. Got it?"

And man, she loved to screw with people. As she released my arm, I couldn't help but admit she was probably doing the same to me.

As we climbed into the Hummer, my phone buzzed with an incoming call from Ma. I started the engine and answered.

"Franco, I'm sorry to bother you, but..."

I groaned. She started all her conversations this way, throwing my busy schedule in my face to make me feel like the worst son on the planet. "Ma, how many times do I gotta tell you you're no bother?"

"It's just that I know you're busy."

Here we go.

Wondering if we'd ever get past this opening and on to what she was angling for, I said the same thing I always did. "Never too busy for you. What's up?"

"A light bulb in my kitchen burned out."

Had Ariana not been with me, I probably would have beaten my head against the steering wheel. As it was, I had to struggle to keep my composure. Ma was far from helpless. Hell, she was one of the most independent women I knew. She wouldn't be calling me for a burned-out light bulb. "Did you call the maintenance guy?" I asked.

"My own son lives in the same city as me, and I've gotta call a maintenance man to replace a light bulb? I don't want to bother him. I'll just climb on the ladder and fix it myself."

The guilt was so thick I could almost see it streaming out of the phone and threatening to choke me. Still, I didn't want her climbing up a damn ladder. Especially not alone. "Where's David?"

"He's at the library, studying for a big calculus exam tomorrow. I'd rather not interrupt him if I can help it."

My useless little brother probably was studying all right… studying one of the girls in his calculus class.

"Franco, if it's too much trouble, I can—"

More guilt. It suffocated me. I cracked my window to get some air. "No, Ma, it's no trouble. It's just that I'm giving someone a ride, and…"

Ariana poked my arm. "I don't mind, Bones. I'd love to meet your mom."

I shushed Ariana, but it was already too late. I could tell by the way Ma sucked in a chestful of air, she'd heard her. Any doubts I had shattered when she launched into a barrage of questions and demands.

"A girl? You're on a date and you didn't bring her by to meet me? Franco, you know I helped your brother Tony pick out his wife, and they were made for each other. You know this. You bring her over and let me talk to her and I'll tell you if she's a good fit for you. I'll whip us up something to snack on while I make dinner."

Ariana snickered. "She sounds like quite the matchmaker."

Yeah, she could laugh. Right up until Ma had our china picked out. I liked Ariana and all, but I wasn't trying to get hitched. I needed to set Ma straight before she dragged me to a jeweler.

"It's not a date. I'm taking a friend home from work. Angel's already making dinner and needs me to pick up Nonna on the way." Probably best not to mention that Ariana would also be eating with us. Of course, if Ma found out Ariana was living with us and sleeping in my bed, she'd have us both saying Hail Marys for Father Barone while she picked out our china.

"But it could turn into a date. You're unsupervised in a car with her, and she sounds pretty. I bet she's a lovely girl."

Ariana batted her eyelashes at me and mouthed, "She thinks I'm lovely."

I really needed to turn down the volume on my phone.

"Franco?" Mom asked.

"No dinner. No long stay, I'm just coming to change the light bulb."

"Yes, of course. I'd never ask more of your time than that. Thank you. You're such a good son."

Right. "I'll be there in about ten." I disconnected the call.

I didn't have to look at Ariana to know she was amused, because I could hear her quiet snickering. We drove the rest of the way in silence while I tried to find a way out of this whole awkward situation. It would have been a good time for the new Tech to call me with the details for Renzo's fence. I could have gone for messing someone up. It'd be a much better way to spend my evening, than hoping Ma didn't get some marriage-material vibe off my boss's girlfriend's little sister.

Still unwilling to accept the meeting as inevitable, I parked in front of Ma's small house and turned to face Ariana. "I don't suppose you'd like to wait in the car?" I asked.

She giggled. "Not a chance."

Damn. "Okay, but not a single word about you and Markie staying with us."

She gasped, looking wounded. "Do I seem like the type of girl who'd rat you out to your mommy?"

I sighed, knowing full well Ariana would do whatever floated her boat. We climbed out of the Hummer and met Ma where she stood waiting on the front porch with a smile spread from ear to ear. Before I could make introductions, she hugged me and then turned to embrace Ariana.

"Ma, this is my *friend* Ariana. Ari, this is my mom, Marcella Leone."

"It's nice to meet you, Ms. Leone," Ariana said.

Ma's smile only widened. "Please, call me Marcella. It is so great to meet you. You're right, Franco, she is gorgeous. He's told me so much about you."

No, I most certainly had not. But since calling out my own mother for lying to make me sound good seemed to be some sort of social faux pas, I shook my head and followed them into the house.

"You need some meat on your bones," Ma said, taking in Ariana's thin body. "I have a lasagna in the oven. That'll do the trick."

I ran a hand down my face. "No dinner, Ma. We don't have time."

"Of course, honey. It was just a suggestion. I'd never expect you to stay."

"I bet you have a hundred baby pictures of Bones, er Franco," Ariana said, grinning wickedly over her shoulder.

Not good. Not good at all. "Yes she does, but we'll have to look at those later. Here to change the light bulb, and then it's back on the road for us. Tight schedule, remember?"

"Nonsense." Ma slipped into the kitchen. "I just pulled some *pizzelles* off the iron. How do you take your cappuccino, Ariana?"

"Milk and sugar, please." She looked at me and added, "Pizzelles?"

"Cookies."

Her brow scrunched up. "Cooked on an iron?"

"Like a waffle iron."

The cappuccino machine whirred to life. "Franco bought me this beast for Christmas last year. Noisy, but it makes a great cup," Ma shouted over the machine.

I scanned the kitchen ceiling, searching for the burnt-out light. "Which bulb, Ma? They all look fine to me."

She gave me a sheepish smile and handed me a cup. "It's been thirty-two days since I last saw your precious face, and I needed to make sure you weren't dead or wounded. Last time you pulled a disappearing act on me, you came home with all those cuts on your chest, and—"

Ariana's eyes grew round.

Needing to derail Ma's train of thought, I jumped in. "I'm fine, Ma. My job's been crazy lately." Since there was no way she'd let me leave without finishing my drink first, I accepted my cappuccino and headed for the table.

Ma asked questions about my job, which I evaded, before switching tactics and pumping Ariana for information. Ariana handled it like a boss, sipping cappuccino and munching on pizzelles while she talked about her job and her dream of singing in a show. But when Ma started questioning Ariana about her family, she excused herself to use the restroom.

I leveled a stare at my mother, knowing she'd never give up. "Her parents are dead, her uncle's an ass, and she lives with her sister."

"Watch your mouth in my house, Franco." Ma glanced at the bathroom door. "And she wants to sing. That's a difficult road. It's a good thing she has you to—"

"To what? We're just friends."

"Now, but I see the way that girl looks at you. She's looking for a lot more than friendship."

I stared at my coffee cup, refusing to meet Ma's gaze. "Well she's gonna have to keep lookin'. Friendship's all I can offer right now."

Ma clicked her tongue and started to say more, but I cut her off.

"What's going on?" I asked. "Why am I really here?"

She stood and started clearing away plates. "Isn't missing my son enough? Why does there have to be a reason?" Now she wasn't meeting *my* gaze. I loved my mother. I took care of her and David financially and there wasn't a damn thing I wouldn't do for them. But we weren't exactly a close family, and hadn't been in several years.

"Ma—"

"I'm dating someone. I'd like you and Ariana to come to dinner with us so you can meet him."

"No."

Ariana picked that very moment to come out of the bathroom. The tension between me and Ma was so thick Ariana didn't even make it to the table before asking what was wrong.

Ma gave her another of those ear-to-ear smiles. "Nothing, dear. I was just inviting you and Franco out to dinner with me and my boyfriend. I think Franco's a little intimidated and—"

"Ma!" I swear the woman was relentless.

Ma winced, and Ariana startled at the harshness of my tone before turning to Ma and asking when the dinner was.

"Well, Tito asked me out this Saturday. Are you free?"

Tito? Great. Mom's boyfriend sounded like a seventies pimp. I put my head in my hands, dreading the inevitable.

Ariana checked her phone. "I'm free. Bones?"

She had me by the balls. Who knew what lies Ma would tell Ariana if I didn't go with her? All I could do was nod.

"Great!" Ma said. "I'll text Franco the location. Tito's gonna be so excited! Can I get you another pizzelle?"

Ariana nodded. "Please. These are amazing."

As soon as Ma headed for the kitchen, Ariana retook her seat beside me. "You okay?" she whispered.

Hell no, I wasn't okay. "Great. Outstanding. Never better." My Saturday night would be spent playing family with Ma and her new boyfriend. I was over-the-moon with anticipation.

Her brow creased. "What's wrong?"

Ma returned, carrying more pizzelles.

"Later," I whispered.

"So, Saturday's a go, but what about the following Thursday?" Ma asked.

Thursday was Christmas. I couldn't remember the last time I'd shared a holiday meal with my mother. "You know I gotta work, Ma."

She looked to Ariana and I about lost my shit. Thankfully she declined before I could blurt out my thoughts on the matter.

"Thanks for the invite, but I gotta work too," Ariana said.

"Well how about tonight? The lasagna is almost ready and—"

It was time to get the hell out of there. I stood, interrupting Ma, and dragged Ariana along with me. "Thanks for the cookies. It's been great, but we gotta jet."

Before Ma could object, we were out the door.

CHAPTER SIX
Bones

BY THE TIME Ariana and I left my mother's house, my shoulders were so tense I thought my head would snap off and go rolling down her front porch steps. Observant as ever, Ariana reached out and gave me a quick massage.

"Hey, you okay?" she asked.

I didn't want to lie, but what could I say to make her understand what Ma was really like? Maybe it was best to let her believe Ma was a sweet old lady who served coffee and cookies. "Yeah."

"Don't lie to me, Bones. What's going on?" Ariana dug her fingers in deeper, working out the knots in my neck. "Something's going on. I've never seen you like this before. What is it? Do you not want me to go to dinner with you and your mom?"

Since I wouldn't put it past Ma to be listening in on the other side of the door, I headed for the Hummer with Ariana in tow. I opened the passenger door and she climbed inside, watching me. The wounded look in her eyes told me she wouldn't accept my silence as an answer. The last thing I wanted to do was bring her into my family drama, but it was too late to avoid that now. I put my arm against the door jamb and leaned into it, looking down.

"This has nothing to do with you, Ari."

She grabbed my hand. "So, what? You have family issues? Tell me about it." When I hesitated, she added, "I would do anything to have my mom back. Please help me understand why you're trying to keep yours away from you."

I looked back at the house I'd bought for Ma. It was no mansion, but it was far better than the tiny apartment we'd squeezed into after Pops disappeared. The car parked in the driveway was the Christmas present I'd bought her two years ago: a hunter green Honda Civic. She had a good life here—one I'd basically paid for, but had never really fit into.

"Talk to me," Ariana pleaded, squeezing my hand.

How could I explain my relationship with Ma? "She's a good woman. Strong. After Pops left, Ma had to get two jobs just to keep us fed."

"Taking care of three boys on her own had to be difficult," Ariana replied.

"Yep. She did what she had to do. We all did." My throat felt dry. I'd never told anyone what I was about to say. Angel knew, but we never talked about it. Talking about it seemed pointless. Words sure as hell wouldn't change the past.

"You all did?" she asked.

I nodded. Silently sifting through the details of my life, trying to separate what I could say and what I couldn't. I didn't have to tell her anything, but for some reason it mattered to me that she didn't think I was a crappy son. So, I took a deep breath and began. "I was ten when I started guarding Angel."

Her eyes widened. Ariana wasn't a Vegas native, but she'd heard enough whispers to know Angel's family was rich and powerful, and she asked enough of the right questions to tell me she knew more about what I did than she should. "Ten?" she asked.

"Yeah. I didn't even know what to do with the money. We'd been living on ramen noodles and mac-and-cheese for months, so the first thing I did was order me and my brothers a pizza for dinner." And that pizza tasted like the best thing I'd ever eaten. "With Ma working all the time and none of us knowing how to cook, I blew a lot of money on delivery those first couple of months. Then we started getting calls from bill collectors. They turned off the phone, then the cable, and when they cut the power, I knew I had to do more than buy food, so I took the bus down to the power and phone companies and paid cash to get our power and phone turned back on."

"Wow. And you were ten? Your mom must have been so proud of you."

That was the reaction I'd expected too. I'd waited up for her that night, but when she came in from her second job and flicked the light on, she didn't say a word about it. She just sent me to bed like nothing had happened. "She never mentioned it."

"But didn't she wonder where the money came from?"

I shrugged.

"Did you talk to her about it? There has to be some sort of explanation." Ariana glanced at the house. "Maybe she thought a family member paid it or something."

I shook my head. "Ma knew what I was doing."

"How can you be so sure?"

"I've been training since I was ten, Ari. I can't tell you how many times I limped home bleeding and bruised. Ma would take one look at me and pull out the first-aid kit. No questions asked. She never grounded me or demanded to know why I came home with stitches."

"But you said she was working two jobs. I bet she was exhausted and unable to deal with you. As a single mom it's not like she could quit and follow you around to keep you out of trouble."

I shook my head, glancing back at the house. "After the second month I paid the bills, she dropped one of her jobs."

"And that proves she knew you were paying them?" Ariana asked.

"No, but it did free up her time."

Ariana's forehead wrinkled. As she watched me, I could almost see her working out what I couldn't say in her head. "And she just let you… do whatever you were doing?"

"Yep." I'd always wondered what Carlo had meant about owing Ma. Had there been some sort of agreement between them? Or was my working for the family something Pops had put into place before he disappeared? "After I got the job, she stopped making me check in with her. She used to be so protective it drove me nuts, but suddenly I could stay at Angel's house whenever I wanted, even though she'd never met his parents. It was like she just stopped caring where I was and who I was with. I almost asked her about it a hundred times, but I couldn't. I wasn't sure I wanted to know the truth."

Ariana studied my face and I wondered what she saw. "What about your brothers? Are they… bodyguards too?"

I chuckled. "No. Tony was thirteen when Pops split. He saw it as an opportunity to start his teenage rebellion early. David was only seven, and he spent most of his time between school and daycare."

Her eyes were watery when she shifted her gaze back to me. "You were all on your own. Kind of like me and Markie, but you were even younger. I'm sorry, Bones. I had no idea. She seemed so great… so involved. She even set your brother up with his wife."

"That was a lie. The only time Trinity came to our house, Tony was sneaking her into his room. Knocked her up in the middle of their senior year. They got married and moved in with her dad in Cali."

"Why would your mom lie about that? She couldn't have known I was listening in on your phone conversation."

"Near as I can figure she didn't like the way it all went down, so she rebuilt the past in her mind… making it sound better." I pulled my hand away from hers and pushed back from the Hummer, shutting her door so I could get behind the wheel. It was almost time to pick up Nonna.

"Guilt does weird things to people," Ariana said, taking one last look at Ma's house. "We've all done crap we're not proud of. At least she's trying Bones."

I turned over the engine, wondering if we were still talking about Ma. "I know. And it's not like Ma pushed me into working or anything. It was my decision. I just wish she would have been a little more… I don't know." Pulling away from the curb, I made a U-turn and headed toward the rich old-folks home.

"Motherly?" Ariana asked.

"Yeah. We didn't talk much after Pops left, first because Ma was always working, then because I was. Now our relationship feels forced… like she's trying too hard to make up for the past, you know?"

"Yeah, I get it Bones, but take it from someone whose mom is gone… you gotta work that crap out while she's still here."

I knew Ariana was right, but I wasn't ready to make any promises. There was one thing I could tell her, though. "I'm glad you're coming to dinner with us. Thanks."

She beamed me a smile. "Don't even worry about it. I got your back."

Nonna lived in an apartment in an upscale retirement home off West Charleston Boulevard. She had more money than anyone could ever spend, but still insisted on personally packing her belongings rather than paying a moving company to do it for her. Ariana and I had to step over boxes to get to the kitchen to help Nonna cart out the dishes she'd prepared.

"I thought you said Angel and Markie were making dinner?" Ariana asked when Nonna pointed us to the containers littering her countertop.

"Oh, they're making the main dish. These are just a few sides," Nonna replied.

Ariana's eyes bulged at the four large containers. She opened her mouth, but I nudged her before she could say something that would offend Nonna. Not like Ariana would insult Nonna on purpose, but she didn't know anything about Italian grandmothers and their need to take care of their kids and grandkids. Based on the spread Nonna had prepared, tonight she planned to do so by stuffing us until we couldn't breathe.

"Smells delicious," I said, handing Ariana a container and stacking the other three in my arms.

We loaded up the Hummer and Ariana climbed into the backseat while I helped Nonna into the front. Then we took off. Nonna was never one for small talk. Maybe because she was old, she figured she only had so many words left in her and had to ration them, using only the ones that mattered most. Before we reached the main road, she turned to me and asked, "How much trouble is Carlo giving you about leaving?"

I cut my gaze to the backseat, hoping she'd get the hint I didn't want to talk about it in front of Ariana.

Nonna clicked her tongue and looked over her shoulder at Ariana. "Men and their secrets. They think they're so clever, hiding what they do like we're too stupid to figure it out. Well, when this one gets himself in too deep, you come to me, dear. They treat me like some powerless old woman, but I helped Angel out of his mess and I'll do the same for Bones here. He'll probably be too pig-headed to ask for my help, though. They usually are."

I glanced in the rearview mirror long enough to watch Ariana nod. "Thank you, ma'am."

"Nonna, dear. Just call me Nonna."

Then, before I could even argue about the way she'd totally dissed me, Nonna shifted herself to face forward and we rode the rest of the way in silence.

CHAPTER SEVEN

Ariana

I'D ONLY MET Angel's grandmother a few times, but she always managed to surprise me. Today was no different. "Men and their secrets. They think they're so clever, hiding what they do like we're too stupid to figure it out," she said. Her words felt like a warning. Like a verbal smack upside the head that said, "Hey Bozo, pay attention. The guy you're crushin' on is into some serious shit." Only I couldn't imagine Angel's grandma saying "crushin'" or "shit." In fact, there was no way she could know how bad I had it for Bones. I didn't even know.

Bones did have a lot of secrets. I was still reeling about the one he'd just shared. Working since he was ten? Coming home all bruised and broken, his mom doctoring him up without saying a word? My mom would have flipped out. What had caused Bones to come home all messed up in the first place? Bodyguard training? That'd be some pretty brutal training for a kid to endure. I'd known for some time there was more to his job by the way Bones often disappeared for "work," leaving Angel—the body he was supposed to be guarding—behind in the condo with Markie. So what was he doing?

If the rumors about the families were true, Bones could be anything… a pimp, a drug dealer, a loan shark, a murderer. All of which made for spectacular boyfriend material. No wonder

Nonna was warning me about him. The guy I was crushin' on *was* into some serious shit.

But he was also sweet, helping Nonna out of the Hummer and offering her his arm while he carried the three hot dishes of food, leaving me the one cool container to carry. And even though he and his mom had issues, he still dropped everything to go change her light bulb. No matter what Bones did for a living that made him pretty remarkable in my eyes.

The condo smelled of sausage, onion, and garlic, instantly making my mouth water. Christmas music blared from the surround speakers, and way too many damn Christmas lights blinked from everywhere. A small but fluffy tree, twinkling with lights, ornaments, and old-fashioned tinsel sat in the corner of the living room. Lights and garland circled the floor-to-ceiling windows and hung from the bar. The tablecloth and runner were red and gold, and coordinating Christmas dinnerware had already been set. A small Christmas village had been set up on the entryway table, and I counted four poinsettias as I stepped into the living room.

"Holy crap, it looks like Santa threw up in here," I breathed.

I heard the deep rumble of Bones chuckling behind me.

"Ari, Bones, Nonna," Markie said. "Come over here and get in on this action." She waved goopy hands, motioning us toward her.

Nonna slipped into the kitchen and hugged both Angel and Markie, skillfully avoiding Markie's hands.

"You didn't do this, did you?" I asked, setting Nonna's dishes down on the bar so I could better evaluate the Christmas nightmare we lived in.

Bones unloaded his arms and joined me.

"I wanted to…" Markie's gaze cut to Angel.

"We called in people," Angel answered.

"I hate not being able to do anything, and I wanted to… I don't know… feel Christmas? It looks great, doesn't it?" Markie asked.

I'd never been big on the holidays—not since mom died—but if Markie had managed to eke out even an ounce of Christmas spirit, I wouldn't be the one who squashed it… even if it made me want to pop anti-depressants. "Yeah, it looks great," I lied.

She beamed me a smile. "Wanna help me stuff manicotti?"

I looked to Angel and asked, "You're letting her cook? I take it her headache's gone?"

"I'm right here." Markie scowled. "It's been over a month since the surgery. Now that my head's better, you all want me to die of boredom."

Angel winced.

"Sorry." Markie put a hand on his arm. "Open mouth, insert foot."

"She's sitting."

I glanced at the bar and realized one of the stools was missing. "Ah-ha."

"Again, right here," Markie huffed.

"And she promised not to overdo it," Angel added, giving her a pointed look.

"Right," I nodded. My sister was an adrenaline junkie. "Overdo it" was her mantra. "Let me know how that works out."

Nonna looked to be taking over anyway, so Bones and I left them to it and headed for the living room. Bones turned down the music and sat on the sofa. I eyed the recliner, but in the end couldn't resist Bones's magnetic pull. I plopped down beside him, sliding my legs across his lap. It was like I needed to touch him and craved the little sparks of electricity his touch ignited. He adjusted my legs and reached for the controller. I watched him, my conversation with Nonna once again playing through my mind.

"What?" Bones asked after a while.

I said the first thing that popped in my mind. "It was nice to meet your mom today. I mean, I realize it's not an ideal situation, but it was still nice, you know?"

He cocked his head and gave me a crooked smile. "Yeah. I'm glad you got to meet her. At least David wasn't home. He'd probably be trying to get in your pants."

Too bad Bones wasn't trying to get in my pants. Hell, he wouldn't even have to try. One more of those crooked smiles and my pants would probably combust. "Well, is he cute?" I asked.

Bones snorted and went back to the television.

"What?" I asked. "It was a reasonable question. Sounded like you were trying to set me up."

"Definitely not," he replied.

Which only made me wonder, why not? Was it because he liked me after all and was just playing excruciatingly hard-to-get? Or did he think I was some sort of man-eater and he was trying to protect his little brother from me? I wish I could say I felt ridiculous for my insecurities, but I knew the truth about myself and everything I was capable of. My mind wandered back to a time when Markie was away at college and I was home alone with our uncle, Jay Lawson, Boise County Deputy Chief Prosecutor. Uncle Jay had been enjoying the single life before his sister—my mom—died and left me and Markie to him. He was all sorts of bent out of shape about taking in two teen girls, and he did little to hide his feelings. For the most part, I slept at a friend's house or stayed in my bedroom to avoid him. That particular night, I claimed a headache and went to bed early so I could sneak out and go to a party with my friend Jasmine.

Jasmine picked me up at the corner and we went to Adam Drinkwater's. I'd always heard that the Drinkwater parties were the best, and the rager we entered that night did not disappoint. Red solo cups materialized in our hands while we were shuffled into the living room where a group of guys were bonging beer. After downing the first drink, we stumbled into the kitchen to retrieve more cups for the newcomers.

The kitchen was cloudy with pot smoke. By the time we found the cups and returned to the living room, I had a pretty strong contact high going and was almost done with my second cup of something they kept referring to as "jungle juice." I didn't know what was in it, but it burned going down and my entire body felt numb by the second cup.

"Let's dance," Jasmine said, stripping off her jacket. Before I could answer, she tugged me into the throng of gyrating bodies.

More people pressed in around us, everyone dancing with everyone. I spun around and almost ran into Markie's boyfriend, Trent Rodgers.

"Hey, Ari," Trent said, tipping his cup at me.

Panic was my first response. "Shit! Oh God, don't tell my sister you saw me here," I pleaded.

He used his free hand to mock zipping his lips. "Don't even worry about it. Your secret is safe with me."

Relieved, I hugged him. "Thanks, Trent."

Trent's eyes were glassy. "But only if you promise me a dance."

I'd had a small crush on my sister's boyfriend since the first time he took us both out for milkshakes. He was way cooler and more laid back than Markie, making me wonder what he saw in her. I nodded enthusiastically.

We danced through a few songs before he draped an arm over my shoulders and led me off the dance floor. "How are you? How's everything going?"

I glanced back to make sure Jasmine was okay without me to find her giving me a thumbs up. Since there was no good way to tell her the hottie I was walking with belonged to Markie, I smiled and returned the gesture.

"School blows. Home blows. Everything's in the crapper right now. But hey, these are the best years of my life, right?" I held up my cup in a toast. "To keepin' it real."

Trent laughed and tapped his cup to mine. We both drained our drinks, and then he headed off to get us refills.

"Dinner's ready," Markie said, bringing me back into the present.

I looked up at her smiling face—noting the tired lines around her eyes—and felt guilty for the memory. My sister was recovering from brain surgery, and I was fantasizing about her ex. I'd never confessed to Markie what had happened between me and Trent, and didn't plan on it. If she knew what a horrible person I was, it would probably break her heart. I loved my sister, and I would choke on my guilt before I'd hurt her. Again. Determined to do just that, I pasted on a phony smile and stood. "Great. I'm starved."

I spent the next hour defending my plate as Nonna kept trying to pile it high with food. She'd apparently taken my starving comment to heart and decided it was her personal duty to solve the problem.

"Eat up, dear. You're too skinny. You'll need some meat on your bones to fight the waves when we move to the coast," she said.

Since I hadn't decided whether or not I'd be moving with them, I cut my gaze to Markie, who conveniently kept her eyes on her plate.

"Markie says you've never been to the ocean. You are in for a real treat. I remember my first time. My mother took me and my sister to Pismo Beach. The sand felt so warm beneath my feet and the surfers… whew… you should have seen the bodies on those boys."

"Nonna!" Angel said, sounding scandalized.

I giggled. Sure, the old lady was trying to fatten me up, but she was funny.

"What?" she asked. "I was young once too. I had all those urges that you kids have now." She leaned closer to me and added, "And I wouldn't mind seeing those surfers again, if you catch my drift."

We all caught her drift. Bones was doing his best to ignore the whole conversation, Markie's cheeks were pink, Angel was shaking his head, and I was doing everything I could not to bust up laughing. My grandparents were stuffy and disconnected, and I'd trade them both in for Nonna.

"We're looking at some locations in southern Oregon," Nonna continued. "Small towns, nice places to raise my great-grandchildren." The pointed look she gave Markie and Angel left no doubt she expected great-grandchildren soon. "I don't know how many surfers will be up there, but the four of you should go up through San Francisco and spend some time seeing the sights."

"The four of us?" Markie asked. "Won't you be driving up with us?"

"Heaven's no, dear. I don't travel well anymore. I'll fly up after the movers deliver everything. That'll give me time to spend a few weeks with Dom and the children beforehand." Nonna patted my hand. "But you all should go and spend some time being tourists."

I'd love to see the sights of California, but there was just one problem with Nonna's plans. "I haven't decided whether or not I'll be moving with you."

She nodded. "Understandable, dear. The lure of the city can be quite intoxicating. Too much of it will kill you, though. More bread?"

It took me a moment to process her offer because I was trying to make sense of what she'd said. She dangled the bread basket in front of me. "Ari?"

"No thanks."

Markie asked Nonna about Christmas dinner. Still unsettled, I looked to Bones. The worried expression he wore reflected my feelings as I listened to Angel's grandmother talk about the gifts she had gotten for Angel's siblings. She sounded like a caring, sweet old woman, but there'd been something more than that behind her words. Had she been warning me? Threatening me? As she patted my hand and reminded me to eat, a shiver of fear went up my spine. Nonna was terrifying, but at least she was on our side.

Or so I hoped.

CHAPTER EIGHT

Bones

ANGEL AND I took Nonna home after dinner. The drive was uneventful until Angel asked Nonna what her comments to Ariana meant.

"Now I'm just an old woman minding my own business, but it seems like there's only two people who survive this city. Those who know everything and those who know nothing. Ariana seems like a bright young person who falls somewhere in between—a little too curious for her own good," Nonna replied.

Angel frowned. "Too curious? You said the same thing about Vinny last year when you told me to keep my mind on him." Angel glanced at me in the rearview mirror. "That was right before Vinny's brakes… malfunctioned and he wrapped his car around a telephone pole."

Nonna nodded.

A shudder ran down my spine, but Angel wasn't finished.

"And Tony… you called him curious right before he got two slugs in him coming out of the movie theater. The cops called it a random drive-by. Never did find his killer."

"You've always been a sharp one," Nonna replied.

If Ariana was in danger, we needed details. I leaned forward and asked, "Is she in danger?"

Nonna turned in her seat to watch me, which I knew was a red flag, but I couldn't keep my mouth closed.

"Have you heard anything?" I borderline pleaded, unable to mask the concern I felt.

"I was beginning to wonder about you, Bones," she said.

Knowing I'd just been played, I forced my pulse to slow down and took a deep breath.

"Nonna, please tell us what you know," Angel said.

She straightened herself in her seat and stared out the window. "There's nothing more exciting than watching a young person chasing a dream. Must have been a hundred years ago, I had a friend named Molly who came to Vegas with big dreams of becoming a dancer. This city chewed her up and spit her out. Couldn't handle the failure. Slit her own wrists." She shook her head. "Such a beautiful, talented girl. What a shame."

"We wouldn't let that happen to Ari," Angel replied, meeting my gaze in the rearview mirror. "We'll help her succeed."

Nonna studied him for a moment before reminding both of us, "*We* won't be here." She let the meaning behind her words hang in the air for a moment before adding, "A person needs more in their life than success to make them happy."

I couldn't help but think about the first time I met Ariana. She was writhing in bed, drenched with sweat, her pulse and breathing erratic, dirty dope poisoning her system. I'd kept enough of an eye on her to know she hadn't used since, but Ariana was impulsive, and I'd be stupid to assume she would never use again.

We dropped Nonna off, and I climbed into the passenger seat.

"We'll help Ari, you know?" Angel asked. "She won't fail. If she decides she wants to stay here, then between the two of us, we have enough contacts to keep her safe."

I wasn't so sure. Without Angel's family, we barely had the contacts to keep ourselves alive.

Angel put the Hummer into gear and motored out of the retirement home parking lot. "In fact, Markie told me Ari's birthday is coming up… January third. We've been talking about possibilities for her gift and I have an idea I want to run by you."

"She's gonna be what? Twenty?"

"Twenty-one. You know she came to Vegas to sing, right?" he asked.

I nodded.

"Well… you still friends with that talent scout?"

"Noah Garner. Yeah, we still keep in touch."

Noah was contracted through several of the local casinos and was always on the lookout for talent. He and I had met years ago, when one of his actors had gotten strung out and owed an insane amount of money to the wrong people. When the actor got the shit kicked out him, Noah reached out to the Mariani family through a mutual contact. Carlo sent me in and I made a few calls and threw the weight of the family around, negotiating the debt to payment installments and an interest rate that wouldn't cripple the guy. Noah and I had kept in contact ever since.

"Cool. You reach out to your contact, and I'll make arrangements at Uncle Mario's restaurant. According to Markie, Ariana has a powerful alto and gave me a list of songs. I'll make sure Uncle Mario's pianist has the music."

My thoughts drifted back to Nonna's warning, and I felt torn. Ariana had come to Vegas to sing. If we got her a gig, she'd be over the moon. She'd stay for sure, and although it would probably be for the best, I didn't want her to. But at the same time, I wanted her to be happy. This was her dream. What kind of selfish jackass would I be for denying her a chance at her dream because I wanted her with me?

Angel put a hand on my shoulder. "Don't worry, bud. We'll make sure Ari gets her big break before we leave."

But that's what I was worried about.

"I'll get Noah there, but let's keep it between us. That way if he doesn't like what he hears, she'll never know," I said.

Angel nodded. "I'll tell Markie you're on board. She's been surfing the Internet for a dress. So we'll make sure Ari looks the part."

It felt strange to hear my friend talk about himself and his girlfriend as a "we" unit. It was so unlike the independent loner Angel I knew and respected.

He turned down a street and I realized we were traveling away from home.

"Where are we going?" I asked.

"I gotta pick something up."

His tone was guarded, which was bizarre since there were no secrets between me and Angel. His safety and our friendship depended on it. Before I could get more information out of him, he parked in the lot of a jewelry store.

"What are we doing here?" I asked. I knew the family had ties with this store, but Angel was no longer in the family business. Whatever he was doing had to be personal. "You getting Markie a Christmas present?"

He gave me a sheepish smile. "Maybe?" He seemed nervous as he got out of the Hummer and headed for the store. I followed him, wondering what he was up to.

We entered the jewelry store, and Angel went straight to the lady standing behind the counter and introduced himself. "I have an appointment with the jeweler," he said.

An appointment? Angel had made an appointment and not told me about it.

"Oh, you must be Angel," she gushed. "So nice to meet you. Give me one second and I'll grab Hugh." Then she disappeared into the back.

"What are we doing here?" I asked Angel again.

"Ring shopping," he said, his attention on the jewelry cases.

"Ring shopping?" I choked out. "As in *the* ring?"

Before Angel could answer, a balding man in a suit greeted us, introducing himself as Hugh Bryant. After shaking hands, we followed him to an office where he had a couple dozen engagement rings displayed on the table.

"Based on our conversation, I took the liberty of selecting the rings I believe you'll be interested in. If you don't see what you're looking for, we can go out front and peruse the rest."

Angel thanked him and began examining the inventory. The hint of a smile tugged at his mouth and his fingers tapped against his leg as he drifted from ring to ring.

I stood there, stunned. These were goddamn engagement rings. Angel was preparing to ask a woman he'd known less than two months to marry him. No wonder he hadn't told me. I'd have told him how crazy he was and done my best to talk him out of it. As his best friend, it was my duty to point it out whenever he lost his freakin' mind, which he clearly had. I should have clobbered him over the head and dragged him out of the damn store.

"This one," Angel said, pointing at his selection.

"A wise choice," Hugh said, setting the ring under a microscopic glass and motioning Angel to take a closer look at it. "Bez

Ambar is the designer. This ring has a fancy pink round center diamond with a blaze frame ring of fire. Note the detail on the band and the perfection of the diamond. This particular band is platinum, but if you'd prefer, we can set it in eighteen-karat rose or yellow gold. Other options include a different cut or color center diamond and—"

"No. It's perfect just like this."

Hugh nodded. "I agree. The round setting paired with the delicate band gives it an elegant feel with the perfect amount of old-fashioned appeal."

"What do you think, Bones?" Angel asked.

I thought he was out of his ever-lovin' mind, but Angel was my boss, as well as my friend. No way would I dress him down in front of an outsider. That was a good way to wind up dead. Instead, I leaned in and studied the ring, giving a low whistle at its beauty.

"Markie will love it. Hell, any girl who's breathing will love it, Angel."

The look of relief on his face made me glad I'd swallowed back my initial response. He beamed a smile at Hugh and confirmed his decision.

"Great," Hugh said, slapping his hands together. I couldn't blame the guy. Based on the rock size, Hugh was no doubt making a killing on this sale. "We just need her ring size and—"

"Crap," Angel replied. "How do I get that?"

Hugh opened his desk drawer and pulled out a chain looped with little brass circles. "Take this. You can measure it against any ring she wears on that finger now, or if she's a heavy sleeper… Do you know when you plan to pop the question?"

Angel shook his head. "I have a couple ideas, but nothing for sure yet."

"Well, we can always size the ring afterward."

Hugh answered a few more questions for Angel before sending us on our way. I waited until we were back in the Hummer before assaulting my friend with my own questions.

"You're gonna propose? Angel—"

He held up a hand. "I know what you're gonna say, Bones. I haven't known her long enough and I should wait, and all the other crap I've been telling myself. But I don't want to wait.

Markie's tumor made me realize how uncertain our lives are. Who knows how much time we have left? Why wait to commit myself to the woman I love?"

"I get that, but—"

"No, you don't. I'm sorry man, but there's no way you could understand what last month was like for me. I didn't even think women like Markie existed, but then here she was. She didn't give a crap about the money or the power. She loved me and saw things in me I couldn't show anyone else. She risked her life to keep the twins safe, and then she was in a coma." His mouth twisted with the memory. "I was holding her hand, waiting by her hospital bed, wondering if she'd ever wake up. You don't know what that's like, and I hope you never do. I wouldn't wish that shit on anyone."

I nodded.

"And now… they got rid of the cancer, but there's no guarantee it won't come back. The only guarantee we have is right now, and I want to spend every possible moment of right now with her. I can't wait to see her walking down the aisle, dressed in a long, white gown. I want my ring on her finger, and my child growing inside her. Every experience… I want to have with her. I know it sounds crazy, but I need your support on this. I need you to have my back."

Now how could I refuse a request like that? Besides, Angel was the smartest guy I knew, and I'd never seen him act impulsively in any relationship but this one. Maybe Markie was the one, if there even was such a thing. Maybe they'd do what fifty percent of married couples couldn't do and actually make it work. Regardless, my friend had made up his mind and needed my support, not my pessimism.

"You got it, bro."

The worry etched into Angel's face morphed into a relieved smile. "Thank you. That means a lot to me. Now, as my best man, I need your help to figure out how to get Markie's ring size."

"Best man, huh?"

"Well, yeah."

I couldn't resist the chance to screw with him. "Aren't you getting a little ahead of yourself? What if you offer her that expensive rock in there and she shoots you down cold?"

He stared at me a second before shaking his head, chuckling. "You're an asshole, you know that?"

"I believe the title is 'Best Asshole.'"

Still chuckling, he started up the engine. "She wouldn't say no, would she?"

Now it was my turn to laugh. "For a genius, you can be pretty stupid sometimes. Hell, Angel, if you offered me a ring like that, I'd be tempted to marry you. She'll say yes, all right. And then you'll have some big-ass wedding that costs more than the average person makes in ten years and she'll start popping out little humanitarian-genius children who will make me want to puke. I'll have to teach 'em a thing or two."

"Great. Stay away from my kids, Bones."

"Uncle Bones. Uncle Bones, Best Asshole. That has a nice ring to it, don't you think?"

I was still worried for Angel, but who was I to keep him from being happy? Even if he wanted to marry some chick he'd only known for less than two months. Hell, I might even help him.

"You can't give it to her for Christmas," I said.

"Why not?"

"Because that's pretty cheap. Like trying to get points for two occasions with one present." I shook my head. "You're better than that, Angel."

He chuckled. "Okay, smartass, what the hell do I get her for Christmas?"

I shrugged. "You're the one with sisters."

"And somehow, I don't think they'd like the same gifts. What are you getting Ari?"

"I have to get Ari something?" I asked. I always sent Ma something, and gave my little brother cash, but there was nobody else I'd ever felt the need to get a Christmas present for.

"Bones, I've seen the way you look at her. Get her a damn present."

There was no denying my attraction to her. Sure, Ariana was fine, but there was so much more than her appearance. "She's a cool broad and all, but you know how things are. I can't…"

Angel knew how the family worked, so I didn't need to say more. He nodded.

"Well, when we get out of here..." He let the promise hang in the air.

"Yeah." I refused to voice the giant "ifs" that inevitably followed.

If I managed to find Matt. *If* Carlo decided to let me go. *If* Ariana came with us.

Before heading home, Angel and I did a little Christmas shopping, while I kept one eye open, watching for Matt.

CHAPTER NINE

Bones

LIGHTS OFF, EVERYONE else in bed, I sat on the couch and struggled to wrap my mind around the idea of Angel getting married. Since he was the son of the Las Vegas *Capo di capi*, or boss of bosses, I'd always expected my friend to be forced into a political marriage. That's the way things were done in the family. Only Angel had broken the mold somehow, and now he'd be able to make his own life decisions. The family couldn't be happy about that, and I wondered what their retribution would be. I was still puzzling out the situation when Ariana ventured into the kitchen to pour herself some water. The clock on the wall told me it was well past midnight.

"The sandman hasn't visited you yet either, huh?" I asked, sitting up.

She let out a little squeak and fumbled her cup, barely catching it before it hit the granite countertop. "Dammit, Bones."

"Sorry. Didn't mean to startle you." I did, though. It was fun.

She filled a second glass, carried them both in, and sat beside me on the sofa. "The sandman's a hater, but he's not the one keeping me up tonight." She offered me the second glass.

Wondering what she meant, I thanked her. Before I could take a sip, she clinked her glass to mine.

"To the stupid decisions that keep us up all night. May they go straight to hell." She downed her water and set her glass on the coffee table before sagging back into the couch.

"What'd you do?" I asked.

She turned her head and considered me for a moment. I watched her as I sipped, trying to look as trustworthy and non-threatening as possible. I got people to open up all the time, but usually I had a baseball bat or a gun in my hand. I'd never tried this method before, but I really did want to understand what was bothering Ariana. Turns out I'm not so good at looking trustworthy and non-threatening, because she turned away and crossed her arms.

"Doesn't matter. It was a long time ago."

"But it still keeps you up?" Meant she had quite the conscience. I filed that bit of interesting information away.

"Are you trying to psychoanalyze me?" she asked.

I shrugged. "Just trying to understand you."

She laughed. "Good luck with that one. Let me know if you figure anything out."

"It would help if you told me more about yourself," I replied.

"Says the man with more secrets than an international spy." Then she huffed and turned to look at me again. "Fine, I'll play. What do you want to know?"

I really wanted to know what was bothering her, but that topic seemed off limits, at least for now. Sticking to a safer subject, I asked, "Why Vegas?"

Her brow scrunched up.

"If you want to start up a music career, there are lots of better choices. New York, Nashville, L.A. I looked up the best places for aspiring musicians online and Vegas didn't even make the list."

"You looked it up?"

After my conversation with Angel, I wanted to know what it took to get discovered in Las Vegas, so yeah, I looked it up. But I couldn't exactly admit any of that to Ariana without disclosing our plans for her birthday. "Yeah, I was curious."

Something in her expression shifted. She tilted her head slightly and asked, "Why?"

This was not at all how I'd imagined this conversation going. I was trying to find out more about Ariana, but somehow she'd turned it around on me. Anything I said would either make me sound like a stalker or clue her into our plans for her birthday. I took another drink, buying enough time to help me realize how to cover this up.

"Because my boss is dating your sister and your story didn't make sense. Came to Vegas to start a singing career? Why?"

Ariana frowned. I got the feeling she was disappointed, but she shrugged it off and grinned. "I don't know. Maybe because I figured I'd have a profession to fall back on here, in case the whole singing thing doesn't work out."

I arched my eyebrows in question.

"Hookers make great money."

"Ari—"

"What, you wouldn't pay to touch this bod?" She ran a hand down her side, drawing my attention to her curves.

Killing me. "Stop."

"Okay, okay, I'm only kidding. Mostly. I don't know why I chose Vegas. Maybe because my mom hated this city and some twisted little part of me expected her to jump out of the grave and stop me from coming here."

She looked so frail and vulnerable for a moment, I wanted to wrap her in my arms and reassure her everything would be okay. But before I could move, she grinned again. "But for real, hookers do make great money."

The next morning I was awakened by the sound of the door opening. I reached for my gun on the coffee table and sprang to my feet, instantly alert. No one was there. I crept to the door and peered out the peephole in time to see Ariana turn the corner wearing gym clothes, with her bag slung over her shoulder. She was going to work out, and she hadn't woken me and asked me to join her. Wondering why, I pulled on a pair of sweats, grabbed my gym bag, and headed out the door. On the way to the elevator my phone buzzed with an incoming text from Tech. Renzo was on his way to pick me up and would meet me outside the building in ten minutes. I swore and headed back into the apartment to dress.

Since Angel and Markie were still asleep, I suited up quietly and took my gym bag with me. If the hit was quick, I would still have time to join Ariana before she was done with her workout. Once I was in the elevator, I messaged Angel to let him know Ariana was in the gym and I was going out on a job with Renzo.

Like most of the family, Renzo drove a black SUV with tinted windows and safety features you couldn't find in any off-the-lot vehicle. It idled in front of the complex doors, kicking out exhaust into the crisp morning. He had one of his security guards—a guy by the name of Paul O'Brian—in the passenger's seat, so I climbed in the back and buckled up. Renzo didn't even look at me when I said hello, which was unusual. He was Angel's cousin, and there was some sort of beef between the two of them, but Renzo had always been cool with me. Wondering what the hell was going on, I kept my mouth shut and my eyes on the men in the front seat.

"What's in the bag?" Paul asked.

I patted it. "Workout clothes. Gonna hit the gym when I get back."

"Search it," Renzo ordered.

In our line of work, you were either paranoid or dead. Trust was an expensive commodity and the richer and more powerful you were, the less you could afford it. I wouldn't expect Renzo to trust me any more than he'd expect me to trust him. He outranked me, though, so I obligingly handed my bag to Paul, who rifled through it.

"Clean," Paul said, tossing my bag back to me.

We drove the rest of the way in silence and parked behind a small restaurant not far from the strip. Renzo climbed out of the SUV, leaving his guard behind, and waited at the curb. Taking his silent stare as my cue to join him, I left my bag in the seat and we headed for the restaurant. Paul remained in the vehicle, also weird since the Marianis never went anywhere without their guards. I spared one more glance toward the SUV, but Paul was staring out the windshield and didn't even look my direction.

Confused, I hurried my steps and caught up to Renzo, who thumbed something into his phone as we walked. Then he said,

"Jimmy's alone in a booth on the northwest corner." His tone was angry and his words were clipped. "He's angled himself so he can see all entrances, but I just sent him a distraction."

"Got it." I clutched the gun in my jacket pocket. "Warn or whack?"

"How about you just stand there with your thumb up your ass while I handle it?"

Venom dripped from Renzo's words. I wanted to find out why, but there wasn't time. He opened the unlocked back door of the restaurant and we filed in. I kept my hand on the gun in my pocket as we passed through a dirty kitchen that smelled of pancakes, bacon, and sausage. The dining room shades were drawn against the rising sun. The muted light made it easy to find the booth in the northwest corner. A waitress stood with her back to us, coffeepot in hand, partially blocking a man wearing a blue cap with an alien on it. Jimmy—whoever he was—appeared to be a minor-league baseball fan. I couldn't see anything below the cap, which meant our target couldn't see us, either.

The booths on either side of Jimmy's were empty. Diner traffic this early was low, but there were still enough patrons to provide a possible witness. Wondering how Renzo planned to play this out, I followed as he slid into the seat across the table from Jimmy and leveled a gun at him. The waitress excused herself and I took her spot, standing to block the view of onlookers. Jimmy was in the middle of taking a bite of his waffle. He stiffened and the color drained from his face. Then he slowly lowered the fork back to his plate and faked a smile.

"Renzo. Hey man, I've been looking for you. My phone broke and I—"

"Cut the shit, Jimmy," Renzo said, gesturing at the phone on the table. "I tracked you through that piece of shit, dumbass. Thought you'd never leave the house. I'm glad you did so I didn't have to go in there after you."

Renzo filched a piece of bacon from Jimmy's plate and stuffed it in his mouth. "Goddammit, I can't believe you put me in this position," he said around bites. "Of all the low-life, scum-sucking, bottom-feeding bastards out there, she had to choose you."

Sweat beaded across Jimmy's forehead. "You gotta listen to me," he pleaded. "I… I made a bad bet, but I'm workin' my ass off to get the money, I promise. I'd have it for you now, but Ellie has to get braces and my insurance doesn't—"

"Shut the hell up," Renzo snapped. He shoved the last bite of bacon into his mouth and then wiped his hands on a napkin. "Stop using my niece as an excuse to be a douchebag."

What? His niece? Jimmy had to be Isobel's husband, and therefore Renzo's brother-in-law. I swore under my breath as all the pieces clicked together. No wonder Renzo was pissed. My presence was a show of disrespect, a slap across his face. Carlo had sent me as a sign that he didn't trust Renzo to whack his sister's husband.

Damn.

I'd worked so hard to make sure nobody saw me as a threat, but in one foul swoop, Carlo had undone all my work. Renzo was pissed, but he couldn't take it out on Carlo. Carlo was disciplining Renzo and putting me in my place. After this hit, I'd be at Renzo's mercy… and Renzo didn't have any mercy.

"If Ellie needed braces, you should have made wiser bets," Renzo said between gritted teeth. "I told Isobel not to marry you. I can't believe I let her talk me into throwing you some business. You got my ass called to the carpet, and now I have to deal with you. You left me no goddamn choice."

Jimmy's eyes practically bugged out of his head. It would have been comical if the situation weren't so deadly. "You c-c-can't d-d-do this. Isobel will n-n-never forgive you."

Renzo calmly slid his gun back into his pocket and pulled on a pair of gloves. When he was finished, he leveled his weapon back at Jimmy, and said, "Get me his piece, Bones."

Taking my cue from Renzo, I released the grip on my Glock to pull on gloves before reaching into Jimmy's jacket pocket and relieving him of his Beretta 92, which I then passed to Renzo.

"Now pick up your phone and text my sister. Tell her you screwed up and you're sorry. Tell her you can't live with the guilt anymore."

Jimmy's eyes went wide. "N-no."

"Think, Jimmy. Don't make this harder than necessary. I can still protect her and Ellie, but I can't protect you. Pick up the damn phone."

Hands shaking, Jimmy did as he was told. His fingers flew over the face of the screen as he composed the message.

"Show it to me," Renzo demanded.

Jimmy held up the phone. Renzo scanned the screen and nodded. "Send it."

Jimmy hit the send key and showed Renzo again.

"Ren, it doesn't have to be this way. You know I'm good for it. Just give me a little more time."

Renzo didn't reply. His eyes were hard when he looked at me—the witness sent by the family to make sure he did the deed—then turned back to his brother-in-law. "You know I don't make the rules, and mercy isn't mine to give." He pulled out his own phone and thumbed a message.

"No, Ren, don't do this." Jimmy turned from Renzo to me, searching for hope.

I had none to give him.

The building's fire alarm pealed, deafening in its steady screech. Renzo tensed. Ignoring our booth, waitresses herded diners toward the exits.

Renzo scooted around to Jimmy's side of the booth. He grabbed Jimmy's hand and positioned it on the Beretta, raising it to Jimmy's temple. Jimmy struggled, but Renzo quickly overpowered him and squeezed the trigger. Jimmy's body jerked. Blood and tissue coated the wall behind him. I stared at the body, knowing I should feel something at the loss of life, but I didn't. Not even a flicker of remorse. Jimmy's gun fell to the seat. Renzo pushed past me and walked back toward the way we'd entered.

Behind us, Jimmy's cell phone rang, the happy tune competing with the high-pitched squeal of the fire alarm. It was probably Isobel, freaking out about Jimmy's text.

By the time we reached the kitchen, the staff had been evacuated. No witnesses. Even had they seen us, no local would be stupid enough to testify. Not in this city. Not unless they wanted to end up just like Jimmy. We escaped through the back door. In the chaos, nobody noticed two wiseguys slinking out of the supposedly burning building. That was nothing out of the ordinary for Vegas.

We made it back to Renzo's SUV before his phone buzzed. He took the call and put it up to his ear. "Hey Izzy, you're up early. Everything okay?"

As Renzo assured his sister he'd find Jimmy and make sure he didn't do anything stupid, I watched the restaurant where Jimmy sat with a hole in his head disappear behind us. The world we lived in was beyond screwed up, and I was thankful Angel was getting out, even if I wouldn't be able to join him.

Much to my surprise, Renzo didn't turn his gun on me. Instead, he dumped me off right where he'd picked me up. I had to admire Carlo's play, knowing even though Renzo had let me go today, he was too prideful to forgive me for what I'd seen. As a made man, Renzo could ice me with very little—if any—retaliation. Unless, of course, I took Carlo's offer and let him turn me into a family man. Then I'd be protected. I'd also be stuck in Vegas and unable to leave with Angel.

I had no good options, and as I watched Renzo pull away, I felt like someone else had eyes on me. Alarmed, I gripped the gun in my pocket and scanned the area. I didn't see anyone, so I slipped inside to get the hell out of the open.

CHAPTER TEN

Ariana

SLEEP AND I had never been on great terms, but our relationship seemed to be getting worse the older I got. When I was with Matt, he'd give me something to knock me out, but Halloween had scared the crap out of me and I hadn't touched so much as a Tylenol since. Exhausted, I stared at the clock on the nightstand, calculating how much sleep I could still get if I miraculously passed out.

Determined to get in at least a few winks, I closed my eyes and attempted to clear my mind. Markie's steady breathing kind of irritated me. I couldn't understand my sister at all. Her boyfriend slept on the other side of the living room and she was here in the bed with me. If I had a guy like Angel—or any guy at all for that matter—I'd be in there wrapped in his arms, doing whatever it took to get rid of this hollow feeling inside me. But Markie didn't seem to crave affection the same way I did, making me wonder what was wrong with me.

Why did I constantly crave to be touched and loved?

My thoughts drifted back to my conversation with Bones. Why had I chosen Vegas? Deep down I knew my chances of making it as a singer were few and far between. But what better place was there for playing the odds? So yeah, I was gambling with my future. Not like I had anything to lose, though. Everything I'd ever had was long gone.

My eyes sprang open again. The clock on the nightstand read 6:12 a.m. Christmas was almost upon us and I still hadn't figured out a gift for Bones. I wanted to get him something special, but didn't want to seem desperate. Cologne? No. I loved the way he smelled and did not want to mess with that. A watch? No way could I afford the type of timepiece a man like Bones would wear. A tie? Too dad-ish. Nothing seemed right.

Frustrated, I threw back my covers. Screw sleep. I didn't need it anyway. What I needed was more time with the punching bag to help me focus. Wondering if there was some sort of workout gear I could get him, I slipped out of bed, pulled on my gym clothes, and crept to the door. Bones was sleeping peacefully for once and I didn't want to wake him, so I slipped out the door as quietly as I could.

About an hour and a half later, I was finished with my workout and still clueless as to what to get Bones. I headed for the elevator and found him standing in the lobby wearing one of his sexy suits with his hand in his coat pocket. Since I wasn't stupid, I knew he kept a gun in that pocket. And like a little kid with a security blanket, his hand was on it every time he left the condo.

Bones's posture was rigid, his lips tight, contrasting the gym bag slung over his shoulder. He faced the front doors of the building, watching something. Curious, I followed his gaze to what appeared to be a typical dry, sunny December morning. Nothing to be all tense about.

"Hey Bones, you okay?" I asked.

He glanced at me before returning his gaze to the lobby doors. "Yeah. Was just on my way to work out with you."

"So you dressed up first?" I asked, gesturing at his designer threads.

"Had to take care of some business first." The way he continued to stare at the door told me it must have been some business.

"Oh. Everything okay?" I asked.

"For now."

When he still didn't move I asked, "So, you heading up? Or are you just going to stand here all day?"

That finally got his attention. His gaze turned on me, taking in my sweaty gym clothes before saying, "I need to hit the gym. You're all done?"

He sounded disappointed, and I didn't want to leave him alone. "Actually… you feel like going for a swim?"

"A swim?" he asked.

"Yeah. You know, with the water and the strokes." I flailed my arms around like I was swimming. Although the complex had a pool, Bones and I had never used it. I wasn't sure he even knew how to swim.

His lips quirked up in a sexy half-smile that made my heart race. "Yeah. A swim sounds good." He cast one last look at the main doors before draping an arm over my shoulders and leading me back toward the gym.

Bones smelled amazing. I leaned into him, inhaling the fresh, clean scent of his body wash mixed with gun oil. I could have stayed under his arm forever, but he shooed me into the women's locker room and headed for the men's. By the time I slipped into my bikini and re-emerged, Bones was already swimming laps. We were the only two people in the pool room, so I stood back and watched the way his powerful strokes ate up the distance from one side of the pool to the next. His trunks hung low on his hips, teasing me with every stroke. For one brief, insane moment I considered getting him a Speedo for Christmas.

Because nothing says platonic like a banana hammock. Ohmigod, get a grip, Ari.

No one looked good in a Speedo. No one. Yet there I was, fantasizing about Franco "Bones" Leone, beautiful specimen of man… Franco. A freakin' sexy name, too. One I could definitely wrap my tongue around… or my legs. And I definitely would the second I had the opportunity. Although, sex had ruined the best of my relationships, and I couldn't afford to lose Bones just because he had a hot body. His hot body chose that very moment to crest the water, and I was caught drooling over him like some sort of pervert. His gaze raked over my body before he cracked another of his sexy, lopsided smirks.

"Did you invite me here just to look at me, or are you gonna jump in and swim?"

Heat shot up my face, and to other parts of my body. I closed my mouth, hoping there was no saliva running down my chin, and dove in.

The water cooled me down immediately. Without giving Bones another glance, I swam until my limbs felt like they were going to fall off. When I couldn't go a single lap further, I headed for the hot tub. Turning my back to the pool so I wouldn't be tempted to gawk at Bones, I closed my eyes and slunk down until the water came to my chin. The jets drowned out the noise of my reality and pounded away at my sore muscles. It was heaven. It lasted all of five minutes. Then the water level rose, covering my mouth and going up my nose to almost drown me. I flailed and coughed, trying to recover.

"Sorry," Bones said, smiling sheepishly. "Most people have a little body fat, so they rise with the water level."

Sometimes he said the sweetest things without even meaning to.

"Aww, thanks."

I resettled and watched droplets of water roll down Bones's chest. It was the first time I'd seen him bare-chested close up, and *da-aamn*, the boy was stacked. Besides the very impressive muscles, though, several scars marked up his pecks and abs. I remembered what he'd said about coming home bleeding from training and his mom not saying anything, but just fixing him up. I nodded toward the marks and asked, "Those the scars from your training?"

"Some." He sank up to his neck, obstructing my view. "Guys have scars. It's a thing."

"Sure they do. Must have been *some* training." I'd seen knife scars before, and Bones definitely had a couple of them. And the sloppy circle on his left shoulder had to be a bullet wound. No way that was from training.

"So…" Bones started, leading into an obvious subject change. "I hear you have a birthday coming up."

I winced at the reminder of my upcoming twenty-first birthday. Old enough to drink and too old to be chasing a dead dream. I could almost hear the clock ticking toward my mid-twenties, and then thirties. When would I be too old to be discovered at all? Uncle Jay used to call my singing "a nice little hobby." Man, I wanted to prove that windbag wrong and show him I could make a career out of it, but after a year in Vegas I was still just waiting tables.

"Ari?"

I shook myself. "Yep."

He chuckled. "What? It's the big twenty-one. You should be at least a little excited."

"Yay me," I deadpanned. Twenty-one, crappy job, always broke, living in my sister's boyfriend's condo, no car, no education; life wasn't exactly turning out the way I'd hoped. I should have listened to my uncle and gone to school. I shouldn't have blown all my money moving to Vegas and renting—and furnishing—the fanciest apartment I could find. I shouldn't have given a cent to Matt. I should have researched him and asked for references. The drugs were also a big mistake. Oh, and all those expensive outfits I bought didn't do a thing for getting me noticed. They just emptied the last of my bank account. Now here I was, washed up before I'd even started.

Boo-hoo. Cry me a freakin' river, Ari. You've got no one to blame but yourself. Idiot.

"You're not the least bit pumped about drinking legally?"

"Nah. Kinda takes the fun out of it for me. It's not like I like the flavor or anything."

He chuckled. It was nice to see him relax after whatever had gone down with his job this morning. Deciding to mess with him, I batted my eyelashes.

"Why do you look so disappointed, Bones? You thinking about getting me drunk and taking advantage of me?"

He stiffened. "Sorry, Ari, but I'm not that kind of guy."

"Don't get your panties in a wad, I know you're the boring definition of a gentleman."

"I wouldn't go that far."

Bones was like a trained bear in this circus called life. He was friendly and knew all the right tricks, but there was something feral and dangerous lurking beneath his skin. The suicidal part of me wanted to taunt him until he lost his cool and showed me the beast within. I wanted to poke him until he broke free and mauled me. Probably not my smartest move, but I leaned forward and said, "Yeah? Prove it."

Then I made the dirtiest play I could think of and stood up. Water cascaded down my bikini-clad body, forcing Bones's attention on my bare stomach, which was right in his face. His eyes widened, and I got the briefest glimpse of his beast. Then he dropped his gaze and looked away.

"Chicken," I said, slumping back down into the water.

"I'm not a nice guy, Ari. I know you're just teasing, but you don't want to do that with guys like me."

"Who said I was teasing?" Frustrated, I crossed my arms and glared at him.

"Come on, don't be like that." He nudged me with a toe. "Talk to me like you did last night. Tell me something about yourself."

"I hate the color pink," I replied. It was the least personal response I could think of.

He cocked his head. "Not what I meant. Tell me something important. Something you've never told anyone else."

"Truth or dare?" I asked.

"But without the dare. I have a feeling you'd beat me every round."

"No fun," I pouted. "Fine, but you go first."

"Okay." Bones looked around the room. I followed his gaze to the two camera bubbles. Whatever he was about to confide, he didn't want overheard. My interest piqued when he turned up the jets on the tub and slid over so the side of his body was pressed against mine. His proximity definitely felt more like a dare than truth. My pulse sped up as he leaned into me, positioning himself to whisper in my ear. Hot breath on my neck made goosebumps sprout across my arms. If he was about to admit he had a thing for me, I could not be responsible for what I did to him in that hot tub. Or what I allowed him to do to me. To hell with the cameras pointed at us.

"I'm sick of watching people die," he whispered.

Talk about killing the mood… Still, curiosity made me seek out his expression. He looked upset—haunted. "What, like family members?" Was he talking about cancer? Trying to relate to me about Markie?

He shook his head.

I searched his face, but it gave me no more answers.

"Your turn."

It felt kind of unfair since he was being all mysterious and elusive, but two could play that game. "Being around Markie makes me feel like a horrible human being."

"That doesn't count. Your sister's not normal. She'd make the Pope step up his game."

I giggled. "Yes she would, but it still counts."

"Give me something else. Did you do something in particular that you feel guilty about?" Bones asked.

His question was a little too on point for my comfort. I raised my chin and looked him in the eye. "Your turn."

He flashed me that heart-stealing crooked smile again. I sucked in another steadying breath as he returned to my ear.

"I've never taken a girl to meet my mom before."

I burst out laughing.

"You can't laugh at my confession!" he said, sounding scandalized.

"I'm not a priest. Not only can I laugh, but I can judge you, and you are so being judged right now. Why haven't you ever brought a girl home, Bones?" My gaze drifted over his body before returning to his face. Lowering my voice, I said, "That body, that smile… I'm sure they were all over you."

His eyebrows rose.

I raised mine in response, challenging.

His leg rubbed against mine, sending little sparks of electricity across my skin. I sucked in a breath and watched him, wondering if he had any idea what he was doing to me. Did he feel this too, or was he just screwing with me?

He grinned. "Your turn."

He was definitely screwing with me. I turned on him, flustered and frustrated. "That so doesn't count. Your mom already told me you never brought girls home."

"Yeah. Dinner with her and her… whatever the hell he is, will be interesting for sure."

I nodded, unsure of how I would react the next time I saw Marcella, now that I knew the truth about her. "Quit trying to change the subject. That still doesn't count. Tell me another one."

"It does count. The rules were something you've never told anyone, and that's something I would never admit aloud."

So he'd never taken a girl home to meet his mom. Did that mean he'd never dated? Slept with a girl? He was twenty-three with a smoking-hot body; no way was he a virgin, but there was something surprisingly innocent about him under his hard-ass exterior. Just thinking about it was setting my body on fire.

"Your face is turning red," Bones observed.

I gave him my best innocent face. "It's warm in here."

He eyed me, no doubt seeing through the lie. "Your turn," he repeated.

Because I needed to show him I could play his game, I dug down deep, searching for something obvious that I'd never say. "I'm afraid of being a big, fat failure."

He eyed me skeptically. "Doesn't count."

"What?" I scoffed. "Why not?"

"Everyone's afraid of failure."

"I've never told anyone." What I didn't tell him was that I was also afraid of success. If I started pulling in decent paychecks, would I use again? Would I be able to get high enough to feel free? Or would the pressure to perform be too much for me to take? Could I handle the critics? I'd read bad reviews and tried to decide how they'd affect me. The outcome was never good. Would the secrets from my past—the reason my uncle hated me—come back to haunt me? Would Markie find out and turn her back on me too? I honestly didn't know if I could deal with any of the possibilities, and my uncertainty scared the crap out of me. I didn't want to become just another drug addicted cliché of an artist. "Your turn."

His expression darkened. Then he leaned into my personal space—creating goosebumps on top of goosebumps—and whispered, "I don't want to get stuck in this city."

My brow furrowed. People didn't get "stuck" in cities. They got stuck in podunk little towns like the one in Idaho I'd fled from. Vegas was full of life and opportunities. I was about to tell him as much when the door opened and a guy in his trunks entered the room. Bones was still pressed against me, his breath still warm on the side of my face. He shifted, and his lips brushed my neck before he stood. He'd kissed me! Kind of. The whole thing had happened so fast, I really wasn't sure. Well, except for the tingling happening throughout my body.

"What about you, Ari?" he whispered, offering me his hand. "When we leave, will you come with us?"

Thinking about Vegas, about my failing dream, about my upcoming birthday, about the sweet, funny, hot-as-hell man asking me to follow him, I nodded. "Yeah. If you want me to come, I will."

He pulled me to my feet and helped me out of the hot tub. Then he released me and headed toward the men's locker room. Instantly missing the contact, I went to change, trying to figure out what had just happened between us.

CHAPTER ELEVEN

Bones

IT HAD BEEN two days since I lost my mind and kissed Ariana. It wasn't even a kiss, really. I barely brushed my lips against her neck before my brain kicked into gear and asked what the hell I was doing. The only problem was that now I couldn't stop fantasizing about doing it again. Her neck, her lips, her cheeks, her eyelids, her forehead, down her arms, her fingertips, I wanted to kiss every inch of her, and the desire was driving me crazy.

Ariana was a good friend and I wanted to keep it that way, which meant keeping my hands—and my lips—off her before things got awkward. Besides, Renzo was pissed at me, Carlo wasn't exactly happy, and I refused to turn Ariana into a liability either of them could use against me. I was in the middle of trying to remind myself of all of these great points when she emerged from my bedroom looking like a magazine cover model. A long-sleeved fitted black suit jacket hinted at cleavage and hugged her torso before turning into a pleated skirt that came just above her knees. Red high heels did amazing things to her legs and ass while elevating her slightly above my six-foot height. Between the outfit and the soft curls she'd added to her chin-length hair, she looked classy as hell. Her neck was bare, calling for my lips once again. I'd never been a neck guy before, but something about Ariana turned me into a goddamn vampire.

"You look stunning!" Markie exclaimed.

"Yeah, you do." When Angel looked at me, amusement flickered across his face. "I hope Bones is taking you somewhere nice."

Ariana ducked her head, brushing off the compliments. "I don't actually know where we're going." She cut her gaze to me. "But I knew Bones would be in a suit, so at least I won't be the only one overdressed."

Angel laughed.

Keeping my hands off her was going to be a bigger challenge than I'd thought. "Yeah, but nothing can compete with that outfit. You look beautiful, Ari. You ready to head out?"

She nodded and slipped her hand in mine. I set it in the crook of my elbow and headed for the door.

"You kids have fun," Markie said.

"Have her home by midnight," Angel added.

"Ha-ha," Ariana replied, giving the two of them a finger wave as we left.

Mom texted me the address of the restaurant, but I wasn't familiar with the area. I plugged it into my GPS and headed into the wrong part of town. My stomach sank as I parked and eyed our destination.

"So, yeah, we may have overdressed a little," Ariana said, studying the diner.

I chuckled. "A little? It's not too late, you know. We can always blow this off and go somewhere nice."

She put a hand on my arm, forcing me to look at her. "Bones, I get that your mom wasn't the greatest, but she's reaching out to you. You're gonna be getting out of this city soon, and who knows when you'll see her next? Don't you want to go in there and make sure the guy she's with isn't some psycho killer?"

Ariana was trying to play to both my sense of duty and my need to protect, but she didn't understand how deep these characteristics were ingrained in me. If Carlo let me leave Vegas, I'd still find a way to look after Ma. Angel and I had run a full background check on Totino Raul Salone the night I found out Ma was dating him, and if he hadn't checked out okay I would have already handled the problem. Still, the concern Ariana showed made me want to wrap my arms around her and take her far away from the situation.

"You're right," I said. "But I'm still not eating here."

She started to argue, but instead of listening to what she had to say I got out of the Hummer and went around to open her door.

"But… we're staying?" she asked, unbuckling her seatbelt.

"Yep. We'll go hang out with them for the meal, then I'll take you somewhere good."

A smile stretched across her face as she let me help her down. "Angel's right, you are a foodie."

I snorted. "Angel needs to shut his damn mouth."

Ariana giggled and followed me into the restaurant where we were assaulted by the stench of cheap food, taking me back to a childhood of hunger, where boxed macaroni and cheese, Ramen, and frozen TV dinners were considered a feast. I'd done everything I could to lock those memories away, and I hated the way something as stupid as a smell could bring them back.

"You okay?" Ariana asked, taking my hand to lead me away from the doorway. Then she stopped me and adjusted my tie in a strangely intimate gesture. Something inside of me stirred at the contact. She released my tie and I grabbed her hands. Her gaze sought mine, questioning.

"Thank you for coming," I said. "It means a lot to me that you're here."

Her eyes softened. "There's no place I'd rather be, Bones." She tugged me forward and her lips turned up in a mischievous grin. "Now come on, let's do this. Then you owe me a really amazing dinner. With an expensive bottle of wine."

I chuckled, following her. "You're underage and I'm not buying you wine."

We found Ma and Totino sitting in a window booth. Ma jumped up and kissed my cheeks, obviously surprised I'd actually came, which made me feel like an ass.

"Ari! You look absolutely beautiful, dear." Ma kissed Ariana's cheeks. "Thank you for coming."

"Of course." Ariana hugged her back. "Thanks for inviting me."

Ma introduced us both to Totino. Because of the background check I knew he was divorced with no children, fifty-seven, drove forklift at a manufacturing plant, owned a paid-off five-year-old sedan, and had a mortgage on a modest two-bedroom home on Cline Street. Angel and I had been keeping an eye on him and searching for mob ties, but so far he seemed to be clean. Coming face-to-face with him, only served as confirmation. Totino had a softness about him that you'd never see in a wiseguy. His eyes were kind and his shoulders, relaxed. He had no problem sitting beside the window, and his attention was fixed on Ma, not scanning the room and watching the doors.

Totino and Ma talked and laughed, sharing the story of how they'd met at the grocery store. No matter how long Pops had been gone, it still made me uncomfortable to hear Ma gushing over the way Totino had helped her reach the soap on the top shelf and listening to how she felt the first time he called her. Still, it was nice to see Ma so happy, giggling like a school girl as she made eyes at him.

Totino was attentive and respectful, helping Ma up and getting her dessert for her. They seemed pretty serious, and although I didn't know how long they'd been together, I was hoping he'd stick around. I'd feel a whole lot better about leaving her behind in Vegas if I knew she wouldn't be alone after my little brother moved out.

Ariana held my hand under the table the entire time, reassuring me that I wasn't alone in this either. It surprised me how much comfort I found in her presence, and as the minutes ticked by, they seemed to release the resentment I'd held toward Ma. By the time Ariana and I left, I felt lighter than I had in years.

CHAPTER TWELVE

Bones

I HELD ARIANA'S hand as we crossed the parking lot, heading for the Hummer. "Thanks again for coming."

"Are you kidding me? That was so much fun. They're adorable." She squeezed my hand.

"Adorable. Sure."

"No, I mean it. It's like Angel and Markie but… different."

"Yeah, because they're older and so it's even weirder."

She shoved me. "No, that's not it. It's like… because I know your mom's not perfect, it's encouraging to see her get a second chance."

I pulled out the scanner and checked for devices. "What do you mean?"

"People like Angel and Markie—who are so freaking perfect they border on nauseating—deserve to be happy. It's nice to see someone who's not perfect get a shot at happiness, too."

I didn't know what to say to that, and the Hummer was clear, so I opened the passenger door and helped her up.

By the time I got in, she had the lit visor mirror down and was applying shiny gel to her perfect lips, the sight of which was strangely erotic.

"Now." She finished and flicked up the visor, shrouding us in darkness. "Let's talk about food and wine."

"Food, no wine. There's a decent tapas bar off Paradise Road." I thumbed on my phone, pulled up the website, and handed it to her. "Here's the menu. We can eat there or get it to go and I can take you to my secret hiding place."

"I recognize that you're probably just using this secret hiding place to distract me from alcohol, but I'll bite." She accepted the phone and tapped a finger to her chin. "Tell me more about this place. Are we talking about an evil lair, or more like Bones's Batcave?" Then she bounced in her seat and said, "Oh, are you storing one of those anatomically correct bat-suits there? Because if the answer is yes, I'm definitely in for checking that out."

I shrugged, enjoying the easy banter. "You asking if I'm good or evil?"

"More specifically, I believe I was asking if you wear spandexy-Kevlar, or whatever that suit is made of, because I've seen your chest and you could definitely pull that look off."

And what the hell was I supposed to say to that? In a matter of minutes, Ariana had managed to completely change my mood and I couldn't help but appreciate that. If she wanted to flick me shit, I'd flick it right back. "Guess you'll have to find out for yourself."

She raised her gaze to the ceiling and leaned her head back as if struggling with the decision. "Oh, what the hell. Tonight, we live dangerously. Take me to your lair."

Feeling a little lighter, I shifted the Hummer into gear. "Food first."

"Right." Ariana looked down at the phone. "Ohmigod this all looks delicious. Can't we go somewhere where I don't want to try everything on the menu?"

"Nope. That's half the fun."

We drove to the restaurant and ordered a little of almost everything they had to offer before jumping onto Highway 147 and heading east. Ariana turned on the radio and searched stations, settling on a Bruno Mars hit. She cranked up the volume and started singing along. Angel often did the same thing, but he didn't sound anything like Ariana. She harmonized perfectly, each note clear and on key, while she tapped her foot to the beat. I watched her in my peripheral, amazed at her voice and pitch. If this was her goofing off, when she really sang, she'd knock the socks off my buddy Noah as well as anyone else who heard her.

When the song ended, I told her how amazing she sounded.

"Thanks. Are we almost there?"

I laughed. "You suck at taking compliments."

"I know, right? I am *the* worst at it. So, how secret is this place?"

"It's on the map, but I've never taken anyone here."

"Really? Not even Angel?"

"Nope. Not even Angel." Local teens sometimes used it as a make-out spot. Not exactly the type of place I'd take another dude—ever.

As we sped out of the city limits she asked, "You're taking me into the dessert to kill me, aren't you?"

"Not tonight. Didn't bring a shovel."

She looked over her shoulder into the back of the Hummer, seemingly unconvinced. "I bet there's something back there you could work with. Oh, I know, you could use the plastic spoons we got from the restaurant."

I laughed. "We need to talk about your lack of self-preservation."

She shrugged. "What? I'm just trying to be helpful."

I slowed and veered off the highway, down a side road.

She plastered her face against the window to read a sign. Then she craned her head around to check out the area. "Sunrise Mountain, huh?" she asked.

I nodded and kept driving.

After a few minutes, she asked, "Uh… where's the mountain?"

The vehicle was inclining, heading toward the parking area at the top. "Here. We're on it."

"This isn't a mountain. This is a slightly larger hill than all the surrounding hills."

"But for Las Vegas natives, this is as big as it gets."

She crossed her arms and sat back. "Disappointing."

"Ouch," I replied.

She giggled.

I parked the Hummer so we were facing the city.

Despite her previous skepticism, Ariana's eyes widened. "Wow. This is beautiful," she said, taking in the view. Lights stretched for as far as the eye could see. "So peaceful. The city seems so far away, but so close." Her smile shifted into a frown. "Like all the opportunities it represents."

My phone buzzed with an incoming message: a code and a name. Everything in the Mariani empire was coded. Drop off and pickup locations all had codes which changed frequently, and I was horrible at remembering them. The codes for orders, however, never changed. They were beaten into me during my training and I'd never forgotten a single one.

Memories of my training resurfaced. I was eleven years old and Carlo and I were in his Jaguar doing surveillance on a target. The code came across the cell phone the family had given me.

"What does this mean?" I asked Carlo.

"Memorize the code and the name, because the message is about to disappear."

Okay. "But what does it mean?"

"Means Nick Jones is hiding from the family and you gotta bring him in."

I'd met Nick Jones. He was pushing six feet tall and had to weigh over three hundred pounds. He was hiding? How would I find him? How would I take him? I couldn't even drive. "Me?"

Carlo chuckled. "Don't get ahead of yourself, kid. You'll be doing that shit soon enough. Those messages go out to everyone on the family network and the first person who sees him needs to take action. There'll be a nice bonus in it for the guy who gets him."

Wondering if he meant what I thought he meant, I stared up at my mentor. Carlo fashioned his hand into a gun and mocked blowing his brains out. Yep, I nailed it.

He gestured at my phone. "See, Tech has already made the message go poof. Can't risk information getting into the wrong hands."

The message was gone. It was a neat trick, but my curiosity wasn't deterred. "Why would anyone hide from the family?" The Marianis kept my family fed and protected. Sure, Carlo was a tough teacher, and my body had a few new scars, but I'd learned how to fight and how to stay alive. The Marianis had done a hell of a lot more for me than my own family had.

He tapped the steering wheel a few times, and I got the feeling he was trying to put his words into kid-friendly speech. He was trying to dumb it down so I could understand.

"Jones is an enforcer," he finally said. "You remember what I told you about enforcers?"

"They enforce the rules of the borgata, *the family."*

"How?" he asked.

They were big, scary guys who only an idiot would screw with. I'd met a couple of enforcers, and they wouldn't have to lift a finger to keep me in line. "I'm not sure."

He lit a cigarette and sucked in a long drag. Then he asked, "What's the one thing I tell you the most, kid?"

I only had to think about it for a second before answering, "Don't trust anyone."

"Good, you're learning. Yes, don't trust anyone. In our line of work, ninety-nine percent of the people you deal with are gonna be honor-less thugs who'll just as soon stick a knife in your back as look at you. The remaining one percent are idiots. That's the world we live in, kid, so the boss makes rules to keep all these greedy, blood-thirsty bastards in check and to keep the cops off our asses. When someone gets out of line, the boss calls in an enforcer to set 'em straight. You understand?"

"They're like hitmen?" I asked.

Carlo smiled and ruffled my hair. "You're a smart kid."

But something still didn't make sense. "But the enforcer's in trouble?"

"It takes a certain kind of guy to be a hitman. Has to be completely devoted to the family and willing to take out anyone the boss orders him to hit. Anyone. Sometimes he'll take too many jobs... do too many hits... and something inside him snaps. Some go numb, some get off on it. Those are the ones you really gotta watch for. Sick bastards. Before you know it, they're making unauthorized hits, whackin' people in broad daylight, wiping out entire families."

I gaped at him, unable to believe my ears, but he didn't seem to notice.

"When the problem solver becomes the problem, we gotta put 'em down. That's the code the boss sent out just now."

"Everything okay?" Ariana asked, pulling me from the memory.

I nodded and slipped my phone back into my pocket, wondering about Tanner Goss, the enforcer who'd slipped his leash this time. Did he enjoy killing? When Carlo and I had that conversation, the idea of making a hit still made me sick. But when Renzo splattered Jimmy's brains all over the restaurant wall I hadn't felt a twinge of anything for the poor bastard. No remorse, no pity, no guilt, no queasiness—nothing. Would Carlo consider me another "sick bastard" who he needed to watch?

Come on, Bones. Jimmy was a dad and a husband. You should feel something.

Trying to manufacture sympathy for his wife and kids just made me feel numb inside. It was a job, and I'd done what I was supposed to do like I always did. My God, what sort of cold-hearted son-of-a-bitch was I becoming?

"Are *you* okay?" Ariana asked.

Was I? Over the years I'd become a damn good enforcer, which made me a pretty shitty human being. It was the reason I stayed the hell away from relationships. Angel was the only person I knew I wouldn't be able to kill. Well, Angel and Ma. Even after everything she'd put me through, I'd defend her with my life.

"Bones?"

"Yeah, just thinking about life."

If the boss ordered me to take Ariana out, I'd be in trouble. What about Markie? Killing Markie would essentially be like killing Angel. Especially once they were married. Shit. When had I picked up so many liabilities?

"Sounds deep."

She had no idea. Desperate to get out of my own head, I picked up the bags. "I got the food. You wanna get the blanket out of the back?"

"I don't know where you're going with this, but it sounds kinky. I'm in." She grinned and hopped out of the Hummer. When she opened the back, she asked, "And why does Angel keep a blanket in his car?"

"Survival. You never know when you're gonna get stranded somewhere."

Or when you're gonna need to wrap up a body.

"You and Angel stranded?" She laughed. "Is that like having to settle for a three-star hotel?"

If she had any idea of the gear stored in Angel's ride, she'd probably think we were terrorists.

I led her to a flat spot off the road where we laid out the blanket, sat side-by-side, and dished out food. Then halfway through the meal she called me a romantic.

"What the hell did you say to me?" I asked.

"Oh come on. You gotta know this is romantic. You can growl and snarl at me all you want—which, by the way, that's hot—but I know the truth, you big softie."

"I was hungry, you didn't want to go home, this made sense," I defended.

"Right. This is totally what all the other big, buff thugs would do."

"Why do I keep you around again?" I asked.

She leaned against me and the soft, sweet scent of her tickled my senses. "Because I'm charming and witty, and you're trying to get in my pants." She looked down at the piece of clothing currently riding up her thighs and corrected herself. "Er, skirt."

After the past couple of days, I was wound so tight I felt like I'd snap and do something we'd both regret. "I told you, I'm not the kind of man you should tease, Ari."

"And I told you, I'm not teasing. You know, you didn't have to go through all this trouble. You could have just—"

"Why do you do that?" I asked.

"Do what? Hit on you?"

"No." I was pretty sure why she hit on me. She liked to drive me crazy. "Why do you sell yourself short? You act like you're not worthy of anyone's time, money, or effort. Like you think the only thing you have to offer is your body. I don't get it, Ari. Yeah, you're gorgeous, but you're also a damn cool chick. Why do you put yourself down like that?"

Her smile slipped away and she stood with her back to me, facing the lights of the city. Knowing I'd upset her, I gave her a minute alone before I joined her. The night was cool, so I took off my suit jacket and draped it over her shoulders.

"There's a lot you don't know about me, Bones," she whispered.

"What? Your past? You think you're the only one who's done shit you're not proud of? You gotta let that go."

She sighed. "I know." Then she leaned against me again. "Thanks for the jacket. And for bringing me to your secret spot.

And for dinner. I'm still pretty pissed about you not getting us a bottle of wine, though."

"I told you, I don't contribute to minors." I draped an arm over her shoulders.

She reached up and laced her fingers in mine. "Yeah, yeah."

We stood like that for a while, watching the lights of the city as our problems faded to the background. It felt comfortable and peaceful to be with Ariana like this, above the world.

Finally, she tugged on my hand. "We're a lot alike, you know?"

"How's that?"

"Doing what we gotta do to survive. Skatin' the edge. Sometimes I feel like I'm about to fall over."

I nodded, knowing full well what she was talking about.

She turned to face me, tugging me closer until our faces were inches apart. Her eyes were dilated and her breathing was heavy. She held me there, searching my face.

"So let's make a deal," she whispered.

"I'm listening."

"You keep me from falling over my edge, and I'll do the same for you."

Locked in the moment, I stared at her, wondering what to say. Sure, she knew how to calm me down, but if I ever stepped over the edge I wanted her as far from me as possible. And what edge was Ariana teetering over? Drugs? Suicide? Beyond the sarcasm and the jokes there was something broken and hurting inside her. I wanted to put it back together.

Still staring into my eyes, she brushed a kiss against my lips.

Before I could think about what I was doing, my hands wrapped around her waist to pull her closer. Our lips met again, this time with hungry intensity. She moaned, letting me past her teeth. My pulse raced as I pressed her body to mine, feeling every curve of her. I wanted more. I wanted to rip off her clothes and stretch her across that blanket and…

My phone buzzed. The vibration in my pocket slapped me back into reality and, breathing heavily, I pulled away to check it.

What the hell am I doing?

I glanced at the display, expecting it to be someone claiming to have bagged and tagged Goss. Instead, one of my contacts finally had a beat on Matt Deter. The reminder of who and what I was cleared my head. *If* I made it out of this city alive and *if* Ariana came with me, then I'd give in to what we both wanted. But until that day, I needed to focus on keeping us both alive.

Lips plump and wet, eyes hooded, breathing heavily, she asked, "What's wrong?"

"Work calls. I gotta get going."

She didn't say anything—just walked over and started cleaning up the food. I joined her, bagging up the leftovers before folding up the blanket and sticking it all in the Hummer. Then, we were on our way back to the city. Ariana still hadn't said a word.

"I'll drop you off at the condo," I said.

She nodded.

Then I'd go hunt down her ex-boyfriend. Ariana thought she could save me, but I was already dangling over the abyss.

CHAPTER THIRTEEN

Ariana

THURSDAY WAS CHRISTMAS. I was actually sleeping in when Markie woke me at o'dark thirty to exchange presents, which I wasn't particularly looking forward to. Knowing she wouldn't leave me alone until we got it over with, I followed her into the living room and sat beside Bones. Markie—giggling with excitement—turned on Christmas music and handed me a small present.

Bones, bless his heart, passed me a cup of coffee. "You're gonna need this," he said. Then he refilled his own cup from the pot resting on the coffee table. Neither of us knew what to do with what had happened on Sunrise Mountain, which meant I was confused and frustrated, but we were pretending like the whole thing never happened.

Markie nudged my hand on her present. "Open it," she urged. Then she sat on Angel's lap in the recliner, wrapping her arm around his neck and looking the spirit of Christmas joy.

I took a gulp of coffee before eyeing the small package. "You should open mine first," I said, still trying to wake up.

Markie deflated, making me feel like a real bitchy Scrooge. Trying to save face, I stood, walked over to the Christmas tree, retrieved the gift I'd gotten Markie, and tossed it to her. She snatched it out of the air and shook it.

"We'll open them together," I said.

Markie grinned, waiting for me to return to my seat. Then we both went to work opening our gifts. She got me a gorgeous leaf necklace and matching earrings. I got her a sweater I'd seen her eyeballing before she'd gone into the hospital.

We shared a moment of happiness and gratitude before things got awkward. Angel, Bones, Markie, and I all looked from the tree to one another, locked in some twisted game of chicken. Who would be the first one to put their gift out there? What if the other person read too much into it? What if they didn't like it? Man, I hated Christmas.

Markie unwound herself from Angel and headed for the tree. She came back with two gifts, handing Angel his before she sat back down on his lap with hers. Then they looked at me and Bones expectantly.

Right. This was clearly gonna be a group thing. I went to the tree and came back with the remaining two presents. After handing Bones his, I studied the package he'd given me. It was big and light, like a box for a pillow or something.

Finally, curiosity seemed to overcome our fear, and all four of us began tearing paper. I held back, waiting to see the other gifts before opening my own. Angel got Markie adoption certificates. Seriously, he gave her a box of cards with photos and information for what looked like half a dozen African kids they'd be supporting together now. My sister turned into a blubbering mess as she sifted through the pictures before trying to kiss Angel's face off. In return, she'd gotten him some sort of electronic gadget that he raved about.

I looked to Bones. He opened the wrapped box I'd given him and paused, staring inside at the contents. On Christmas Eve and still without a gift for him, I'd panicked and spent way too much money on a gift certificate for a foodie tour for two. The certificate was wrapped around a gun-shaped hair comb I'd also included because it reminded me of him: dark, sleek, well-groomed, and deadly.

He arched an eyebrow, unwinding the gift certificate to reveal the comb. His eyes were laughing when he looked at me.

"What?" I asked. "Come on, that is so you. And the gift certificate… it's for two, but totally not meant for me to go with you."

He read the certificate and cocked his head. "You don't want to come with me?"

"Not what I meant. I just don't want you to feel obligated to take me because I bought it for you. I want you to be able to take whoever you want and..."

He didn't answer. Did not say one damn word.

And I was rambling, trying to fill all the blank space between us. Desperate for a topic change, I ripped the paper off my gift and plunged into the box. It was a beautiful Coach bag.

"I noticed yours is getting worn," Bones explained.

He'd noticed my bag and spent a grip of money to replace it, which was thoughtful, sweet, expensive, and yet somehow still impersonal. A purse? What did a purse mean? It sure wasn't romantic.

"If you don't like it, we can take it back," Bones said. "Get you something else."

"No, it's great. It's perfect." It just didn't tell me a thing about how he felt about me. I'd gotten him something I knew he'd love and hoped he'd share the experience with me, and he got me a freaking purse? "I love it. Thank you."

I was getting ready for work when Markie came into the bathroom, collapsed on the side of the bathtub, and gave me a pathetic sigh.

I rolled my eyes and pulled the straightening iron through my hair. "No."

"Oh, come on. It's one night. Christmas. You can call in and spend one holiday with family, can't you?"

Probably, but there was no way I would. And thankfully, I had an easy out. "I forget, tell me again what happened the first time *you* had dinner with Angel's family," I said.

"That was different," she said, lowering her gaze.

Different didn't even begin to describe it. From what I'd heard, she'd practically been strip-searched for trying to get into Angel's Hummer for her migraine medicine. I didn't need that kind of attention in my life. There was only one suited stud I wanted ripping my clothes off, and he didn't seem to be interested in the task.

"No. This is your mess. You're the one dating the spawn of the big bad wolf."

"And you're my sister. You're supposed to hold my hand and walk with me through the dark and scary mansion."

I cracked a smile. "I'm pretty sure the girl in the red hood is a solo act. One girl. Definitely singular."

"You could play the grandma?" she asked, sounding hopeful.

So what if I couldn't use my years of drama class to get an audition? At least it still provided sound information so I could argue with my sister. I set down the iron and leveled a stare at her. "The grandma gets eaten, remember? No thank you."

She threw her head back dramatically, almost falling into the tub. "Don't make me do this alone."

"I'm not. You'll have Angel and Bones with you. And be careful, would you? I'm pretty sure you're not supposed to be throwing that recently-operated on cranium around like that."

She grunted. "You sound like Angel. I'm fine. Feeling so much better. The headaches are almost gone." She righted herself on the tub and leaned forward, all conspiratorial. "Bones got you such a nice gift."

"Yep."

She frowned. "But you're not happy about it. Why?"

Because I'd gotten him a tour I desperately wanted him to take me along on, and he'd gotten me a purse. And I was overanalyzing the gift and would feel like an idiot if Bones ever found out how much it was messing with me. I was confused and a little hurt, and probably bordering psychotic for feeling that way. I dabbed concealer on my face and lied through my teeth. "I am. It's a good friend gift."

"Friend gift? You think he's friend-zoning you?"

Gah. I'd already told her too much, but now that it was out there, I couldn't take it back. "I know he is."

"Why? What happened?"

The concern in her voice made me feel even more like an idiot for some reason. Trying to play it off as no big deal, I admitted, "He… kinda shut me down."

"What?" Markie asked.

"No details. I don't wanna talk about it."

"But… but… I'm sure it's not you, Ari. His job is—"

"Complicated. I know. I get it. And we're cool."

She eyed me.

"Don't look at me like that. It's fine. We're all good. Still going to the gym every day. Best buds." I forced a smile.

Although we hadn't spoken about what happened on Sunrise Mountain, Bones had plenty of other things to say to me, like "Raise your hands," "Protect your face," and my personal favorite, "Don't drop your shoulder." He seemed obsessed with making sure I could defend myself. We'd graduated from the punching bag, and he was now letting me take swings at him. I had yet to make contact, but sometimes I really wanted to. Finished with my makeup, I stuffed it into my new bag and turned to face Markie. "I have to get to work."

Her face scrunched up and she looked at her phone. "But Angel and Bones aren't back yet and you have plenty of time."

I shouldered the Coach bag I was trying really hard not to hate. The purse was beautiful, but every time I looked at it I couldn't help but wish it was something else, something more personal or meaningful. I wanted something that shouted Bones's everlasting love for me, or even something that told me to go jump in a lake because he wasn't interested. I just needed to know where I stood with the guy.

"Not if I plan on taking the bus."

"They don't want you taking the bus. Angel says it's not safe right now."

"'Angel says,'" I mimicked. "What are you? His pretty little parrot? Listen, I have ridden the bus thousands of times. Sure, there's the occasional creep, but it's public transportation and full of… well, public. Nobody's gonna do anything in broad daylight on a crowded bus. On Christmas Day. Besides, I need a little time to myself. It feels like the four of us are living on top of each other and I have no time alone."

Markie frowned, which admittedly played on my conscience, but this wasn't about her. This was about me, needing to get my head screwed on right.

She started to object in that annoying older-sister-filling-in-for-an-absent-mother way of hers, but before she could nag me to death I counter-attacked. I went in for a hug, and said, "Make sure you don't overdo it tonight. Do not get on the floor with the kids."

Her mouth gaped open, giving me the time I needed to get out the door. It had been so long since I'd gone anywhere alone, fleeing the building before Angel and Bones returned felt like *Mission Impossible.* The theme song even played in my mind as I crept down the hallway and slunk into the elevator. Knowing Markie was probably already on the phone ratting me out, I half-expected to run into my jailers the instant the elevator doors chimed open. When they weren't there, I was so relieved I almost laughed out loud. Feeling free and like I was getting away with something, I hurried for the exit. The guard in the lobby gave me a puzzled look, but didn't try to stop me.

Pulling my jacket tight against the cool December air, I made my way toward the nearest bus stop. My phone buzzed in my pocket, but since I had a pretty good idea who it was, I ignored it until I was safely on the bus. Only then did I check the text message from Bones. It asked me to please wait for him but it was too late. The bus was already en route. Smiling as I sent the text to tell him this, I sat and waited for his reply.

Minutes passed with no reply. I felt a pang of regret and wondered if he'd see my defiance as immature, because now that the high of escaping was wearing off, it did kind of feel that way. But then I came to my senses. I was riding a bus to work, not doing something dangerous or illegal. People lived through the experience every day, and I was pretty sure the odds of surviving were in my favor. Yes, bad guys had gone after my sister, but only because she was protecting her boyfriend's little siblings. I, on the other hand, had no boyfriend and was a nobody. Bones was paid to be paranoid, but I couldn't let his madness affect my independence. I refused to be sheltered from the big bad world by anyone. Even if that anyone happened to have a smokin' hot body and could melt my panties with a kiss.

Despite the concerns of my paranoid roommates, I lived through my bus ride to work just fine. Bones never did reply to my text, and I couldn't decide if I was disappointed or relieved about his lack of communication.

The combination of garlands, lights, and the smell of ham and mashed potatoes made me painfully aware this was the third Christmas in a row I'd spent alone. Four years ago Markie had come home from college during the holiday, determined to make it a little less sucky by trying her hand at Mom's old recipes. We did our best, but holiday dishes were well beyond our expertise. The ham was dry, served with runny mashed potatoes and chunky macaroni and cheese. The only edible course was dessert, thanks to the store-bought chocolate cream pie.

Despite the ruined food and the lack of additional family, Markie and I had a blast that year. And as I delivered the dinner special to two little old ladies—sisters—guilt gnawed at me. Markie was the only real family I had left, and I should be spending every holiday with her. So why wasn't I? I could have requested the time off or called in sick. Hell, Piper wasn't on the schedule today and she'd volunteered to take my shift for the time-and-a-half pay. But I'd said no, not because I was afraid of Angel's family, but because I didn't want to spend the holiday with Markie. I couldn't. I didn't deserve another family Christmas. Not after what I'd done to her.

The day dragged on, taking much longer than any day should. Bones was waiting for me after my shift, leaning against the wall of the casino where he could watch the main entrance, the floor, and the restaurant entrance. He looked irritated, so I approached with an apology.

"Sorry about earlier. I was already on the bus when I got your text."

He pushed off the wall and headed for the main door. "You knew I was coming back to take you to work." Since I couldn't deny that, I followed him out to the parking lot. Once we were in the Hummer, he asked, "Why'd you take the bus?"

A thousand excuses formed on my tongue—everything from needing to buy tampons to meeting with a guy for coffee—but I didn't want to lie to Bones.

"You've been avoiding me. I thought I'd make it more comfortable for both of us."

"Fair enough." He started up the engine and headed out of the parking lot. "But don't do it again."

That pissed me off. "Don't do what? Take a bus? Ohmigod, Bones, I am a grown-ass woman. You can't keep me off public transportation and make me depend on you for a ride. Or for anything else for that matter. Who do you think you are?"

"I'm the guy trying to keep you safe."

Something inside of me snapped. I opened my mouth, and all my confusion and frustration came rushing out.

"Safe from who? Because as far as I can tell, the only one I really need protection from is you. You know I like you, and you screw with my feelings and make me think you actually give a damn about me, too. You tell me all this shit about your mom… your past… you take me to your secret spot and... fine, I probably read too much into the situation. Romantic dinner, honest conversation, sue me for believing you wanted the same thing I did. I gambled our friendship for a chance at something more, and clearly that was the wrong play. I screwed up, and I am hurt and upset about it, and—" My voice cracked. I wanted to ask him what the Coach bag had meant, but even thinking the words made me feel ungrateful. I swallowed them back. "—and you can't *make* me ride with you every day, pretending none of that happened."

Stupid tears leaked down my face, making me feel even more weak and vulnerable. I turned toward the side window and brushed them away, hoping he wouldn't notice. He did, though. He put his hand on my shoulder and told me he was sorry.

I choked back a sob, straightened, and stared out the window. "Don't worry about it. I'm fine," I lied.

We rode the rest of the rest of the way in silence, and when we got to the condo, Bones dropped me off and left again.

CHAPTER FOURTEEN

Bones

SATURDAY NIGHT, ANGEL'S parents were going to some sort of charity dinner and the nanny was unavailable, so Angel and Markie dragged me and Ariana with them to keep an eye on Angel's siblings. Worried about Ariana, I spent the ride coaching her on what to say and how to act when she met the Marianis. The last thing we needed was for her to accidentally insult them.

"You know I'm housebroken, right?" Ariana asked. "I promise not to pee on their carpet or hump anyone's leg."

"Thank God for small favors," Markie said, giggling.

I wasn't amused. "This is serious, Ari. You don't know how important respect is to the family. They don't tolerate any disrespect."

"And I'm mouthy. But I'll be on my best behavior. You'll see. Parents love me. And ohmigod is this 'The Fortress'?" she asked, gaping out the window.

Angel chuckled at Markie's nickname for his dad's home.

"Holy crap, the guards really are carrying semi-automatics," Ariana said.

I had to admit, the sight of the boss's house still unnerved me. Armed guards waved us in while security cameras tracked our vehicle. A maid let us in to a gorgeous foyer, decorated in the browns and oranges of autumn, where we waited to be received. A curvy redhead wearing a low-cut glittery green gown and a jewelry store worth of diamonds came down the wraparound staircase and greeted us with all the forced joy of a mall Santa.

"Angel, Bones, Markie, thank you for coming," Rachelle said with her signature plastic smile. "Are you sure you're feeling up to this, Markie?"

"I'll make sure she doesn't overdo it," Angel said, squeezing Markie to him.

Markie gave him an annoyed look. "Yes ma'am. I'm feeling much better. As I told everyone at Christmas."

The hair rose on the back of my neck when Rachele turned her attention onto Ariana. "Markie's sister. Yes, I remember seeing you at the emergency room, but I don't believe we were introduced."

Angel stepped in. "Rachele, this is Ariana. Ari, my stepmother, Rachele."

"It's a pleasure to meet you," Ariana replied. "Beautiful gown, by the way."

I eyed Rachele's dress, wondering if Ariana was being serious. The thing was cut down to almost her belly button, revealing an eyeful of augmented cleavage.

"Thank you. It was a gift from a local designer, Fabio Meda. The man is a genius and this little number is his generous contribution to tonight's charity ball." Then she dismissed Ariana and turned back to Angel. "Dom is almost finished, and then we'll head out. Angel, I trust your father sent you the new security specs?"

The house had been attacked only weeks ago. Although the damage had been extensive, all evidence of it was gone. Seriously, not even a trace of new paint smell. If I hadn't seen the bullet holes firsthand, I'd never believe it had happened.

"Yes."

"Good. Please call immediately if there's any trouble."

"Where are Georgie and Luci?" Markie asked, looking around.

"Hiding," Rachele said with a huff. "Constantly. It's their new favorite game. Makes it nearly impossible to get anywhere on time."

A bigger, older, intimidating version of Angel came down the stairs. Power and money wafted from Dominico Mariani, their presence as real as the fat luxury watch he secured around his wrist as he descended. He acknowledged us with a nod before ushering Rachele out the door. The second we heard their car start, Angel started prowling around the house.

"Now we hunt down the beasts," he said.

Young laughter came from the hallway.

Angel headed in that direction with Markie on his heels. He turned and frowned at her. "Not you. You should go sit in the family room. I'll round them up and bring them in."

"Right." Markie sighed. "I'll go stare at Rachele's fascinating magazine collection while you have all the fun."

He and Markie took off while I patted Ariana on the arm. "You did great. You can breathe now. They're gone."

She blew out a breath. "That's Angel's dad, huh?"

I grinned. Not only that, he was the *capo dei capi,* the boss of the Las Vegas families, but Ariana didn't need to know that bit of information. "Don't worry. He has that effect on everyone."

She was about to say something else, but I hushed her. "You hear that?" I asked, listening.

"Wha—"

I put a finger to her lips and pointed toward the kitchen before slipping my oxfords off and creeping that direction. Ariana followed. When we stepped onto the tile floor, I dropped to my hands and knees and crawled to the island, glancing over my shoulder to make sure Ariana was still behind me. I had a pretty good idea of who we were stalking, and if I was right, I'd need backup.

I rounded the corner and let out the loudest roar I could. Luciana jumped three feet in the air—almost doubling her height—before squealing and sprinting past me. I reached for her, but the little booger was fast. She ran around the long dining room table once, twice, a third time, and each time, I gained on her.

"Are you gonna help me?" I asked, looking to Ariana who was laughing at the sight.

"I can't," she said between fits of giggles. "This looks too much like a Tom and Jerry episode."

Realizing she was right, I eased up. Luciana took advantage of the break and dove under the table. I groaned, knowing I'd have to go in after her.

"Good move, Luci!" Ariana cheered.

"Who are you rooting for here?" I asked. "You're supposed to be helping me."

She shrugged, trying unsuccessfully to wipe the grin from her face. "Sorry. I meant get her, Bones. Yeah, that's it."

Luciana giggled.

I lunged for her.

"Help me, Ari!" Luciana shouted.

Ariana rushed in, but I had no idea which side she was on. I fell back, and Luciana sprinted out from under the table to join up with her brother, who was still evading Angel. We chased the little curtain-climbers around the house until they were good and tired. Angel's other two sisters, Sonia and Sofia, emerged from their rooms, phones in hand, and let us know they were starving half to death and expected us to rectify the situation. They were thirteen and eleven going on twenty, wearing makeup and leggings with sweaters, but ate like college-aged boys. We ordered pizza and settled around the table. Georgio and Luciana gave us the rundown on the days since Christmas.

"Has father stepped up your training?" Angel asked.

Sonia nodded, flicking mushrooms off her slice of pizza. "Yep and it's been brutal. He brought in a trainer who's literally trying to kill us."

"You mean figuratively, and I doubt it. He's literally trying to keep you alive," I said. "Sometimes it's hard to tell the difference."

"But check out the guns I'm getting," Georgio said, standing and posing to flex his biceps and chest.

"That's nothing. Mine are bigger," Luciana said, joining him.

"What's the trainer been working on?" I asked.

"Pressure points," Sofia said. "Where to hit people to make them stop breathing. How to use pepper spray. Stuff like that."

"Hey, that's what my trainer's been working on, too," Ariana said, eyeing me.

"Wanna spar?" Luciana asked.

"Spar?" Ariana's eyebrows shot up her forehead. "You know martial arts, too?"

Luciana grinned.

"I would, but you'd definitely kick my butt."

Angel laughed. "You're probably right. They've had years of conditioning, and I know their trainer is way better than Bones."

"Ha-ha, funny boy. I'm good enough to keep your sorry as—butt alive."

"Where's Dante?" Angel asked.

"Dante's sad," Luciana said.

"He stays in his room most of the time," Georgio added. "Dad told us not to bug him. He needs time to be alone right now."

Angel's expression fell. He and his seventeen-year-old brother used to be close, but over the past few years their father's manipulation had driven a wedge between them. Most recently, Angel had threatened to blow up Dante's car. The car did blow up, and although neither Angel nor I had been involved in that mess, it had been too much of a coincidence for Dante to ignore. The collateral damage had been enough to sever their relationship for good. Angel was probably the last person Dante wanted to see right now.

"I'll go check on him," I said, piling an extra plate with pizza.

"Thanks, man," Angel said.

I found Dante in his bedroom, lights off, curtains closed, reclining in a gaming chair in front of his television. I tapped on the door as I pushed it open, but he didn't acknowledge me. The sound of gunfire drew my attention to the screen; Dante was deep into some sort of first-person shooter game. I stood back and watched, waiting until he finished the round before setting the plate of pizza down at the base of his television.

"Hey," I said. "Got another controller?"

He handed me one and queued us up for a game.

My family was never big on discussing our emotions. When Pops disappeared, I would occasionally hear Ma crying late at night when she thought we were asleep, but we never talked about it. Like normal people, we bottled our emotions and kept putting one foot in front of the other. But I could tell by Dante's greasy curls, dirty, rumpled clothes, and bloodshot eyes he'd stopped moving forward. The kid had watched his girlfriend blow up along with his car. He probably needed a professionally-trained counselor to help him deal with that kind of shit. A counselor would be seen as a sign of weakness, though, and there was no way Dominco Mariani would allow his son to be seen as weak.

So we handled it like wiseguys and let the elephant take up the whole damn room as we blew faces off.

"Sniper in that building to your right," I said, ducking my character behind a car as bullets rained down on me.

Dante sneaked around and shot the guy in the head. "Got him."

"Thanks."

We played three rounds before I returned the controller and stood to leave.

"What? You're not gonna lecture me?" he asked.

Confused, I asked, "Why would I lecture you?"

"Because she was a… a whore." His face contorted. "She was using me for my money and position. She was too old for me. Why can't I see that I'm better off without her?" His voice choked up. He swallowed. "The Pelinos did me a favor, and I'm up here pining away for her like some lovesick puppy."

My chest ached for the kid. I could almost hear his parents reciting this shit over and over, willing him to accept the truths about the woman he loved. His pain was so heavy, so encompassing, I couldn't even look at him. I was afraid of being sucked into it. "You're not stupid, Dante. She couldn't have been all bad."

It was the best I could do. I couldn't defend her against the accusations of his parents. Especially not when everything they said was true. Still, he was just a boy in love with a girl. He needed to know how normal that was.

His expression softened, once again revealing the persistent little boy who used to follow me and Angel around. "Thanks," he whispered, turning back to his game.

"When was the last time you slept?" I asked.

"I can't sleep. Every time I close my eyes I see her reaching for the door." He choked up again. "We were fighting. I did what you guys wanted. I called it off… told her I couldn't be with her anymore. I was trying to protect her from you, from Angel, from the family. But I get it now. There is no protection from the family." His voice dropped. "The family takes everything."

I couldn't argue with him, because every word of it was true. Nothing I could say or do would make him feel better.

"You ever been in love, Bones?"

Ariana's face immediately came to mind. She was standing on top of Sunrise Mountain, my jacket draped over her shoulders as she watched the lights of the city. Then sitting beside me in the Hummer, wiping away tears I'd caused because I couldn't tell her I had feelings for her. I didn't even know what I felt.

"I loved her, so they killed her. I watched her die, and there wasn't a damn thing I could do about it. She was dead before I got to her. I didn't even get to tell her I was sorry."

What would I do if something happened to Ariana? What if I could never hear her laughter or see her smile again? Would I end up like Dante, locked away hiding from reality? No. I'd go after the son-of-a-bitch who did it and make sure they never hurt anyone again. But if I was really smart, I'd keep Ariana as far away from the family—and me—as possible.

Dante jumped into another game, so I headed downstairs. Everyone had finished eating and the kitchen was empty. I searched the house until I heard sounds coming from the den. They were crowded on the sectional, watching an animated movie on the eighty-five-inch screen. Markie was teaching Sofia how to braid Sonia's hair, while the twins were snuggled against Ariana. Angel was standing behind them, but broke off and joined me at the door.

"How's Dante?"

His question pissed me off, not because of the question itself, but because of the necessity of it. Dante's girlfriend hadn't died of natural causes or some accident. She'd been murdered because she was dating Dominico Mariani's son. That was the world we lived in.

"What'd you be like if you lost Markie?" I asked.

Angel's eyes narrowed. His gaze cut to the sofa, as if reassuring himself she was still there and unharmed. He shook his head. "I don't know. I can't think about that right now."

He wouldn't be able to think about it ever, but it was always a possibility, especially while we were still in Vegas.

"We need to get the hell out of this city," I said.

Angel nodded. "I worry about my brothers."

I worried about them, too. With Angel gone, they'd be completely under their father's influence and he'd do his best to make sure Dante and Georgio grew into family men he could use. "Maybe we can come back for them or help them in some way. When they're older." I couldn't see how, but Angel was a smart guy. He'd think of something.

He nodded and leaned against the doorway, returning his attention to his siblings in the room. "Maybe we can come back for Christmas and the other holidays to visit. Maybe they can spend some time with us when school's out."

I nodded, agreeing with him because he needed it, but I doubted the boss would let Angel anywhere near his children once he left. The boss never negotiated, but Nonna was the wild card. Since she'd be living with us, she could request the kids. Would the boss keep his own mother from seeing her grandchildren? We were in unchartered territory, and I had no idea what would happen. No need to crush Angel's hopes.

"The twins are getting big," he observed, drawing my attention to them.

They seemed to be focused on the movie. Ariana must have felt us watching, because she looked up and grinned. She squeezed their shoulders and kissed their foreheads. I'd never pictured Ariana as a kid-person, but watching her with the twins made me reconsider. I wondered what kind of mom she'd make. What kind of wife.

"What's up with you and Ari?" Angel asked.

And that was the million-dollar question. She liked me, we had chemistry, she made me laugh, she had my back, she was gorgeous, and the taste of her kiss had made me hungry for so much more. Yet there was still a very big problem.

The family takes everything, Dante's voice said in the back of my mind.

I knew it was true. As long as I belonged to the family, any relationship I had would be doomed. I'd always known it, which was why I'd stayed clear of anything that could turn romantic. But somehow Ariana had gotten in past my defenses. I still didn't know if I loved her, but I liked her too much to find out. So I looked my best friend in the eyes and lied to both of us. "Not a damn thing."

I could tell he didn't believe me, but he let it go. "You been out a lot lately. Still looking for Matt?"

"Yeah. I got a bead on him last night, but he split before I got to him."

"Weird. It's almost like he knows when you're coming," Angel said.

I'd been thinking the same damn thing. But I'd been scanning the Hummer every day and I wasn't being tracked. If Matt was getting tipped off, it had to be from someone in the family. Two months ago, I wouldn't have even considered the possibility, but a lot had happened in the past sixty days. And I was running out of time. As an enforcer, I was only as good as my job performance. Up to this point, I'd gotten every man the family had sent me after. My record was spotless, making me look like a valuable, capable soldier. But if I didn't burn Matt, people would start wondering if I was slipping. Or worse, they'd wonder if I was in cahoots with the junkie. And assumptions like that would lead to the boss sending someone after me.

"You'll get him, Bones. You always do," Angel said, patting my shoulder.

I had to get Matt. Killing him was the only way I could stay alive.

CHAPTER FIFTEEN

Ariana

MY SISTER HAS always had a soft spot for kids, which is like saying casinos have a soft spot for money or SUVs have a soft spot for gas. Markie seems to need kids around her to survive, almost like she thrives on helping them and doing things for them. Growing up, she was one of those weird kids who would break plans with her friends to babysit, and not because she needed the money. She was crazy. Which was why—on a night when I was finally exhausted enough to sleep—she was talking my ear off, agonizing about Angel's siblings and wondering how she could possibly drag him away from them.

"Drag him away?" I asked. The visual her words created made me giggle. Angel towered over Markie, and outweighed her by a good fifty pounds. "If he's the type of man you can 'drag' anywhere, you need to dump that loser. Yesterday."

She sighed. "You know what I mean."

"Uh, I don't even think *you* know what you mean, because you just insinuated that your boyfriend is some spineless jellyfish, who's abandoning his family to be with his girlfriend. And that's not the type of guy my sister would date."

"Angel's not like that at all," she defended, rolling over to face me.

No, he wasn't. Angel wasn't as tough or scary as Bones, but he wasn't a pushover either. He was perfect for Markie, and he practically worshiped the ground she walked on. "Don't look at me. *I* didn't say he was."

I watched her out of the corner of my eye. It felt so weird to share a bed with Markie again. After our mom died and we moved in with our uncle, I used to sneak into her bed every night. It was silly and immature since we were in high school, but after losing both of our parents, I was afraid I'd lose her, too. But I didn't lose Markie. She left, first to college, and then to Africa. I was angry when she moved into the dorm, and devastated when she got onto the plane. Especially since I knew she had cancer and I would probably never see her again. Now here she was, healthy, madly in love with Angel, and trying to take care of kids who weren't her responsibility.

"I wish there was something I could do to help them," she said.

"You can't help everyone, you know?"

She frowned. "Yeah, I know. I need to get back to the orphanage. That'll make me feel better."

"I don't think you're quite ready for that yet. When do you go to the doc next?"

"Friday the fourth."

The fourth was the day after my birthday. If the doctor gave Markie a clean bill of health, she, Angel, and Bones would be clear to leave Vegas. I didn't want them to leave, which made me feel needy and co-dependent. Did Bones even want me to go? Sometimes it seemed like he didn't even want to be in the same room with me. I missed our easy friendship and wished I'd never kissed him on Sunrise Mountain and screwed it up. But he had kissed me back, full of passion and need as his greedy hands roamed over my body. Was that just hormones and testosterone? At the time, I'd been certain there was more, but now I wasn't so sure. I was still trying to puzzle him out when I drifted off to sleep.

The next morning's workout was particularly grueling. Bones had stepped up my training to a point where he was now swinging the punching bag at me. I didn't know whether to dodge or hit and several times I tried both. That didn't go so well, and I spent more time trying to keep my balance than anything.

"Hey! What's your problem?" I asked after he slammed the bag into me so hard it ended my war with balance by knocking me off my feet.

Bones leapt into action, steadying the bag as he scanned my body for damage. "You okay?"

I nodded, still breathing heavily. Boxing was no joke on the cardio, especially when your trainer was acting like a muscle-bound sadist.

"Sorry. I was distracted. I didn't mean to swing it that hard."

Well that confused me since there were only the two of us in the gym. "Distracted by what?"

"I just got a lot on my mind."

No way was I gonna let him get away with such a crap-lousy excuse. "Join the party. But you don't see me trying to put you on your ass."

He cracked a smile. His gaze roved over my body as I lay on the mat, lingering at the hem of my shorts before drifting to my sports bra, assessing, challenging. "Think you can?"

It was the most attention he'd shown me since the mountain, and I craved it like sunshine after a hard winter. Not to be outdone, I returned the favor, my own hungry gaze floating up his baggy sweats to the T-shirt stretched across his six-pack and pecs. The beast was back, feral, lurking behind his eyes, and I wanted to unleash it—to let it roam and conquer—even though the smart thing would be to run and hide. My senses played a quick game of rock, paper, scissors, and courage crushed brains, forcing me to my feet. Eye-to-eye with the predator, I breathed him in deeply before answering, "Yeah, I do."

We stood locked in that moment for what seemed like forever, and I really thought he'd take me up on my offer. I hoped. I prayed. I wanted to set him free, but Bones was too caged, too controlled. His expression shifted from hunger and lust to pain and torment, and then finally, resignation.

He released the bag. "I know what you want from me, Ari, but I can't give it to you. I'm sorry." Then he walked away. I watched him through the glass wall as he sat at a weight machine, back to me, and began lifting.

That was it. I was done. If Bones deflected one more pass I made at him, my fragile ego would shatter into a million pieces. I could tell he wanted me, but something held him back—something much more important to him than I'd ever be. Whatever. I was over it and over him. Picking up what was left of my pride, I got out of there.

I showered and got ready for work in record time, determined to take back my life and remember who I was. Dammit, I'd promised myself I wouldn't let another jerk screw with my head, but here I was, pining after another one. I was so absorbed in my self-loathing that I almost ran into him on my way out of the apartment. Bones was suited up and leaning against the wall waiting for me, keys in hand, determination etched into his face.

Screw his determination. I was never ever going to put myself in a position to be alone with him again. I needed time to build walls. Walls not even his sexy crooked smile could knock down. "I'm taking the bus today."

He sighed, rolling his head to the side and looking at me like I was the one acting all hormonal. "Come on, I'll give you a ride."

He couldn't even look me in the face and he was still insisting on taking me? No way. Angel and Markie were perched on the sofa in the living room, eyes on their laptops, but I could feel their attention on us. I didn't care. I took a deep, steadying breath and tried again. "I'm an adult, it's a free country, and I'm taking the bus." Then, because I'm a smartass who couldn't seem to stop challenging him, I added, "Unless you're prepared to physically force me to ride with you."

Then he did look at me, and I swear to God, he considered it. The little thrill that went up my spine was all the evidence I needed that I could never let that happen. Every ounce of self-preservation I had left was screaming at me to put as much distance between us as I could.

"Don't touch me, Bones," I warned. "You do, and you will never see me again."

"Ari—" His voice was deep and soft, whispering to the crazy in me… the crazy who wanted him no matter how much he was unwilling to give me.

I turned to Angel and Markie, who were now openly watching us. "'Bye guys." I waved. Then I stepped around Bones, careful not to touch him, and fled.

Bones didn't follow me.

I don't know what I was expecting. Maybe some sort of romantic scene where he ran down the stairs to meet my elevator only to throw his hot, sweaty body at me and profess his undying love. But when the elevator doors pinged open, he wasn't there. I clearly wasn't worth him running down the stairs for.

Sighing, I went to catch the bus with all the other loners.

As if my day wasn't crappy enough, Matt was back in my secret hiding spot, waiting for me when I took my lunch break. This time he wore jeans, sneakers, a baseball cap, and an old sweatshirt. Not even trying to impress me anymore. Good, because I didn't feel like being impressed. Still pissed about Bones, I didn't have enough energy to deal with Matt. My heart had been run over too many times. Prince Charming himself could have shown up at that very moment and I would have put one of my heels through his eyeball. I was done letting guys sweep me off my feet only to drop me off a cliff into a garbage heap.

"What do you want, douchebag?" I asked.

"Whoa, rough day?" He stood and took a step toward me. "I got something that can help you with that. Take the edge off."

"I've been clean since the night you almost killed me." I backed up for his protection, not mine. I was more than willing to try out some of the fighting moves Bones had been teaching me. "How do you even know when I'm working? And when I take lunch? I swear, if you put some sort of tracker on me, I will shove it so far up your a—"

"Whoa." He put his hands up. "Chill, babe. I missed you and came to see if you've thought any more about my offer."

"Your offer? Whatever you're selling I sure don't want it."

"About the audition," he clarified. "I just got off the phone with the guy and he's got an opening in an hour and—"

I had to hand it to the guy, he was persistent. Like a cockroach or the plague. "I'm working, Matt."

"Working a dead-end job that you should blow off for this chance of a lifetime."

"Blow off my stable income for a gamble?" I laughed. He was so unreal it was almost funny. "Been there, done that."

"This time's different. This is for real."

Why wouldn't he just go away? "Look, I don't know what your game is, but I'm not playing. I gotta get back to work."

Matt's calm facade melted away, revealing concern, then anger. He switched tactics, grabbing my arm. "I'm trying to help you, babe, or are you too stupid to figure that out. Now come on, we have a meeting to get to."

Then he started walking toward the door, yanking me along behind him. Shocked, it took me a lot longer than it should have to realize what was happening. But when everything clicked, I went ballistic.

"NO!" I screamed, jerking my arm away from him. I didn't care if I made a scene, I was over men thinking they could tell me what to do.

His eyes widened in shock. He glanced around to the few people who were watching us. "Stop it. You sound like a crazy bitch." He reached for me again. "What the hell's wrong with you?"

He hadn't even begun to see what a crazy bitch I could be. "Keep your hands off me, Matt!" I backed up. "No means no, you freaking horn dog."

That earned us a healthy dose of attention. People stopped what they were doing to catch the show we were putting on. One of the security guards made eye contact with me, silently questioning. All I had to do was nod or yell, and he'd rush over to help.

Matt looked from side to side, forcing a don't-mind-me-I'm-harmless smile while raising his hands in surrender, like this was all just some big misunderstanding. "My bad. Sorry. I thought I was doing you a favor. Thought you were serious about gettin' on a stage."

I was serious—more serious than I'd ever been about anything in my life. Singing was all I had left. It was the only thing that hadn't broken my heart or left me. I needed to commandeer a stage and a microphone, release all my pent-up passion and frustration, and let the crowd shower me in love and adoration. If I could just get a shot, I knew in my heart they wouldn't reject me. Maybe they wouldn't even leave me. But Matt had already had his chance to get me noticed, and he'd failed. He'd taken everything I had and left me with promises. Now that I had nothing more to give, he was back. Why?

"What's in it for you?" I asked.

He startled. "What do you mean?"

"Cut the crap. You know what I mean."

He shrugged. "The satisfaction of knowing I finally came through for you, that I—"

Bullshit. I started walking away.

"Fine. I get a fat finder's fee. If you're the girl they're looking for."

That sounded a lot more reasonable. "I'll think about it," I said over my shoulder, without breaking stride.

"Think fast. Time's runnin' out."

CHAPTER SIXTEEN

Bones

ARIANA SLAMMED THE door on her way out. She was pissed and hurt, and I wanted to help her, but there wasn't a damn thing I could do about it. No matter how smart and funny she was, no matter how good she looked or how amazing she smelled, or how she licked her lips and invited me to kiss her, I couldn't risk her safety for a hookup. I wouldn't let her end up like Dante's girlfriend, caught in the crossfire of the mafia life-style. I needed to be strong and push her away, but I was so damn frustrated I felt like I was going to burst.

Markie and Angel sat on the sofa in open-mouthed awe, eyes darting from me to the door, no doubt dying of curiosity over what had happened between me and Ariana. I didn't feel like going into it with them, so I put my hand on the doorknob, preparing to make my own escape.

"Bones, wait," Angel said.

"Uh…" Markie stood, depositing her laptop on the coffee table. "I'm gonna go… take a bath. And read a book. I'll be right in here if you need me." She stepped into my old room, pulling the door closed behind her.

"I need to take a break from staring at this screen," Angel said, setting his laptop next to Markie's and turning on the television. He picked up two controllers and offered me one. "Join me."

Coping skills at their finest. I accepted the controller and sat beside him. We didn't talk—didn't need to—Angel knew me well enough that I didn't have to say a word, and that in itself was calming. By the time he went back to work, I felt much better.

"You heading out?" Angel asked.

"Yeah."

"Still looking for Matt?"

I nodded. The bastard had been spotted multiple times over the past week—with a date at a diner, alone in a grocery store, with a couple of friends in a bar, warming up a slot machine at the Rio—but always managed to disappear before I got there. It was almost like he was screwing with me. Like everyone was trying to drive me out of my mind. Maybe the new Tech was as dirty as the old one. Or maybe Carlo was keeping Matt one step ahead of me to prove my incompetency. Or maybe all the families had teamed up to keep Matt out of my reach.

Or maybe I'm losing my touch.

"If you pick up that tail again, try to get the license plate. Call me with it."

The first time Ariana had taken the bus, Angel and I made a quick run to the jewelry store. On the way there, we'd picked up a tail—a black Camry. I was pretty sure it was the same tail I'd picked up leaving Carlo's a couple weeks ago. We were able to slip it and doubled back around to get the plate, but it vanished. Since Angel wanted me to call him—instead of Tech—with the plate, he must be doubting Tech's loyalty as well.

The fine line between cautious and paranoid grew thinner by the day.

"Be safe out there," Angel said, returning his focus back to his laptop.

The keys to the Hummer were in a dish on the entryroom table. My hand hovered over them while I thought about all the near misses, all the times I should have caught Matt. Beside the Hummer keys was another set, a set so rarely used that it still had the dealer tag attached. A dark-blue 2015 Jeep Wrangler. It had less than ten thousand miles on it and had cost me a small fortune, but it didn't have any of the outrageous safety features of Angel's Hummer. On the other hand, very few people knew about it, and Tech did not have direct access to it. It was the closest I could get to going out incognito, but if bullets started flying, the Jeep wouldn't stand a chance. If I didn't catch Matt soon, I didn't stand a chance, either. Resolved, I left Angel's keys where they were and took mine.

"Stay in contact," Angel said as I walked out the door.

My Jeep was in the far corner of the parking lot, where it had been sitting for months. I scanned the vehicle, finding a tracking device under the rear bumper. All trackers looked the same to me, but Angel could usually tell when one belonged to the family. I considered running it up to ask him, but why? What difference would it make? The device could have been on the Jeep for months or hours. I stuck it to the cement wall, hoping whoever was monitoring it would believe my Jeep was still in the garage.

I drove around for a few hours, making calls and checking in with contacts. There was still no word on Matt, but I did find out some interesting information about Ma's boyfriend, Totino. There were rumors he was working for one of the families, but nobody seemed to know which one. He was known for selling furniture—but didn't have a storefront—and for spending hours at the Mirage, betting on horses and taking advantage of the drink tickets.

Curious, I stopped by the Mirage and talked to my buddy Ross in the Sports Book. He couldn't tell me much about Totino, but did give me a few names, locals Totino had been seen chatting it up with. I thanked him, and got back on the road.

Then, my big break finally came. A contact who worked security for the Tropicana called and said some douchebag who matched Matt's description was harassing a girl.

Ariana's restaurant was in the Tropicana.

"What does she look like?" I asked, already turning around.

"Tall, maybe five ten, five eleven. Brown, chin-length hair, waitress."

It had to be Ariana. "Shit. I'll be right there. Call me if he leaves."

I was ten minutes from the Tropicana, but I made the drive in seven. The afternoon light was quickly fading by the time I parked. My contact called back to tell me Matt had left alone through the front doors. Determined not to let the little chooch slip through my fingers again, I put my hand on the gun in my pocket and ran for the entrance.

Matt was talking on his phone and crossing the street, heading for the parking lot, when I saw him. I ducked behind a truck and watched. I wasn't close enough to hear his conversation over the roar of traffic and passersby, but his gestures were animated enough to show his anger. He had to be arguing with someone about something. Tracking his movements, I slunk closer, waiting for him to end the call. When he finally did, I jumped out and wrapped my arm around him, pulling him close enough to settle my gun into his side without being seen.

"Hey, buddy, how you been?" I asked.

It took him a moment to register what was going on. Then he glanced from me toward a newer red Chevy sedan, no doubt gaging the distance. I nudged my gun into his ribs.

"You'd never make it."

"Bones, I—" The asshole reached in his pocket.

He was fast, but I was faster. I blocked him, twisted his arm back, and retrieved the little Walther nine millimeter he was packing. "Cute little pea shooter," I said, pocketing the gun. I half-dragged him to the Jeep and tossed him into the front, climbing in behind him and shoving him to the passenger's seat where I relieved him of his cell phone, an ounce of cocaine, his wallet, and a pocket knife too dull to cut an apple. I pointed my gun on him and told him to buckle up. Now that I'd finally gotten my prize I wasn't about to let one of Las Vegas's finest stop me for some stupid traffic infraction.

"I-I-I'll get you the money, Bones. I p-p-promise. There's a couple hundred dollars in my wallet. You keep that."

"Oh, I plan on it, but you might want to shut your mouth and stop insulting me."

At this point, no amount of money could purchase Matt's life back from Carlo. Matt's stupidity had long since sealed his fate. Keeping my gun trained on him, I started the Jeep and headed out of the parking lot.

"I-I-I have some stuff, too. That packet you took from me… that's quality blow. The street price is—"

"I don't deal, and I sure as hell don't want the shit you're selling now. Who's your supplier now that you burned the family?"

No response. Fine. We could do this the hard way. In fact, I was looking forward to it. The idea of him being anywhere near Ariana had made my blood boil.

The family had several hidden locations we used to handle business. Under normal circumstances, I'd call Tech and ask where I could take Matt. But circumstances were far from normal, and I didn't want Tech—or anyone else—knowing where I was. So I drove north of the city, following Moccasin Road until the pavement ended. Then we veered onto an unnamed dirt road that wound through piles of construction gravel until the lights of the city were a distant memory.

Matt didn't say anything. He watched out the windows, sweating a little more with every mile we drove. When I came to the end of the dirt road, I parked, leaving on the lights so I could see in the growing darkness.

"I'm not telling you anything," Matt said.

He'd talk. They always did.

"Get out and keep your hands where I can see them." I had all the weapons and there was nowhere for him to run or hide. Nothing but flat land for miles. Still, protocol needed to be followed.

"Don't do this, Bones," he pleaded.

"Don't make me repeat myself." I pressed my gun into his side. "Out."

Matt creaked open the door and slowly slid out. I followed him, watching him every second.

"You're gonna kill me anyway," Matt said, hands in the air, fear etched into his features.

Yes, I was. But I needed information from him first. "Why were you at the Tropicana?" I asked.

"Might as well kill me now. I'm not talkin'."

I laughed. Men like Matt thought death was the worst thing that could happen to them. They had no idea how much pain a person could live through before he passed out. I knew. It was my job to know just how far I could go before it was game over. Death would be easy. It was the other things I could do that Matt should be afraid of.

He shuddered.

I took a deep breath, grabbing hold of the tension, frustration, and anger I'd been bottling, and released them. I lunged, once again the ten-year-old boy going after the bully who wouldn't shut his face about my father. My first hit clocked Matt in the jaw. He spun around and fell on his stomach with a grunt. I'd knocked the air out of him, but he was conscious. His body shifted from side to side, and then he pushed up until he was on his hands and knees. I ran at him and kicked him in his stomach. He flipped over, landing on his back.

I circled him as he curled up like a giant armadillo, protecting his stomach. Like he could protect anything from me.

"Here's how this is gonna go down. I'm gonna ask a few questions. You can either answer me and die quickly with as little pain as possible, or you can hold back and I can draw this out for days. Weeks. Months. After what you did to Ari, I'll enjoy it. Your call."

His jaw was crooked and swelling. "Go to hell." He winced.

"It's like that, huh?" I kicked him again, this time in the back. Matt swore. He writhed in pain, trying to guard both his back and his stomach.

"It's the shoes. They're deceivingly painful," I explained.

I was twelve when Carlo started training me to be an enforcer. He'd already taught me to fight and shoot, ensuring that I could do my job and protect Angel, so these lessons were for the details like how to walk, talk, behave, and dress. I'll never forget the way he eyed my sneakers and shook his head. The next day he presented me with my first pair of steel-toe wingtip oxfords. Then, he showed me how to use them. My body still bore the scars from that lesson.

"It'll get more painful as we go," I promised Matt.

He didn't respond.

My adrenaline spiked. I wanted to hurt him. I wanted to make him bleed… to see how far I could stretch him before he snapped. I grabbed him by the shirt and pulled him to standing, forcing him to look me in the eye.

"Why were you at the Tropicana?" I repeated.

"You… you know why," he said.

"You screwin' with Ari?"

"No. Yes. It's a job."

"What job? Who hired you?"

"I don't know. Some woman said she'd give me two large if I took Ariana to her."

"Two thousand? You sold Ari out for two thousand?"

He didn't answer.

No one in the family would send a woman after Ariana. "What did this woman look like?"

Again, no answer.

I brought my knee up fast, shoving Matt's head down into it. Dazed, he wobbled, only remaining on his feet because I was still propping him up. "Tell me."

"Long dark hair. Dark eyes. Maybe five six? About a hundred and fifty pounds. Nice rack. Big ass."

He'd just described most of the Italian women in Vegas. And several non-Italians. "What does she want with Ari?"

"She didn't say, and I didn't ask. Now, can you take me back to town? If something happens to me, a lot of people are gonna come looking."

Story of my life. If I didn't get out of Vegas soon, this would be my legacy: broken bones and buried bodies. At least until someone's pissed off family member pulled the revenge card and put a bullet between my eyes. "Yeah, sure, I'll take you back to town," I lied. "Just answer a few more questions for me first. Tell me where you're getting the dope from."

"You're lying. You're not gonna take me back. Even if I tell you."

The second lesson Carlo had taught me was to know the target's weaknesses and be ready and willing to exploit them. "You're right, Matt. You're gonna die and I'm gonna bury you right over there." I pointed at the ground. "The million-dollar question is whether or not you'll be alone in that grave."

His face scrunched up. "You planning to bring me company?"

I shrugged. "That's up to you. Family should be buried together, right? What about your sister. What's her name again? Jenny? She's in Texas now, isn't she?"

His eyes grew round.

"Yep. In Amarillo. Going to school at West Texas A & M. I bet your family's proud. It would be a pity if she just up and disappeared, wouldn't it?"

Blood seeped into his eyes from the cut on his forehead. He wiped it away and stared up at me, looking uncertain. "You wouldn't."

I showed him my teeth. "You don't have any idea what I'd do."

We stared each other down for a moment before he lowered his head. "I don't want to feel anything else, you hear me?" he asked.

"Deal. Name your source."

"And you'll leave Jenny alone?"

"I promise. Unlike you, Matt, I'm a man of my word."

"Durante. Joey Durante."

Well, that was unexpected. The Durante family ruled the city before the Marianis defeated them and took over. Most of the family had been killed or ran off, leaving it too small and weak to be productive. They weren't even part of the local commission anymore. They couldn't piss in Vegas without authorization. Weaseling in on the drug trade would be suicide.

"Why?" I asked.

"What do I look like? Their goddamn business planner?"

Matt was seconds from death, so I let that little outburst slide. "Next question." This one wasn't for the family. This one was for me. "I've been all over you all week. Who's been tipping you off?"

He chuckled. "I can't answer that."

"I thought we were done playing games."

His chuckle turned into a cough. He held his stomach until he was finished. "No, I really can't tell you. I have no idea. I get a text… a different number every time. Tried to text it back but it goes to a landline. Same thing when I call. Check my phone. You'll see."

There'd be plenty of time for checking that later. Our current business had already gone too long. Lesson three: Get in, do the job, get out. The longer you take, the higher the risk of getting caught. I scanned the area, confirming that we were still alone, and pulled out my Glock and its silencer. Matt watched as I screwed on the silencer. Then the coward looked away when I aimed. I squeezed the trigger. Twice. Matt collapsed.

"Two in the head. Make sure he's dead," I whispered to myself.

That had been lesson number four. I'd felt so tough the first time I said it, but now adrenaline was wearing off and I felt weak and hollow, a slave to the system. Matt's body relaxed, filling the night air with the telltale smells of death. I hadn't been lying when I told Ariana I was sick of watching people die. Sick of making them die. This wasn't what I wanted to do for the rest of my life, and I needed to get out of Vegas before my future was set in stone.

But that was a problem for another day. Focusing back on the here and now, I retrieved Matt's cell phone from the Jeep and thumbed it on. No password. The idiot was probably too baked to remember one. I took a couple pictures of his body to prove the hit. Then I grabbed the shovel out of the back and went to work. After Matt was safely tucked six feet under, I climbed back into my Jeep and thumbed through his texts. Sure enough, multiple texts from multiple numbers had sent Matt running every time I was onto him. Had to be someone with access to technology decent enough to hijack lines. Angel could do it. Hell, anyone in the Mariani family could. All it would take was a quick call to Tech. I thought about calling the new guy to see if he'd slip up and tell me what was going on, but instead dialed Carlo.

"You got him," Carlo said before I could even say hello. "Good. I'm sure you have some questions."

I always had questions, but I was too smart to voice them. Lesson five: Keep your mouth shut, your head down, and get your goddamn job done. The less you know the better.

"Meet me at Tony's in two hours. We need to have a conversation about your future." He disconnected.

My throat went dry. Carlo knew I wanted to leave with Angel. By icing Matt, I'd finished my last job… the last task Carlo had given me. So now he wanted to talk about my future? Was he gonna let me leave with Angel? Or was he going to insist that I sign on for good when they opened the books? My refusal would be seen as an insult. He'd have to kill me. I stared at my phone, wondering what to do. I had two hours to figure it out, and a sneaking suspicion that if I met with Carlo, I'd be leaving Tony's in a body bag.

CHAPTER SEVENTEEN

Bones

TWO HOURS. IT was about a quarter after seven, so I needed to be at Tony's shortly after nine. Matt was dead and buried and I'd removed my fingerprints from his personal items—all except for his cell phone since I wasn't done with that quite yet—and stored them in a plastic bag for Carlo. I didn't know what else to do, so I put my hands on the wheel and drove. Before I'd even registered where I was going, I pulled into the Tropicana parking lot and cut the engine.

Snippets of information drifted through my mind as I tried to form some sort of connection or pattern. Carlo wanted to promote me. Someone had been helping Matt evade me. A woman had hired Matt to pick up Ariana. Markie's doctor appointment was steadily approaching. When she was cleared, Angel would want to take her and get the hell out. Would I be able to go with them? Would Ariana? Would I even make it through the night?

I could leave now.

All I had to do was turn over the ignition and drive, and I could be well out of the state by the time anyone realized I was gone. Angel's father would protect him. Nonna would make sure nothing happened to Markie.

What about Ariana?

Someone was after her. Who? Why? Ariana's nose had been clean since she'd moved in with us. I was almost certain of it. So who the hell wanted her? Was it someone trying to get at me? Possibly. If Nonna could tell how I felt about her, other people could as well. I'd been stupid and careless.

And what about Ma?

I found a little comfort in knowing Totino would look after Ma, but the guy was soft, and if the family came for her there'd be nothing he could do to stop them.

There were too many factors I couldn't run from. I had to stay and accept whatever Carlo had in store for me. But first, I needed to see Ariana again. Stupid, careless, but I couldn't stop my feet from crossing the parking lot and heading for the casino.

Food smells mingled with cigarette smoke as I lingered in the diner entrance, watching Ariana deliver plates to patrons. Her uniform black shorts, barely longer than the apron covering them, and fitted V-neck top—logo in the middle of her chest—were designed to draw attention. The waitresses here were all knockouts, but she was leagues above the rest of them. My gaze raked over her body as she slid an empty tray under her arm and stepped to the side, taking the order of some asshole whose gaze kept dropping to her breasts. He said something and she laughed. It was a fake, hollow sound, nothing like the real sound of her laughter.

Man, I missed that sound. It had been days since I'd even see her smile.

"Will you be dining alone?" someone asked.

Irritated by the interruption, I nodded at the hostess. "Yes, but give me a sec." I pulled my phone out of my pocket and slipped out into the casino. I knew one surefire way to make Ariana smile again. I'd been putting off making the call, because I was a selfish son-of-a-bitch, afraid to see her succeed. Afraid she'd show Vegas everything I saw and the city would love her and keep her for good. I wanted her to leave with us, but more than that, I wanted her to get what she wanted. I owed her that much. I scrolled through my contacts and dialed when I found the right one.

"Noah Garner," he answered.

"Noah, it's Bones, how are you, man?"

"I'm good, bud, how are you? Been a while."

"Yeah, I've been busy. Hey, are you still recruiting for that talent agency?"

"Yep. Why? What can I do for you?"

I appreciated people who got right down to business, and Noah was never big on small talk. "You know that favor you owe me? I need to cash it in."

"I'm listening."

I went through my spiel, explaining Ariana's circumstances and inviting him to come listen to her sing.

"Tomorrow night?" he asked.

"Yeah. Sorry this is so last minute." I'd dragged my feet to the very end, planning to make some lame excuse for Noah not being able to make it.

"You know I can't promise to place her, right? These things are tricky. I have a couple of shows looking for vocalists right now, but they're all searching for a specific sound. A specific look."

"Yeah, I get it. Ari wouldn't want me pulling anyone's strings to make this happen. She's just lookin' for a legitimate shot."

"That, I can give her. I'll be there, Bones."

"Thanks, man." Feeling like I'd done something right for once, I disconnected the call, reentered the restaurant, and requested a table in her section.

When she saw me sitting at one of her tables, she stiffened. Another waitress—one with dark spiked hair and several piercings—said something to her. They both looked at me, spoke a little more, and then Ariana shook her head and finally wandered over.

"I still have a couple hours to go. And even then, I'm not leaving with you." Her tone stung, but not nearly as much as the guarded, hurt look in her eyes.

"I'm not here for you. I'm thirsty."

"Okay." She eyed me skeptically. "What can I get you?"

I opened the menu the hostess had given me and scanned the drinks. "How's the strawberry lemonade?"

"Better with vodka."

I smiled, thankful she seemed to be lightening up. She looked away.

"I bet it is." And I could seriously use a stiff drink, but it'd be suicidal to meet up with Carlo with liquor on my breath. I needed to stay sharp, just in case I had a chance to get out of this mess alive. "I gotta work tonight, though, how about a cup of coffee instead?" I tapped a dessert on the menu. "And bring me one of these lemon squares to go with it. Please."

She nodded and hurried off, giving me a great view of her fabulous ass. When she disappeared into the kitchen, I pulled out Matt's cell phone and examined the disposable, cheap piece of shit. Scrolling through his messages, I searched for clues. Other than the messages warning him about me, there'd been very little activity. A couple of texts from someone listed as "Contact" who kept asking if Matt had picked up "A" yet. The thought sent a chill down my spine. Who the hell was this person and what did they want with Ariana? And how could I warn Ariana she was in danger without telling her I'd tortured her ex-boyfriend into admitting it?

Ariana returned, interrupting my search. I palmed the phone as she set down the coffee, lemon bar, and creamer.

"Thanks," I said, dropping the phone into my lap so I could fix my coffee.

"Can I get you anything else?" she asked, watching me.

"This is good. Thanks."

Ariana stayed where she was, her face a mask.

"You wanna sit down?" I asked, gesturing at the seat across from me.

"Nope."

Okay. I took a bite of the lemon bar. It was good, but I'd had better. I pushed it away.

Ariana was still standing there, staring me down.

"Can I help you with something?" I asked.

"Waiting for you to cut the bullshit and tell me why you're really here."

I shrugged. "Coffee and a lemon bar aren't compelling enough reasons?"

She put her hands on her hips and gave me a full once-over, focusing on my coffee cup when I took another sip. "What happened to your knuckles, Bones?"

They were bruised and a little bloody, probably from when my fist had connected with Matt's jaw. I hadn't even noticed until she'd pointed it out. I shrugged. "Must have gotten a little rough with the punching bag."

She snorted. "Sure, we'll go with that. Still doesn't explain why you're here."

I held up my coffee cup. "Long night ahead of me. Needed some caffeine."

"Right. Matt was here a couple of hours ago. Did you know that?"

Damn, she was too smart. Since pretending to be surprised would only insult her intelligence, I nodded. "Why didn't you call me?"

"I handled it. I told him to get lost, and I think you should do the same."

People were beginning to watch us. The spiky-haired broad from earlier hurried over and asked Ariana if she was okay.

"Yeah. Just one of my temporary roommates bummin' around," she said.

Bummin'?

The broad sized me up and asked, "You need to take five? I'll cover your tables."

"Please. Thanks Piper," Ariana said, taking off her apron.

"Anytime. Let me know if you need me." She looked me over again before heading off to refill water.

"Let's go somewhere and talk," I said after the broad was out of earshot.

Ariana tossed her apron into the booth and sat. "I don't have anything to say to you."

Fair enough. "What did Matt want?"

"Same thing guys always seem to want these days. To screw with my head."

I probably deserved that one, too. "Well did he say—"

She held up a hand, stopping me. "Didn't listen to him, don't plan on listening to you."

Piper showed back up, coffeepot in hand. Annoyed at her persistence, I put my hand over my cup. "Everything okay?" she asked Ariana.

"Peachy." Ariana gave her a tight smile. "Thanks."

Piper drifted toward the next table and Ariana kicked me. "Stop scowling at her."

"She's got her nose in our business, and I don't like it."

"She's a friend. She's concerned because I have shitty taste in men."

Ouch, but yeah, deserved that one as well. "I'm sorry, Ari. There's some stuff going down right now and it's—"

"Complicated." She frowned. "And you're always sorry. But it doesn't make it any better. Piper has a room for rent. I'm going to move in with her after my birthday."

"Ari I—" I needed to tell her she was in danger, and that she couldn't move out, but the words stuck to the roof of my mouth. She'd want to know why. Then she'd get pissed and probably move out anyway, after she called the cops. Instead, my mind drifted back to a question she'd asked me a while back. I'd been thinking about it ever since, and I finally had the answer. "I'd go back to school, maybe become a personal trainer or something. I enjoyed working out with you and teaching you how to hit a bag. I think I'd like to do that."

Her forehead scrunched up. "What are you talking about?"

"You asked what I would do… if I wasn't Angel's bodyguard." It wasn't like it mattered, and I didn't know why I even mentioned it, but with this thing with Carlo hanging over my head I wanted Ariana to know I did have a dream. I wasn't just some schmuck with scars and bloody knuckles.

The lines of her face softened. Her eyes scanned my face, searching. Finally, looking exhausted and defeated she crossed her arms and said, "I hope you make it back to school, Bones. I really do. I think you'll be a great trainer. But now I need you to stop screwing with my head. "I'm finally in a good place. I'm clean. I'm trying to keep it together and all these little games you're playing are really… I can't take them anymore." She looked away, but not before I caught the glint of moisture building in her eyes.

"Ari—"

Tears flooded her eyes. "Please leave."

I realized how all this must look to her and it disgusted me. I never should have kissed her, never should have led her on. No wonder she was pissed. Desperate to fix things before I left, I said, "I am sorry, Ari. I never should have… we never should have… it was a mistake."

A tear slid down her cheek. "A mistake. Great. Got it. Awesome."

Confused, I stood. I wanted to hold her, to comfort her, but she wouldn't even look at me. "That came out wrong."

"Listen, I don't know what you're trying to do to me, but I need you to stop. If you ever decide to stop being a dick, we can talk. But until then, my break is over and I need you to leave." She stood.

"Ari, wait."

Piper reappeared, stepping between us. Ariana fled to the back of the restaurant and there wasn't a damn thing I could say or do to stop her. Every word out of my mouth had just made the situation worse.

"Sounds like you're done here," Piper said. "Need me to show you to the door?"

"Why don't you mind your own business?" I asked.

The skinny little broad puffed up her chest at me. "I work here and Ari's my friend. This *is* my business."

"Yeah, yeah, fine. I'm out." Before more stupid shit could tumble from my mouth, I tossed a fifty on the table and bounced.

Once I was back in the Jeep, I made two phone calls. The first was to Ma. She was so shocked at my random phone call she must have asked me what was wrong at least a half dozen times, making me feel even worse. By the time I got off the phone with her and called Angel, it was almost time to head to the restaurant. I told Angel Matt was dead, someone was after Ariana, and then I came clean about everything that happened between me and Ariana.

"Wow," he said when I finished.

"Yeah." Wow was pretty much all I could say, too. "I'm heading to meet up with Carlo right now and I don't know how this is gonna go down. No matter what, I need you to promise me something, Angel."

"Sure. What do you need?" He didn't even hesitate, and he always kept his word. I knew he would now, too.

Feeling comfort in that, I started up the Jeep. "Whatever happens tonight, promise me you'll get Ari to that restaurant tomorrow."

"You got the scout to commit?"

"Yeah. Noah will be there. Just make sure Ari will be too, okay?"

"Of course, bro. You know I've got your back."

Just like Ariana had my back, and look at how well that went for her.

“I don’t want you to go down for this, Angel. You stay clear. And do what you can to protect Ari, will ya?”

“You know I will. No idea who’s after her?”

“Not a goddamn clue.”

“Well, that makes it interesting. What about Uncle Carlo? Did you get a beat on him? Is he pissed?”

I thought back to our conversation. “Said he wants to talk about my future, whatever the hell that means.”

“Maybe he’s gonna let you off. Let you leave with us,” Angel said, forever the optimist.

“Maybe, but I’m covering my bases just in case.”

Neither of us had to voice what that meant.

“I get it. You should have told me what was going on sooner.” I heard the frustration in Angel’s voice. If he was a made man, no one would dare come after me, which was why I’d waited so long to have this conversation. No way I was going to let him agonize over that decision. Not to save my ass.

“I’m not sorry. Take care of Markie, okay? Take care of both of them.”

Before he could answer, I hung up and pulled out of the parking lot. I had a meeting to get to, and I sure as hell didn’t want to be late.

CHAPTER EIGHTEEN

Bones

CARLO'S FAVORITE HAUNT was a classy, off-the-strip Italian restaurant with floor-to-ceiling windows, dark wood paneling, low-hanging chandeliers, and red-and-white tablecloths. The hostess led me to the Barolo Room, which seemed to be permanently reserved for the family. It had wine racks on both sides, a table for twelve running down the center, and a floor-to-ceiling window with dark drapes at the end. She passed me off to two of Carlo's goons who asked for my weapons. I disarmed myself, placing everything into a box, which was promptly covered and set aside. I'd added Matt's phone to his bag full of belongings, and I removed the bag from my pocket and handed it to the closest guard. He set it on the table beside Carlo and resumed his post by the door.

Carlo sat at the end of the table where he could see the rest of the restaurant out of the windows while staying hidden in the shadow of the drapes. Two more of his goons stood around him. Carlo sipped from a glass of red wine, occasionally picking at the plate of calamari in front of him. I approached slowly, waiting to be acknowledged. Some capos were power-tripping assholes who liked to make their people sweat it out for hours. But as the underboss, Carlo didn't need to flex for anyone.

He greeted me and motioned for me to sit. "Bones, it's good to see you. Can I get you a drink?" His tone was pleasant enough, but then again, I'd seen Carlo compliment a soldier with one breath and order his hit with the next.

Outside the window, people talked, glasses clinked, plates were served, all reminding me we were in a very public location. If Carlo had plans to off me here, he'd have to do something to keep the crumbs from noticing. Renzo had used a fire drill, but Carlo was much classier than that. I wondered how he'd do it. Poison? That was possible.

"No, thank you. I'm good." I joined him at the table, my hands trembling. I wanted to hide them under the table but that was a good way to get killed. Better for him to see me nervous than to assume I was going for a weapon. Last year a soldier got iced for scratching his ankle. When he leaned down, his capo thought he was going for a knife and did him up good right there.

"How's my nephew?" Carlo asked.

"Good, healthy."

"But still determined to leave."

I nodded. "Yes sir, as soon as Markie is cleared."

"Soon. Her appointment is the day after tomorrow."

It wasn't a question, so I didn't answer. He frowned and watched the restaurant for a few beats, taking another sip of wine. Carlo dismissed the guards standing nearest him. They joined the other two at the door, too far to eavesdrop, but close enough to rush in if they were needed.

"Relax, Bones," Carlo said, lowering his glass of wine. "I've never been big on theatrics. If I was going to take you out, you'd never see it coming."

It was a promise, both comforting and alarming.

"You should know me better than to think I'd do it here." He sipped his wine, never taking his eyes off me. I wondered what he saw, what he was looking for. Did I measure up? Was I everything he'd hoped I'd become that fateful day when he stopped out in front of my school and offered me a job?

Carlo put on a pair of latex gloves and opened the bag his bodyguard had brought him, sifting through its contents as if the items would reveal their secrets. Finally he pulled out the phone and powered it on.

"Joey Durante, huh?" Carlo rubbed his chin, staring at the screen. "He's gotta be out of his goddamn mind to start shit now.

What could he possibly hope to accomplish with that handful of bastards of his?"

The question wasn't directed at me, so I didn't answer. We sat in silence as Carlo searched the phone, seeing the pictures, reading the texts, getting all the information I had.

"Who is this woman they're talking about grabbing?" Carlo asked.

My stomach sank. I knew he'd see the texts and ask the questions, and all I could do was be honest and hope for the best. Anything less would be suicide, since Carlo probably already knew at least part of the truth.

"Markie has a sister by the name of Ariana. Matt used to date her and was seen today at her place of employment. The two were arguing. That's how I got the lead on him."

Carlo nodded. "Who wants the girl?"

Here's where things got tricky. "Matt didn't know. He said he was contacted by a woman."

"Did he give you a description?" Carlo watched me. I knew from his teachings that he was monitoring things like my breathing, how many times I blinked, whether or not I looked him in the eye… all the tells of a liar.

Careful to show him my honesty, I stared right back at him. "Long dark hair. Dark eyes. Maybe five six? About a hundred and fifty pounds. Nice rack. Big ass," I repeated word-for-word, just as Matt had said it.

Carlo's brow furrowed. He put the phone back into the bag, took off his gloves, and pocketed them before announcing, "This has nothing to do with Angel."

"You know who's after Ari?" I blurted out. It was a stupid mistake, and I realized it the moment the words left my mouth. But they were already out there, drifting in the space between us. My tone, the nickname, the worry in my voice, had all revealed too much.

He steepled his hands and instead of answering me, he asked a question. "How long have you been working for me, Bones?"

I wanted to demand answers, not spend time telling him what he already knew. But because I valued my life, I did the math in my head and answered, "Thirteen years, sir."

"And in all that time have you ever had any complaints with your compensation?"

My pay? What the hell does this have to do with Ari?

"No, sir. You've been very generous."

"Have I been cruel? Have my tasks been too difficult? Have I not given you adequate training?"

As far as capos went, Carlo was probably the best one to work for. Sure, he was a hard son-of-a-bitch, but he was fair. "No. None of the above."

He laid his hands on the table and straightened his back. "And yet you're planning to leave with my nephew, aren't you?"

It was a direct question, requiring an honest answer. Lying to my capo would most assuredly lead to my death. But telling him the truth could also be lethal. I took my chances with honesty and nodded. "Yes sir."

"Why?"

I thought about my life, about the way Carlo had saved my family from starving, about the pride I'd felt in being able to help Ma provide, about how useful protecting Angel made me feel. I got paid well to have my best friend's back, and I loved that part of my job. But then there were the other tasks. Matt's face came to mind, two holes through his head. Blood. Pain. Threats. Shakedowns. Beatings. Murders. I used to hate the way the job made me feel. I hated it more now that I felt nothing; no remorse, no shame, nothing, and I hated myself for it. But since I couldn't tell him any of that, I focused on the part of my job I loved.

"I remember the day I met you, sir. You showed up out of nowhere and you saved my family. We wouldn't have made it through these years without you. Without the family. But that day, you gave me my first order… you told me to befriend Angel."

My mind drifted forward about a year, to the day when Angel found out about the arrangement I'd made with his uncle. We'd gotten close. I liked Angel. He was a good kid—smart and funny. Most weekends I stayed at his house, playing video games, working with his trainer, or running through his father's family safety drills. No one questioned my almost constant presence. Then one afternoon we were in the swimming pool recovering from an especially grueling workout when Angel started asking me about my family's finances. He'd noticed we were doing better and couldn't understand why.

"Did your mom get a raise?" he asked in that open, direct way he's always spoken to me.

"Not exactly." I didn't know what to say... how much I should tell him. Would he be pissed? I didn't want to lose my best friend, and my family couldn't afford to lose my paycheck.

Angel watched me. "What changed then?"

I respected him too much to lie, so I came clean. We both treaded water as I recounted what had transpired between me and his uncle the day I got suspended for breaking a kid's arm. Angel listened, his face a mask as I admitted I'd been paid to befriend him.

When I was finished, he asked, "So Uncle Carlo pays you to hang out with me?"

"Yes. But I'd be your friend even if he didn't." I'd grown to really like Angel. He wasn't like the other rich kids at the school. Sure, he was some geeky whiz-kid, but he was also a genuinely nice guy. He brought me food and helped me with my homework. His family was the most powerful in the city, but Angel was never cruel nor condescending. "You've become like a brother to me. If my job ended today, I'd still want us to be tight."

He nodded. "And your family needs the money, so it all works out."

"Yeah."

"You had to do what you did to survive. I get it." I'd expected him to be angry or hurt, but he looked almost relieved. He stretched backwards, floating on top of the water. "Besides, it could be worse."

I gaped at him, wondering what could possibly be worse than finding out your best friend was being paid to hang out with you.

He cracked a smile. "One of the other families could be paying you."

Angel had never had a friend before. Not a real one, anyway. Everyone in his life wanted something from him, so he'd assumed I did too. My family could suddenly pay our bills, so he was worried I was a traitor, probably selling information about him. That was the first time I got a full look at how screwed up his life really was. My family was dirt poor, but at least I had friends. None of them were like Angel, though.

"I didn't even know what friendship was, until I met Angel," I told Carlo. "He's more of a brother to me than any of my blood and he's leaving the protection of the family and going God-only-knows-where to do God-only-knows-what."

"Angel's made his decision," Carlo said.

"Yeah, he has." I lowered my voice. "But he's still family, and you know he's not like us."

Carlo raised an eyebrow at me.

"Don't get me wrong, he'll protect his broad and his job, and he'll fight for whatever's his, but he needs someone there who's got his back."

"And you want to be this person?" he asked.

I nodded.

"You'll be off the payroll."

"Yes sir. I have some money saved up, and I'll be living with Angel. He's already offered me a job."

"But it won't pay nearly as much. How do I know you'll stick with him and not bounce the second you get a better offer?"

"If I was in this for the money, I'd be staying in Vegas."

A waiter entered the room, water pitcher in hand. Carlo waited until he left to start in with more questions. "You're prepared to leave your mom? Your brother?"

"They can always come visit us," I replied.

He tapped the table a few times before leaning back in his seat. "Here's what's gonna happen. You'll be allowed to leave the city with Angel, but only after you do one more job for me."

He was going to let me leave. I'd be free… out of this place for good after I did just one more job. There was always one more. "Thank you, sir. What do you want me to do?"

"Find Joey Durante and do him up."

This job, I'd been expecting. "Yes sir."

"Oh, and Bones… this woman who's after your girl… that's your problem. She's not after Angel. You better keep my nephew out of it, or you and me… we're gonna have beef."

I froze, taking in every clue Carlo gave me. After my girl, my problem, Angel wasn't involved, keep him out of it or die. Sure, no problem.

Angel was tearing up my phone by the time I made it back to the Jeep. I returned his call and filled him in on my meeting with Carlo.

"How you gonna find Joey Durante?" he asked. "The Durantes have been underground for years. Hell, I didn't even know any were still in Vegas."

If only I wouldn't have killed Matt. I could have put a tail on him and waited until he led me to his new boss. "I don't know. Matt couldn't have been his only dealer, though. There's gotta be more out there, and I'll get a line on one of them."

"I'll see if I can track down a digital footprint for any of the Durantes."

"Thanks, Angel."

"Hey, no problem. What are you gonna do about Ari?"

Now that I knew someone was after her to get to me, I couldn't let her bus it and possibly get nabbed. I had to find a way to protect her. But since she currently hated me, I wasn't sure how I'd accomplish that.

"Shit."

"Flowers," Angel suggested. "Here, wait a second. Markie wants to talk to you."

"Hey, Bones," Markie said. "If you want to get on my sister's good side, don't get her roses, okay? Get creative."

"Creative. No sweat." How the hell was I supposed to do that? "Any pointers?"

Markie giggled. "Walk into the floral shop and pick out something that makes you think of her, like lilies or orchids or something. Then talk to her. Be real with her, Bones. I know there's a lot you can't tell her, but she has to know she's important. Here's Angel."

"You get all that?" Angel asked.

"Yeah, sure. Get the girl flowers so she'll let me protect her and take out the bad guy. What could possibly go wrong?"

He chuckled. "Everything. Just be careful, okay?"

"When am I not?" I asked. Then I hung up before he could answer.

I didn't have time to chat with Angel. Ariana would be getting off work soon, and apparently I had to buy her the perfect bouquet and spill my guts in order to save her life.

"No sweat," I repeated to myself, but I was definitely sweating.

CHAPTER NINETEEN

Ariana

I WAS IN the back of the restaurant trying to compose myself when Piper showed up. She handed me a tissue and said, "That's the guy who's been messing with your head? The ex?"

"No. We're just… I don't know. It's complicated." It seemed everything in my life was complicated apparently. "That's not the ex. That's the one I currently live with."

"But you're not dating?"

I wiped my eyes, blew my nose, and threw the mess away. It was time to get back to adulting. "Nope. See? Complicated."

"Well, that explains why you're interested in the room I have for rent."

I started to protest. Yes, Bones was definitely part of it, but it was more about getting my independence back. Okay, it was about chasing down my dreams *and* leaving the asshole boys alone.

Piper held up a hand, silencing me. "Don't get me wrong, he is fine. Something about a man in a suit. Mmm-mmm. Especially when you can tell he's stacked beneath it. But I don't care how hot he is, you gotta take care of you."

I nodded, knowing she was right, but she hadn't seen the other side of Bones like I had. She didn't know the kind, sweet, loving Bones who still took care of his mom even though she'd basically sold him to the wolves so they could survive. A guy afraid of losing himself and falling over the edge into whatever the world wanted him to be. I understood that Bones. He was suffocating beneath the thick neck and bruised knuckles, and I wished I could get him air.

"Oh honey, men are assholes," Piper said.

"They sure are." And yet I couldn't keep myself from hoping Bones was different. Even now.

Done airing my relationship laundry to Piper, I glanced in the mirror long enough to wipe away any smudged mascara before getting my butt back to work. The restaurant stayed busy for the last couple of hours of my shift. Thankful for the pace, I went on auto-pilot, bottling my confusing emotions so I could deal with them later.

My shift ended, and I clocked out and headed for the exit.

"You want a ride?" Piper asked before I reached the casino. "I can take you by my place so you can check out the room. Make sure it's gonna work for you."

My last apartment had been one safety hazard away from being condemned, so I was fairly certain I could live with whatever space Piper had to offer. I still hadn't officially told her I'd take the room, but after today, I knew I would. I just needed some time alone to think. "Thanks, but not tonight. I'm dead on my feet. Can I give you a call tomorrow?"

"You're not working? Oh, that's right, it's your birthday. Yeah, grab your phone."

We swapped numbers and she made me promise to give her a call after her shift so she could take me out for a drink.

"I mean it, Ari. I don't even care how late you call. We're going for that drink."

"Thanks," I said, feeling a little better. I'd committed to a birthday dinner I was now regretting since Bones would be there, but no matter how much it sucked, at least drinks with Piper promised to be a good time.

Piper took off, and I lingered inside the restaurant, hesitant to head home. A couple asked me for drink refills, and I knew it was time to bail before the manager put me back to work. I rounded the corner and found Bones, still dressed in his suit, holding the most unusual bouquet of orange and purple flowers I'd ever seen.

Deep down, I knew the smartest thing I could do was to turn and run the other direction. But then Bones met my gaze and gave me that crooked smile of his, shredding my resolve. I was nowhere near ready to forgive him, but I was curious enough to approach.

"What are you doing here?" I asked.

"Funny story. I was walking through a flower shop, and I saw these and thought of you. The florist said the orange ones are called birds of paradise and the purple ones are tiger lilies. They're beautiful and unique. Kinda like you."

His words were like flint and steel on the dying embers of hope inside of me. Afraid to let him ignite this thing between us again, I stood back, my arms across my chest. "What were you doing in the flower shop, Bones?"

He swallowed. "Thinking."

"About…?"

"About that night on the mountain. About what you said… I'd keep you from your edge and you'd keep me from mine." Something flickered in his gaze. It was like his mask slid off, revealing a young, vulnerable Bones beneath. "I know I haven't been doing a very good job of it, but I need you. You still up for the task?"

How could I say no? How could I walk away from that? The tough badass I couldn't get out of my head was asking for my help, and I'd have to be the biggest bitch in the world to deny him.

Tears stung my eyes as I nodded. "Yeah."

We stood there staring at each other, each of us too afraid to move and wreck the moment. Finally, Bones asked, "You gonna take these? I feel kinda funny holding them."

Laughter bubbled out of my throat and a tear ran down my cheek. I wiped it away and accepted the flowers. They *were* beautiful and unique, their fragrance sweet and alluring. More tears threatened to fall, but I blinked them away.

"Let's go home," Bones said, draping an arm over my shoulder. "We've got a lot to talk about."

I nodded, not trusting myself to speak. He led me to a blue and black Jeep Wrangler. The shiny chrome wheels alone were probably worth more than my entire wardrobe.

"Whose ride is this?" I asked when he opened the passenger door for me.

"Mine."

I didn't even know Bones had a car, and I was surprised he hadn't showed this baby off. Leather seats, sunroof, tinted windows, buttons and controls for days, a stereo system that thumped. As if his looks and bulging muscles weren't enough, this car would definitely get him laid.

"Do you like it?" he asked.

I nodded. "Is it new? Did you just get it?" It still had the new car smell.

"No. I've had it for a while, but we keep it stabled. Not many people know about it."

"Ah. So this is your incognito ride. Your girl on the side?"

He chuckled. "Yeah. I guess you could say that."

I began to wonder what Bones was up to today that he didn't want to be spotted doing. Something told me it wasn't buying flowers. My gaze drifted to his knuckles. I wanted to ask him, but knew he'd tell me when he was ready. "How'd it go? Did everything turn out okay?"

"Yeah." He started up the Jeep and turned the radio down. "A lot better than I thought." He turned to face me, and smiled. "Look, Ari, I like you a lot."

"But…?" I asked, feeling my heart plummet.

"But I had some stuff I had to deal with first."

"Had to? As in past-tense?"

His smile widened. "Almost completely. I have one more thing I gotta handle." His smile fell. "But in the meantime, I have to know you're safe. There are people who'd use you to get to me if they knew how much I cared about you. You understand?"

I looked from Bones to the flowers in my hand, my heart plummeting. "You care about me? Because it really feels like I'm being handled."

His brow scrunched up. "Wait, what?"

"I'm not an idiot, Bones. I see exactly what you're doing here. You're some control freak who thinks he can lead me on with promises of tomorrow if I just do what you want today. You say you care about me, but that's not how you care about someone. That's—"

Before I could finish, Bones lunged at me. His lips greedily sought mine as his hands slid behind my head, keeping me captive. He smelled of metal and musk, and I breathed him in and let his scent make me crazy. His tongue explored my mouth, claiming me. I grabbed his suit jacket, holding him against me as his hands roamed down my back, around my waist, and under my shirt. I knew I should pull away, but his passion stole the oxygen from my brain. I lost the will to think, to move, to breathe. All I wanted was him.

By the time we finally came up for air, the windows were foggy. Bones kissed my cheek and drifted down to my neck. "I'm not handling you, Ari. My feelings are very real. You're right, though," he whispered against my neck, sounding as breathless as I felt. "I am a control freak. But you drive me crazy. I'd lose my mind if anything happened to you. That is what would send me over the edge. That is what I need you to protect me from."

My eyes burned at his words. I closed them and let the vibration of his deep voice against my skin soothe me. This felt so good—so right. Like nothing in my life ever had.

He moved from my neck to trail kisses across my jawline, ending back at my lips. "You have no idea what you do to me. What I want to do to you. We just gotta get out of this town first."

Out of this town and away from my dream. A dream I was no closer to than when I'd arrived in Vegas over a year ago. Could I give it all up for a chance to be with Bones? Probably. Would he break my heart and make me regret it? Probably. Was I stupid enough to do it anyway? Yes.

"Okay," I whispered.

He kissed me one last time—a soft and gentle promise—before putting on his seat belt. I picked up the flowers, slightly embarrassed at the way I'd tossed them down to grab onto him, and he defogged the windows. Then, he held my hand and drove me home.

The next morning, Bones was gone before I got up. Markie was in the kitchen teaching Angel how to make crepes filled with fruit and whipped cream for my birthday breakfast, just like the ones

Mom used to make. It was a sweet gesture, but it made me sad. Made me miss all the things we'd lost. She and Angel cleaned up the dishes while I went to the gym alone, wondering where Bones was.

About two hours later I got back and he still wasn't home, so I showered then lounged on the sofa watching television and waiting until it was time to get ready.

Markie and I had shared a bathroom growing up, but it had been years since we'd been crammed into a space getting ready for a big event around each other. Not like Bones's bathroom was small, but unlike Angel's bathroom, it only had one sink, which meant the mirror was made for one person. The third time Markie elbowed me—and apologized—I dropped my curling iron into the sink, gave up, and sat on the toilet seat.

"There's room. Get back over here," she insisted, scooting until she was pressed against the wall, eyeliner still in hand. She glanced down at my curling iron in the sink, and a flash of sadness rolled over her expression before she smiled it away. She never complained about her hair, but every once in a while I could tell she missed her long golden locks.

"Nah, I can wait. It's not like we're in a huge hurry."

I watched her finished lining her eyes. She looked tired.

"You sure you're up for this?" I asked. "You've been doing a lot, you know?"

"Ohmigosh, you sound like Angel. We're taking a cab to a restaurant and eating dinner. We're not going out dancing or painting the town red."

I smiled. "I never understood that expression."

Markie paused, mid eyeliner stroke and looked at me. "Yeah, I have no clue what it means."

I left her to her makeup while I snooped around Bones's bathroom. Opening a cabinet, I found an unopened bottle of body wash, popped the top, and gave it a good sniff. It smelled like heaven.

"What are you doing?" Markie sounded scandalized, like I'd stolen the crown jewels or something.

"Barely resisting the urge to rub this all over my body." I closed my eyes and breathed it in again. Suddenly we were back in his Jeep with his lips on my neck.

"Get out of his personal stuff, you freak," Markie scolded.

I laughed.

"You seem better today," she said. "Did you and Bones make up last night?"

"You'd know all the details by now if you hadn't been bumpin' uglies with your boyfriend last night."

Markie's brows shot up her forehead and her face turned red. "We were not bumping anything. We fell asleep watching a movie in his room."

I eyed my blushing sister, trying not to laugh at how scandalized she sounded. "Poor Angel. Are you ever gonna give it up for that guy?"

"We're not talking about me. We're talking about you and Bones."

I grinned. "Oh, well I would give it up for Bones in a second. Shoot, all he had to do was kiss my neck and my panties melted off. I didn't even care that we were in the parking lot."

"You did it in his car?" Markie asked, her eyes widening.

"No. Unfortunately we didn't get past second base. The boy can suck face like nobody's business, though. I can't wait until—"

"Ari!"

My big sister was still so freaking innocent. It made me want to mess with her even more. "What? Did you see the flowers he got me? Tell me you wouldn't have your hands down Angel's pants if he brought you that bouquet."

Her eyes bulged out of her head.

"And have you seen Bones's body? All those muscles to nibble." I took another whiff of his soap. "And smell this. Tell me you wouldn't want to jump the sexy guy wearing this."

"Ohmigosh you're ridiculous. Stop it."

"Fine." I popped the cap back on the body wash and searched through the rest of his cabinets, finding a giant medical kit stocked with more supplies than the average pharmacy store. "Holy crap, check this out," I said, riffling through the contents.

Markie glanced down. "What? It's just a medical kit."

Reading package labels, I asked, "With chest seals? Tactical tourniquets? And what's a LOKSAC? This looks like it belongs in a trench, not in a bathroom." I thought about the scars on Bones's chest and back, wondering how many of these kits he'd been through.

"Angel's family isn't exactly safe to be around," Markie reminded me.

That was the understatement of the century. Angel had a legitimate job now, but what about Bones? He worked an awful lot for someone who didn't actually go to a job. And what was this "one more thing" he had to take care of? How dangerous would it be? Would he need this kit before he was through?

No time for worries like that now. It was my twenty-first birthday, I had a hot date, and nothing was going to bring me down. Determined to lighten the mood, I opened a package of gauze and wrapped it around my chest.

"Hey Markie, look. I think I figured out what I'm wearing tonight."

She giggled. "What are you doing?"

I stood, twirling so she could get the full effect. "What? You don't think this looks hot? Oh, just wait till you see it with my shirt off."

"Oh no, please."

"It's my party. I can dress like a hoochie if I want. Hey, think I can get Bones to go all the way if I show up like this?"

Markie laughed, throwing her hands in the air. "What am I going to do with you?"

Her question plunged me into a memory.

I was drunk, sitting in the middle of the floor at the Drinkwaters' party because I could no longer stand. Markie's boyfriend, Trent, stood over me laughing, drink in hand. "What am I going to do with you?" he asked.

"Uh... help me up?" I slurred.

Still laughing, he hefted me to my feet and into him. I wrapped my arms around his chest, willing the room to stop spinning. Trent felt warm and hard. I snuggled in, enjoying the feeling. The next thing I knew, we were dancing slowly. He put a finger under my chin and angled my face up until my lips met his. Something in the back of my mind screamed that what we were doing was wrong, but it all felt so good to my body. I wanted this. I wanted this hot, older guy to want me. I didn't care who we'd hurt, I wanted to feel loved and valued and beautiful. Trent made me feel all that and more.

Without breaking the kiss, he led me out of the living room until we were alone in a bedroom. He locked the door behind us and kept kissing me, leading me to the bed.

"I know just what to do with you," he said.

"Ari?" Markie asked, the concern in her voice breaking through my memory. "You okay?"

"Yeah," I lied, pulling the stupid gauze off my chest, disgusted with myself. "We should hurry and get ready. The guys are probably waiting at the door and we're not even dressed."

I replaced the first aid kit and closed the cabinet. I could feel Markie's gaze boring into me, but I didn't say more. I couldn't. I needed a drink. I needed the whole damn bar to be numb enough to forget.

On my way out of the bathroom, I remembered why I hadn't yet dressed. "How nice is this place we're going?" I asked.

"Swanky," she replied, seemingly happy I'd recovered enough to talk to her. "And you need to dress especially nice."

"Uh…" I glanced in Bones's closet that we'd, for the most part, taken over. "I don't know that I have anything that would qualify as especially nice."

"Sure you do." She set down her mascara, returning with a garment bag. She held it out to me and waited.

"What's this?"

She smiled. "Your outfit. Check it out." When she realized I wasn't going to take it, she laid it across the bed and walked back into the bathroom.

Curious, I unzipped the garment bag and peeked inside to find a long black dress.

"Try it on," Markie called.

She didn't have to ask me twice. I pulled it from the garment bag, unzipped the back, and stepped in. It was sleeveless, floor-length, fitted through the waist and hips, down to the calves, where it flared just enough to walk comfortably. I stared at myself in the mirror, shocked.

"How does it look?" Markie asked.

"Like *Jessica Rabbit* meets *Audrey Hepburn*. Check out my curves. Ohmigod, I look like a lounge singer. It's so perfect. Where did you find this thing?"

Markie whistled her appreciation at me. "Angel knows a guy. You look gorgeous, Sis."

Angel knew all sorts of guys, but they seemed more likely to design guns than dresses. The thing fit like it was made for me. I'd never felt so beautiful. "This is too much."

"It's exactly enough."

"Markie, this must have cost a fortune."

She waved me off. "You only turn twenty-one once. Angel and I wanted to make sure you had something you could leave an impression in."

"It will definitely make an impression," I said, imagining Bones's eyeballs rolling out of his head in his best *Roger Rabbit* impression. "Thank you."

"Don't forget the gloves," she said.

The gloves came above my elbows, adding mad levels of glamor. I didn't deserve something so nice, not after the things I'd done and the people I'd hurt.

No. Happy thoughts only. Tonight's gonna be amazing.

Determined to make it so, I finished adding waves to my hair, stuffing back the guilt, worry, and fear, and becoming the confident performer I saw in the mirror.

CHAPTER TWENTY

Bones

"HEY BUD, LONG night? Busy day?" Angel asked, dipping his razor into a sink full of water.

"Yeah to both." I hadn't seen Angel since yesterday afternoon. He was already in bed when I dropped Ariana off last night. I went back out to get the supplies for her present, and spent half the night working on it. Then I got a call from one of Carlo's soldiers early this morning, with a possible lead on Joey Durante. Ready to get this thing done and over with, I jumped at the chance to meet with the contact, and rushed right out.

The contact was an older guy named Martin who worked at a convenience store a few blocks from Circus Circus. When I arrived, Martin took one look at me and told me I looked like my old man.

"You knew my pops?" I asked, surprised.

Martin nodded and told the kid working with him he was taking a break. Then he led me out back to an enclosed area with a plastic picnic table. He lit up a cigarette, leaned against the building, and started in on the tale about the Durante family.

"Back when the Mariani family took power, Maurizio Durante was killed. Three of his sons were also iced, but Joey—the youngest—disappeared. The kid must have only been about four or five back then, so the Marianis didn't look too hard for him, if you know what I mean."

Angel's dad had won the war, and needed to secure his throne. He hadn't been willing to waste time and money to hunt down a kid. Now that Joey was back, I wondered if the boss was regretting his decision.

Martin took a drag from his cigarette and continued. "Rumor has it that the Marianis got the drop on the Durantes because they had a guy on the inside. An enforcer who was feeding information back to Dom. Old Maurizio had a niece named Ambra who was quite the looker, and the Mariani enforcer fell for her. Hard. They got married, and had a little girl. All while he was carrying Durante secrets back to Dom. When the shit hit the fan, the enforcer got both Ambra and their young daughter out of there."

"How did Joey escape?" I asked.

Martin shrugged. "Ambra was Joey's babysitter, so she'd be my best guess."

"What happened to Ambra and the child?" I asked.

"Nobody knows." Martin took another drag.

"And the enforcer?"

Martin let out a breath of smoke and looked away. His hesitancy to answer raised a red flag in my mind, but I waited for him to answer. "He led a double life for a few years, going back and forth between his other family and Ambra and their daughter. Then about thirteen years ago he up and disappeared for this good. To this day, nobody knows where he is… which family finally got wise to him and put him under."

Ice filled my veins. Dreading the answer I feared he'd give me, I asked, "Who was the enforcer?"

Martin put out his cigarette in the ashtray by the door and looked me in the eye. His expression—a mixture of pity and understanding—only confirmed my fears. He didn't give me a name, though. Instead, he frowned and said, "I believe you already know."

Then he went back inside, leaving me alone with a truth I refused to accept.

I drove around for the next several hours, trying to reconcile a man I could barely remember with the enforcer from Martin's story. By the time I got back to the condo my body was exhausted, my mind was numb, and my heart was torn.

“What’s wrong?” Angel asked, turning to stare at me. “What happened?”

I opened my mouth to tell him, but Carlo’s warning sounded in my ears.

“This woman who’s after your girl… that’s your problem. She’s not after Angel. You better keep my nephew out of it, or you and me… we’re gonna have beef.”

Carlo knew. He’d known all along and he’d kept the truth from me. Now, after all these years, he sent me to Martin as his twisted way of coming clean. This was *my* fight, my family, and Carlo should know better than to think I’d ever drag Angel into it.

“Nothing. Just tired and running late.” I scooted past him to the second sink, turned on the water, and splashed my face. The cold blast did little to wake me up, but it did keep Angel from asking more questions. I pulled out my razor and cleaned up the two-day shadow on my face, then grabbed a fresh suit from the side of Angel’s closet I’d taken over and headed to his bedroom to dress.

“You pick up that Camry again?” Angel asked, pulling on his suit.

“Nope. Haven’t seen it since I started driving the Jeep.”

“Well, that’s… something, I guess,” he said. “Did you find out who wants Ari?”

“Nope,” I said. “I’ve got a lot of feelers out there, though. I’m sure I’ll hear something soon.”

“You and Ari better?”

“Yep.”

“You wanna talk about it?” he asked.

“I’m good. Unless, of course, you want me to lie on your bed and tell you all my deepest, darkest desires like you’re some sort of damn shrink.” I smoothed down his blankets, as if I was considering it.

“Stay off my bed!” Angel snapped. “And keep that shit to yourself. Nobody wants to hear your desires. Don’t even say that word in my presence.”

I laughed, feeling lighter. “Oh come on. Please give me advice on my love life. You know, since you’re such a pro and all.”

He flipped me off. We finished dressing and hung out in the living room, waiting for the girls.

"Wanna shoot some faces off?" Angel asked.

Since he wasn't exactly the violent type, I knew he meant in-game. We fired up the television.

"Dante's on. Want me to invite him?" I asked.

Angel shrugged. "Sure. He'll probably ignore the invite anyway."

Despite his attitude, I knew Angel missed his little brother. I threw Dante an invite, but he never accepted. After a few minutes we gave up and started without him. About an hour of mindless gameplay turned out to be exactly what I needed to chill the hell out. By the time the girls finally emerged, my mind was almost blissfully blank.

"Is this what we're doing tonight?" Markie asked.

Angel turned to look at her and was immediately shot dead in the game. "Damn," he breathed. "You look… damn."

Markie was a knockout. Her inch-long blonde hair only made her blue eyes look bigger and more intense, and her lips look fuller and more pronounced. The dress she wore pulled attention to all the right places, but she only held my attention for a moment, because Ariana stepped out behind her, wearing a floor-length gown that fit her like a glove. I was immediately torn between wanting to see her on the stage dressed like this, and wanting to lock her away where no horny assholes could molest her with their eyes.

"It's not too much, is it?" Ariana asked, sounding hesitant and self-conscious.

In the background, I barely registered my character being riddled with bullets. I couldn't look at that, though. Everything I wanted to see was right in front of me. Was it too much? Yes, definitely, because the sight of her caught my skin on fire.

"No, don't be silly," Markie assured her. "You look gorgeous. Doesn't she, Bones?"

I stood, officially on the spot. My gaze thirstily drank her in as I tried to compose a reply which didn't include my tongue rolling out of my mouth.

"I can change," Ariana offered. "Wear something a little less—"

"No." I finally found my voice. "You look… wow… amazing. Don't change."

She blushed.

"It looks great on you. I'm glad you like it," Angel added.

Ariana spun around. "*The* nicest birthday present I've ever received. Thank you so much!"

"My pleasure," Angel said, opening his arm to Markie, who slid in and hugged him. "Our pleasure, really."

I wondered how my stupid homemade present could compete with the dress Angel and Markie had bought her. But before I could think too much on it, Markie ushered us out the door, reminding us we had reservations.

Markie wobbled a little in the hallway, unsteady on her legs after the surgery followed by more than a month of sitting. "I think my muscles are atrophying," she said.

"I still don't know if this is a good idea," Angel replied.

"I told you, I'm not missing my sister's twenty-first birthday dinner."

He tightened his hold around her. "Yes, but a wheelchair—"

"Is ridiculous. I'll be fine."

Angel didn't look so sure, but he let her make it almost to the elevator before scooping her up in his arms like they'd just gotten married and he was carrying her over the threshold. I couldn't help but wonder if my friend was getting in practice. He hadn't mentioned the ring since we'd picked it up, but the gesture was a glaring reminder he had it.

"I *can* walk," Markie replied. "You don't have to do this."

"But I want to."

She smiled and leaned against him, making herself comfortable.

We took a cab to Uncle Mario's restaurant, where we were escorted to the table with the best view of the stage. Because of its central location, it left us exposed. No matter where I sat, there were occupied tables at my back. Feeling uneasy, I looked to Angel, who shrugged and pulled out a seat for Markie. Reasoning that we were in Uncle Mario's restaurant and he wouldn't have put us where he couldn't protect us, I gave up and pulled out Ariana's chair for her.

The waitress went around the table collecting drink orders, and when she got to me I asked for water.

Ariana put her hand on my thigh and leaned in. “It’s my birthday, and I want you to relax and have a good time.”

“I am relaxed,” I objected. Well, as relaxed as I could possibly get, knowing she was in danger, Joey Durante was still breathing, and I was running out of time to fix both problems.

She handed me the drink menu. “Pick one, or I’ll pick for you.”

That sounded dangerous, so I played it safe and ordered a beer. Shortly after the waitress brought our drinks and took our food orders, the pianist wrapped up his set. A second microphone was set up in the center of the stage, and the pianist removed it from the stand and spoke into it.

“Tonight we have a very special treat for you,” he said. “One of our honored guests is celebrating her twenty-first birthday, and I’d like to get her up on the stage.” He looked right at our table. “Ariana, will you be a doll and join me for a moment, please?”

Ariana’s jaw dropped. “What did you do?” she asked Markie.

Markie grinned, looking all too guilty. “I have no idea what you’re talking about, but you better get your butt up there and show the world why you deserve to be on that stage.”

As Ariana stood and headed up, I scanned the restaurant, searching for the talent scout who promised me he’d be there. When I spotted him leaning against the back wall, Noah gave me a mock salute.

Ariana’s hands shook as she accepted the microphone from the pianist.

“Ariana is quite the songbird,” the pianist said. “And tonight, she’ll be performing for us.”

Ariana’s eyes grew wide. “I will?”

The pianist chuckled. He whispered something to her and she nodded, still looking uncertain.

The pianist sat. Then clean, crisp piano notes competed with the chatter of the room. The intro came and went, but Ariana did not raise the microphone to her lips. Her eyes were full of fear as she took in the room. My stomach sank. I looked back at Noah, but his attention was on his phone.

“Come on, Ari, you’ve got this,” Markie muttered.

The pianist slowed his notes and came back around to repeat the intro. This time, Ariana raised the mic and sang the first line of the verse, sounding hesitant and barely audible. The chatter of the restaurant grew, drowning her out completely.

Markie leaned forward in her chair, as if to run up and rescue her sister.

Ariana stopped midnote and said something to the pianist. He nodded and wound down again as she replaced the microphone in the stand. She was giving up. I turned back to look at Noah, and he shrugged at me before turning to leave. The intro restarted, and Noah looked up at the stage and froze. I followed his gaze to find Ariana staring back, her eyes glowing with determination. She took a deep breath, and this time, when she opened her mouth, there was zero hesitation.

Ariana's strong, powerful alto owned the room, snapping all conversations to a halt as it dipped and rose, flirting and promising. The entire restaurant fell silent, captivated by her voice. By the time she reached the chorus, we were enslaved. She grabbed hold of the microphone stand and belted out soul-filled notes, riding the bluesy-jazzy edge of the song like an orphan raised on the streets of the deep south.

I watched her glow with passion and power, realizing I was seeing her for the first time. Beyond the sarcastic, struggling orphan girl who almost died trying to escape reality, she was this woman—this perfect, enchanting, passionate woman, and I loved every damaged inch of her. Like the rest of the crowd, I gobbled up the sight and sound of her, like an addict shooting up after a long dry spell. She entered my veins and lingered, soothing, calming, enchanting. The song ended too soon, leaving me wanting. I peeled my gaze from her and sought out Noah. He paused his wild clapping to give me two thumbs up.

He loved her. Everyone in the restaurant did. She got a standing ovation. It was exactly what I'd wanted, what Ariana wanted, what we all wanted. So why did I feel so apprehensive about it?

Ariana handed the pianist back his microphone, but he only accepted it long enough to ask the crowd if they wanted to hear more. Enthusiastic cheering encouraged Ariana and the pianist to put their heads together and come up with two more songs. She performed them just as perfectly as she did the first.

The kitchen held our food back until Ariana thanked the crowd and the pianist and rejoined our table. She sat and sipped her cocktail, looking unaffected by what had just happened.

"Stop it right now," Markie said, laughing. "I know you're freaking out inside. That sounded amazing, Ari. You nailed it. You made that song your b."

Ariana laughed. "My bitch? You can say it, Sis. We're all adults here." She tipped up her cocktail again, this time draining it. "I don't know how you guys made that happen, but thank you. Seriously. Talk about an incredible birthday."

I glanced back to where Noah had been standing, expecting him to descend on the table and make her night a hell of a lot better, but he was gone.

"I need another drink. A shot," she announced, flagging down a waiter. When he reached our table, she ordered four Kicks-in–the-Crotch.

Before the waiter could leave, I stopped him and said, "I don't know what she ordered, but if anyone comes at my junk, we're gonna have an issue."

Color drained from the waiter's face.

"Don't worry, he's joking." Ariana said, smacking me. "Simmer down, Bones, you'll scare the poor man."

Markie scanned the drink menu. "That's not on here. How do you even know about it?"

Ariana's smile morphed into a grimace. "You probably don't want to know."

"You're right. But at least tell me what's in it."

"I don't know. It's purple and yummy, and it's my birthday, so do it and like it."

Angel shrugged. "It's a good thing we took a cab. But you know Markie can't drink right now, right? Not with the medicine they have her on."

Ariana scrunched up her face. "Crap. I forgot about that. Oh well, I'll drink hers. And I was trying to help you get lucky, Angel. So much for that idea."

Markie turned bright red, and I had to cough to hide my laugh.

The waiter headed off to get our drinks and I continued to search the crowd for Noah. Still no sign of him. I pulled out my phone and saw I'd missed a text, telling me he had to leave to get to a meeting, but would call me later.

We were in the middle of dinner when the shots arrived. I wasn't a drinker. As an enforcer—and Angel's twenty-four-seven bodyguard—I couldn't afford to have my senses dulled. Sure, I indulged in the occasional beer, but hard alcohol was off-limits.

"One shot on a friend's birthday won't kill you," Ariana said, nudging my leg with hers. The lusty way she watched me spoke of a lot more than friendship, though.

Feeling my pants tighten, I accepted the shot and held it in the air.

Angel and Ariana joined me with their own shots, and Markie raised her glass of water.

"To Ari," I said. "May you rock every stage you step on and make this town your bitch."

"Happy birthday," Angel and Markie added.

Then we all tipped our drinks back.

CHAPTER TWENTY-ONE

Ariana

I SANG, AND the crowd cheered! Feeling on top of the world, I floated back to the table—back to the people who'd somehow made it happen—trying to play it cool. The crowd smiled at me, complimenting my performance as I walked past them, and each one made my heart soar. By the time I made it back to the table, I had to force myself to sit so I didn't run around the room, high-fiving everyone and screaming like I'd just won the Super Bowl.

They freaking love me!

And man it felt good. I thanked Angel, Bones, and Markie, for whatever they'd done to make it all happen. I could have asked for details, but I was afraid knowing would take away the magic of the night. So instead, I ordered us all shots, determined to settle my nerves and maybe conjure up enough courage to throw myself at Bones again. The way he was looking at me was practically searing off my clothes anyway. Emboldened by the alcohol, I gave those looks right back.

We ate, had dessert, and stood to leave. Bones dropped a hundred-dollar bill on the table. I looked from it to him and arched an eyebrow.

"That's not gonna cover the bill, Bones. I can pitch in." I opened my purse and reached for my wallet.

Bones chuckled. "That's the tip."

That was the tip? Da-am, I needed to pick up an application for this place. "But what about the bill?" I asked, searching the table. Sure, I'd been drinking, but I wasn't drunk enough to miss the bill. Especially because I intended to pay my share.

"Don't worry about it," Bones said, draping an arm over my shoulder and turning me toward the exit.

Before I could argue with him, Angel literally swept Markie off her feet. My sister didn't say a word, just snuggled closer to him. She must have really been exhausted.

"I'm gonna get a cab," Bones said, hurrying to get in front of Angel.

"You okay?" I asked Markie.

"Oh yeah, I'm… I can't believe how much this has taken out of me. I feel like such a wimp. I don't want to ruin your birthday though."

"You won't," Angel reassured her. "They can drop us off and go back out."

Nobody even suggested Markie and Angel leave without us. I'd never seen Angel outside of the condo without Bones attached at his hip. A cab stopped. We all climbed in and headed toward home.

"If you're not feeling well, I can stay," I suggested as we stopped in front of the building.

Angel stiffened. "I'll take care of her," he said. Then he got out and went around to open her door.

"I'll be right back," Bones said, following them.

Moments later he returned and slid in beside me, squeezing my hand. "This party is far from over," he promised. Then he gave the cabbie directions to our next destination.

We were deposited in front of a nightclub with a line wrapped around the building. Bones paid the driver and then joined me at the curb.

"Check out that line," I whined.

He chuckled, grabbed my hand, and tugged me straight for the two muscle-bound bouncers guarding the door. "Hey, Aaron, how's the fam?" he asked.

"Bones, hey, they're good. How are you man?" the blond answered, doing some sort of handshake before tugging Bones in for a quick hug.

"Good. Stayin' busy. This is Ariana. Ari, my friend Aaron."

Then Aaron seemed to realize Bones's other hand was attached to mine. His eyes widened in surprise for a second before he recovered and offered me his hand. "Good to meet you, Ariana. You two get in out of the cold. Max is workin' the bar tonight, so be careful of the drinks."

Bones laughed.

Before I got a chance to ask what that meant, we were ushered through the door. Bones wrapped his arm around me and tugged me through the throng of people where he found Max and gave him a hard time before ordering our drinks.

"Do you know everyone?" I asked.

Bones cupped his ear, signaling he couldn't hear me over the music.

I leaned against him so I could yell in his ear, at the same time he turned. Our lips collided. Before I could even process what was happening, he wrapped his arms around me, settling his hands on my lower back. We made out for a moment before he slowly pulled his lips away and rested his forehead against mine.

His eyes squeezed closed and the masculine scent of him encircled me, wrapping me in a cocoon of his scent: body wash, gun oil, and alcohol. Time stopped as we stood there, breathing in the same air. The moment felt strangely intimate and personal, surrounded by bodies bumping into us as they tried to get to the bar.

"I'm sorry," Bones breathed. "I shouldn't have done that."

"Yes, you should have."

In fact, I could think of several more things he should be doing. I thrust my pelvis against his, feeling the hard length of him through my dress and his pants.

He groaned. "You're killin' me, Ari."

"I don't know. Feels like you're enjoying it."

His eyes popped open, and I got a glimpse of the beast lurking within. He was passionate and intense, and his heated stare threatened to boil me alive. I held his gaze as his hand slid up my back until his fingers combed through my hair. "You're so gorgeous." His gaze flickered down my neck, following the line of my breastbone down to my cleavage, before returning to my face. "You make me want to lose control."

A shiver went through my body. "Control is overrated." I licked my lips, thrusting against him again.

Bones's eyes widened and both of his hands landed on my hips, forcing me still. "Stop that."

I felt a smile tugging at my lips as my hips fought against his hands. "Make me."

Some drunk asshole bumped into Bones, jarring him out of our moment. Bones looked around and when his eyes landed back on me, he'd regained control. Disappointed but unwilling to give up, I snatched my drink off the bar and drained it. Bones watched me, his smirk firmly in place. Holding his gaze, I slowly ran my hand below my mouth, wiping away the condensation the outside of the glass had left on my lip.

Bones's composure cracked again.

Come on. Come out and play with me, I silently pleaded. Aloud, I nodded toward his drink and said, "Your turn."

He cocked his head, considering me as he lifted the beer to his lips. I put a finger on the bottom of it and helped him along. His empty bottle landed beside my glass.

"Good, now dance with me."

"I don't—"

"You do. It's my birthday, and I want to dance."

His mouth hung open for a moment before he shut it and shook his head, no doubt appalled that I would use my special day to get whatever I wanted from him.

Believe it, buddy.

He led me to the dance floor and held me at arm's length. I stepped in, turning until my butt pressed against his crotch. I grinded against him for the rest of the song. When the next song started, he held my body still and—through gritted teeth—said, "We gotta get out of here."

About time.

Satisfied and bubbling over with anticipation of finally getting what I really wanted for my birthday, I let him tug me out of the club and into a cab. We were on our way home and headed for bliss, when he got the phone call.

Bones glanced at the screen and grinned at me as he answered. "Hey Noah. Yeah, it's a great time. What did you think?"

I tried to listen in, but he must have lowered his receiver volume after the call with his mom.

As Bones listened, his smile stretched further across his face. "I told you she was good." He chuckled. "Yeah, she's a knockout."

I felt my cheeks heat up under Bones's stare. But then his smile started to fade. I searched his face for clues as to why, but saw nothing.

"Yeah, I get it. Sounds good. I'll pass along the information and let you know," he said before hanging up and pocketing his phone. His jaw tightened.

"What's wrong?" I asked.

"Nothing." He smiled. "It's all good. Great news."

I couldn't tell which of us he was trying to convince. "What is?"

The cab pulled up to the curb.

"I'll tell you inside," Bones said, paying the cabbie.

We hurried upstairs, and I went straight to my room to check on Markie. She wasn't there, so Bones tapped on Angel's door. Markie had fallen asleep watching another movie. I leaned past Bones to see my sister passed out in her pajama shorts and top, a peaceful smile spread across her face.

"She looks really comfortable," Angel said, sounding reluctant to move her.

"Yeah. I'm glad she has you, Angel. You guys are amazing together."

He smiled. "She's my world."

I choked up at his words. Sure I was happy for my sister, but man, I wanted what she had. I needed someone to love me like Angel loved Markie. I wanted to be someone's world. Markie deserved it, though. I didn't.

Angel went to bed and I went looking for Bones. I found him coming out of the bathroom, wearing a black tank top and pajama pants.

"You ready to tell me about this great news?" I asked.

He looked over my body. "Wanna get comfortable first?"

Uh, no I didn't want to change. Especially not after the way he'd just looked at me. "I am comfortable."

I followed him to the sofa and sat beside him, making sure our thighs were touching. Bones tensed and scooted away, turning to face me. Before I could call him out on his standoffish behavior, he gave me a forced smile.

"So… great news. I didn't want to tell you this until after you performed, but—"

"Performed? Oh, you mean after you guys set me up to sing at dinner?" I couldn't help but smile at the memory. "That was a really great birthday present, by the way."

His gaze flickered to something behind me, and then back to me. I turned to look, but nothing was there but the closet door. Feeling unsettled, I asked, "What were you waiting to tell me?"

"There was a talent scout at the restaurant. He's a friend and I asked him to—"

"Ohmigod! There was a scout there? And you know him? What did he think? This is great news! Why aren't you freaking out with me? Oh God, did he hate me?"

"No, no, Ari." Bones patted my shoulder. "He thinks you're amazing. You are… amazing."

Heat flooded my cheeks again. "Thank you, Bones. But why do I get the feeling there's some huge ass 'but' that you're holding onto?"

He rubbed his chin and looked away, as if trying to figure out how to word what he needed to say.

I wanted to shake him. "Come on, this is me. Give it to me straight. Tell me what's up."

"More good news. He has the perfect opportunity for you."

I groaned. "I've heard that line before."

"No, he's legit. I trust this guy. We go way back. But here's the thing… you take the job and you can't leave Vegas for at least six months."

"Okay." I shrugged. "So I try this thing out and catch up with you guys when it's finished." I leaned forward and gave him a peck on the lips before nodding toward the empty bed in Bones's room. I had a great buzz going, Markie was bunking with Angel, and I'd just gotten the best news of my life. If I could get Bones out of his pajamas, my birthday would be perfect. "We should go celebrate."

Bones's eyes dilated. I took it as a good sign and gave him another kiss, this one longer. He didn't kiss me back. I leaned into him, but his hands shot up to hold my shoulders away.

Feeling rejected, I lowered my head. "What's wrong?"

"We can't. It would be a mistake."

A mistake. Sex with me a "mistake"?

That hurt. "Why?"

"Because I don't want to complicate things. This is the opportunity of a lifetime for you and Angel, Markie, and I will be leaving soon and—"

Ice filled my veins. "And you don't want me to join you after the six months is up."

"No, it's not like that. You'll need to stay in Vegas a minimum of six months. Maybe longer. And what if this leads to something bigger? Something more? Then what? You're just gonna throw away your dream job to come live with us?"

"Maybe."

"Ari, this is the reason you moved here. It's what you want. You should stay here and take this shot."

He was right. I wanted to sing. But I also wanted mountaintop picnics with my gym buddy. I needed to see his sexy smirk every morning and to smell his delicious scent every night. I longed for the feel of his hands on my lower back and his lips working their way down my neck. But more than all that, I wanted to be his world.

And I could tell he wanted the same thing, but he was willing to walk away. He'd start a new life somewhere without me, and I'd be here alone. I don't know what I expected him to do about it, but my stomach twisted at the thought. Tears blurred my vision as I pushed myself off the sofa and stared down at him.

"You don't have a clue what I want, Bones."

I walked into the bedroom and closed the door behind me.

He'll come. He'll follow me. He won't leave me in here alone.

I sat on the bed waiting to hear a tap on the door that never came. The only sound I heard was the main door opening and closing.

Bones left.

My heart felt like it was being shattered into a million pieces.

It hurt so bad I wanted to die. I needed to fix the pain… to numb it. Tears rolling down my face, I picked up my phone and called Matt. His phone went straight to voice mail. The hollow ache in my chest grew, threatening to consume me.

I needed to get out… to go somewhere… but where? A notification blinked on my phone—a missed call from Piper.

Piper!

Desperate, I called her back. She picked up on the third ring, sounding way more chipper than a person should.

"Hey, Ari! Happy birthday, girl!"

Yeah. Happy freakin' birthday.

I swallowed back a sob and tried to sound normal. "Hey, I know it's late, but you still wanna go out for those drinks?"

"Yeah, sure, of course. What's wrong? You sound… is everything okay?"

"Just a shit day. Can you pick me up? In fact, can I go ahead and move in with you now? I have my share of the rent."

"Oh shit, that sounds like a story. Yeah, of course. Pack up what you need and I'll come get you. What's your address?"

I gave it to her, grabbed my jacket and purse, and headed out, texting Markie to let her know I moved in with a coworker—in the middle of the night—because why not? Hopefully she'd write it off to my impulsiveness.

Since I didn't want to deal with the nosy doorman, I slipped out the back entrance and ran around to the front of the building. Half expecting Bones, Markie, Angel, and the entire National Guard of mobsters to come bursting through the doors any minute, I waited in the shadows until a car pulled up to the curb.

The passenger door swung open and I peeked in.

Piper's smiling face greeted me. "Get in. It's freezing out there," she said.

"Thank you so much for picking me up," I said, sliding into the passenger seat. I turned to pull the door shut behind me, and felt a prick in my left arm. Startled, I turned to see what had stuck me just in time to see Piper pulling a syringe out of my arm.

"Sorry, Ari, but someone's offering a lot of money for you."

Then everything went dark.

CHAPTER TWENTY-TWO

Bones

I HAD EVERYTHING I wanted sitting in front of me—her big, beautiful brown eyes practically begging me to accept her, but all I could think about was something Pops once said. We were in my bedroom looking down at a glass jar stuffed with grass and leaves. I'd punched small air holes into the lid of the jar, so the little side-blotched lizard I'd caught could breathe, but not escape.

"Well, where is he?" Pops asked, leaning over my shoulder to get a better look.

I tapped on the glass, but my lethargic little lizard did not come out of his hiding spot.

"You know, lizards don't like to be bottled up like that," Pops said.

"But I want to keep him."

Pops put his hand on my shoulder. "I know you do, Son, but do you want him to die? They're not meant for captivity." He frowned. "People aren't either. Never believe you can keep anything or anyone by bottling them up. They'll only fight harder to get away from you."

Pops had disappeared less than a month after that conversation. I'd never connected the dots before, but after hearing Martin's tale at the convenience store, I realized how many childhood details I'd repressed—entire weeks Pops never came home, fights between him and Ma, school functions he never showed up for. Pops had left long before he'd disappeared.

Why? Hadn't we been enough for him?

My gaze roamed over Ariana's flawless body. She nodded toward the bedroom and I almost lost my mind. But if we hooked up, it would only mess with both our minds. I wanted more than one night. Hell, I wanted to bottle her and keep her forever, just like that damn lizard, but she wasn't meant for captivity either.

She was meant for the stage, her soulful voice enchanting the crowd. She might settle for me, but she'd never be happy. I loved Ariana, and I'd do anything to make her happy. The only way I could do that was to set her free to follow her dream.

The anger and hurt in her eyes told me this time she wouldn't forgive me. I'd finally managed to blow it with her for good. It was what I wanted, right? Then why did I feel like shit?

Unable to sleep, I slipped on socks and sneakers, grabbed my gym bag, and headed downstairs. I needed to work the rest of the alcohol out of my system so I could think clearly.

I hit the weights, punishing my body until I could barely move. After a quick shower, I returned to my bed on the sofa where I must have passed out, because the next thing I remember, I was being shaken awake. I reached for the gun on the coffee table as Angel jumped over the recliner and positioned himself between me and Markie, putting his hands in the air.

"Bones, everything's okay. No gun," Angel said.

I dropped the gun and sat up, wiping sleep from my eyes.

"Everything is not okay," Markie said, pushing her way out from behind Angel, phone in hand and tears streaking down her face. "What happened between you and Ari last night?"

I tried to shake the cobwebs from my head. "Why? What's going on?"

"She's gone. Said she moved out. In the middle of the night. Why?"

Angel draped his arm over Markie's shoulders. "I'm sure there's a good explanation. Let's calm down and get a cup of coffee, then we'll get this all figured out."

Markie pulled away from him, holding up her phone. "She's not answering my calls. She was drunk, and I don't even know when she left. What if she did something stupid? Did you hear her leave? Why didn't you try to stop her, Bones?"

Last night's events filtered through my mind. "She came onto me. I… I… I got a call from Noah. He was impressed with her. He can place her as long as she plans on staying in Vegas."

Angel nodded.

"I tried to explain why we couldn't… but she was pissed. She stormed back into the room and I thought that was that. I felt like shit, so I went to the gym and worked out. She must have slipped out while I was gone."

"Crap." Markie blinked back tears and stared at the ceiling. "She doesn't take rejection well. What if she's back with Matt and"—she swallowed back a sob—"what if he kills her this time?

"She's not with Matt," I blurted out before I could clamp my mouth shut.

"What? How do you know that?" Markie asked.

Since I couldn't tell her Matt was worm food without explaining how I knew, I looked to Angel for help.

"No." Markie folded her arms across her chest. "You're not gonna do some sort of bro-code thing and keep me out of this. She's my sister—the only family I have left—and you two are gonna get your crap together and tell me what's going on here."

Angel rubbed his temples and stared at the ceiling.

"I'm serious. Start talking," Markie demanded.

Angel gave me the nod, and I collapsed back onto the sofa and broke into the abridged version. Markie leaned against Angel, and he massaged her shoulders as she listened. She took it surprisingly well, without reaction or outward signs of judgment. After I finished, she blew out a breath and asked, "Any idea who this coworker is that she moved in with?"

A girl's face came into my mind. "Dark, spiked hair with blue tips, piercings, maybe five-foot-seven." Angel once said that remembering people was my superpower. I could usually put a face with a name, but I was struggling with this girl. I closed my eyes and let my memory drift down to her name badge. "Her name starts with a P."

"A P?" Markie asked. She thumbed a few keys on her phone and started reading names. "Paige, Pamela, Pandora, Patricia, Phoebe, Piper, Portia—"

"Piper. It was Piper."

Angel was already at the table with his laptop open. "Great. I'll hack their payroll system and find a last name and an address.

Call Tech and have him pull up the building's security footage and see if Ari was picked up in front. Maybe he can get us a make, model, and license plate."

Tech could hijack any of the cameras in Vegas, but since the Mariani family owned the building we lived in, he would have easy access to the footage from last night.

"I'll call the restaurant and see if they've heard from Ari or Piper," Markie said, dialing.

Since Angel and I were no longer officially in the family business, I didn't know how Tech would respond to my request, but either nobody told him not to help us anymore, or he was bored, because he promised to get right on it. I poured myself a cup of coffee and sat at the table beside Angel, wondering what else to do. It felt like I was missing something… some giant clue that would tie this all together. Maybe that was it. Maybe this Piper chick was somehow connected to Joey Durante. Only Piper couldn't have been the long-haired, curvy beauty who contacted Matt. Nothing up.

Still, I couldn't just sit there and do nothing, so I did the one thing I could think of. I called Ariana's phone. It rang once, twice, three times, and then the phone clicked. Expecting her voicemail message to start, I was about to hang up when a woman answered. "Franco, thought you'd never call."

Only Ma called me Franco, and this definitely wasn't her, nor was it Ariana. Didn't sound like that Piper girl either. Gesturing at Angel and Markie I put the phone on speaker and set it on the table. Markie and I crowded the phone as Angel's fingers flew over his keyboard, setting up the trace.

"Who is this?" I asked.

"Firstly, rude. You should at least start with hello. And secondly, I'm a little disappointed you haven't figured that out yet."

"Please, enlighten me."

"Well since you asked nicely, my name's Natalia. My dad named me after his mom."

Not random information, it was a clue. Not a clue, a confirmation, but I refused to say anything which would draw Angel into this mess. "Is Ariana there?"

"Wow."

"Please, I need to know she's okay." I sounded desperate, but Natalia already had Ariana, so she had to know how I felt about her. Pretending not to care wouldn't change the situation at all.

"Now you're just being offensive. I haven't heard from you in… well, I've never heard from you, and all you want to do is talk to this little skank? She was leaving you, Franco. I did you a solid by picking her ass up."

Markie started to reply, but I gave her a look and she clamped her mouth shut.

"Is she okay?" I repeated.

Natalia sighed. "Still worried about the girl. How goddamn romantic. Makes me want to barf all over her. Yes, she's okay. And as long as you do what I tell you, she'll stay that way."

"How do I know you're telling the truth? That you really have her and she's alive?"

I heard another sigh, followed by rustling noises.

"Say something. Tell him you're alive."

There was silence and then a slap, followed by more rustling. Then Ariana cried out, "Ow, ow, ow, get your hands off me, bitch!"

Markie turned into Angel, burying her head in his chest. He held her and whispered something in her ear.

Natalia came back on the phone. "She's fine. And so classy."

And Natalia was doing god-knows-what to her. The thought of it turned my blood to ice. "You have her, you want me. Where and when do you want to do the swap?"

She clicked her tongue. "You have no talent for small talk, you know that?"

"Where and when?"

Angel signaled me. Tech had tracked the call and we had a location. He grabbed our coats and tossed me mine.

"I'm still really disappointed in you. Be a doll and figure this one out on your own."

"But—"

"Chill out, Bones. I'll even leave you a note. Prove you're competent and find it, will ya?"

The line went dead.

Angel tossed me his shoes and started putting on his own.

"You can't come, Angel," I said, steeling myself for a fight.

"Like hell I can't."

"This doesn't concern you. It's my fight. I can't bring you into it. Carlo said—"

Angel wriggled his foot into his sneaker. "I don't care. I'm coming."

"Me too," Markie said, putting her jacket on.

I stared at Angel. "You're gonna get me killed. You know that, right?"

He frowned. "We'll take separate cars. You tried to stop me. I followed."

"You think he'll care? He told me to keep you out of this, and you've already pulled Tech in. This could all be a test, you know? You leave this condo, you're signing my death warrant."

Angel ran his hand through his hair. "So I'm just supposed to sit here and let you walk into this alone?"

He had to. They both did. "I'll get her out of there, Angel." But I had no idea what would happen to me.

"What's going on?" Markie asked. "Why aren't we out the door looking for my sister?"

Angel swore and kicked the chair into the table. Markie jumped.

"I'll let you know where to pick her up." I hugged him, then Markie.

"What? Why are we hugging?" Markie asked. She tried to follow me, but Angel grabbed her hand. "No. Bones, no. Why are we letting him go by himself?"

I grabbed my keys and ran out the door.

The trace on Natalia's phone led me to a gas station parking lot on South Wynn Road. As I parked my Jeep in front of the air and water pump, Tech called. He'd pulled the condo's security footage and saw Ariana leaving in a beat-up Subaru. He'd even gotten a license plate number, but the plates had been lifted off a totaled vehicle owned by an insurance company. He promised to keep an eye out for the vehicle and let me know if and when he got a visual.

I got out of the Jeep and scanned the area. The gas station and mini-mart took up a corner lot with a used-car lot to the north, and across the street to the east and south were mixed-use buildings. Natalia said she'd leave me a note, but I searched the ground by the pumps and the parking lot and came up empty-handed so I headed into the mini-mart.

The slender man behind the counter stood about five-foot-nine and was balding. I grabbed a stick of jerky and waited in line between two people paying for gas. When it was my turn, I leaned across the counter and introduced myself.

"Uh, hello." He pointed to his name badge. "Tom."

"Nobody gave you anything to give to me?" I asked.

He shook his head, looking at me like I was a lunatic.

"It would have been a note or a letter. A brunette would have left it for me."

He shook his head and rang up the jerky. I paid him and headed back outside, wondering what the hell to do.

I had to be missing something, but what? Natalia wanted me here. She'd stayed on the phone long enough to make sure I'd get her location, so there had to be something here.

"Chill out, Bones. I'll leave you a note."

Was that a clue? I glanced back at the mini-mart and got an idea. Starting with the drink coolers, I searched every refrigerated unit I could find—nothing. Unwilling to give up, I asked the sales clerk if there were any other cool places I could look, but he shook his head before giving it so much as a moment of thought. "Not that I can think of, sorry."

I was about to head back outside when a little kid yelled, "Someone dropped a phone in the ice cream!" He stood in front of the small freezer wedged between two shelves of snacks. I'd missed it completely. I thanked him for finding my phone and powered it on.

There was a note app open that read, *Come alone and relax at the old cozy hub. We'll pick you up at noon in the docking bay and leave your little skank behind. Your friends can pick her up at twelve fifteen. Don't show, she dies. If I see them before twelve fifteen, she dies. Don't be stupid.*

Noon. According to my watch, I had a whopping twenty minutes to figure out where the old cozy hub was and get there.

The old cozy hub.

It sounded familiar, but I couldn't place it.

"You ever hear of the old cozy hub?" I asked the clerk.

He rubbed the whiskers on his cheek. “Sure. Years ago there was a jingle on the radio… How’d that go, again? Come on down to the old cozy hub, the coziest seats around,” he sang. “Damn thing’ll be stuck in my head all day now.”

Hub Furniture. Of course. “Where is Hub Furniture?”

“Gone,” the clerk replied. “Been closed down for years. They used to have a warehouse not far from here, though. On South Highland Drive. Just north of that barbeque place.”

I thanked him and ran for the Jeep. As soon as I was on my way I called Angel and told him where and when to pick up Ariana. I hoped this wouldn’t count as involving him, but chances are it wouldn’t matter anyway. I didn’t know what Natalia had planned for me, but she’d gone through a lot of trouble to catch me. She probably wasn’t planning to let me go.

I screeched to a stop behind the warehouse, parked, and climbed up on the loading dock with three minutes to spare.

Before I’d fully regained my breath, a nondescript white van came around the corner. It stopped in front of the dock, and the side door slid open enough to reveal a big man holding a semi-automatic.

I held my hands up, trying to look as harmless as possible.

“Get in,” he said, gesturing with the rifle.

“Where’s Ariana?” I asked.

A muffled cry drew my attention. The rifle-wielder opened the door enough to show Ariana sitting in the far back. There was a gag in her mouth and her hands and feet were zip-tied. Her eyes were wide and she looked like she’d been roughed up a bit, but she was breathing.

“You okay?” I asked.

She tried to say something around the duct tape, but I couldn’t make out what it was.

“They’ll be here to pick you up in fifteen minutes.”

“Enough talking.” The guy waved his rifle around. “Get in or I’ll shoot.”

I moved slowly into the vehicle and waited as he patted me down and zip-tied me. He picked Ariana up and tossed her onto the loading dock. With her hands and feet zip-tied, she had no way of catching herself when she landed. Her body slammed into the concrete as the door slid shut.

“Hey, you bastard!” I stood, trying to get free.

I barely registered the back of the semi-automatic connecting with the base of my skull before darkness took over.

CHAPTER TWENTY-THREE

Ariana

THE VAN SMELLED of old pizza and stale beer, making my stomach clench. I hadn't eaten since last night. Was my birthday dinner last night? It felt like an eternity had passed since I'd been on the stage singing for the crowd. No, singing for Bones. The lyrics of my favorite song had been so perfect, I'd belted it out at him, telling him he was the only one I wanted. Had he even noticed? Even cared?

It seemed like a stupid thing to be worried about while my hands were zip-tied in my lap and the business end of a semi-automatic followed my every move. I'd probably be freaking out about it if I wasn't still so groggy from whatever I'd been drugged with. Between that and the alcohol from my birthday, my mouth tasted like the inside of a communal barf bag on an international flight. Not like I'd ever flown internationally—or licked the inside of a barf bag for that matter—but I was pretty sure my mouth would pass for one in its current state.

"Do you have any gum?" I asked Natalia.

She shook her head no and glanced at her cell phone, her legs bouncing up and down. She had to be barely out of high school, but her dark eyes were way too serious for someone so young. I wondered what sort of messed up crap had put her here with a gunman and a driver, using me to bait Bones into a trap.

"He won't come for me," I said, partly from fear that he wouldn't, partly just to get her to talk.

The look she gave me in response told me she thought I was full of crap. "Yes he will. Trust me."

"That's kind of a weird thing to say to someone you had kidnapped and drugged," I pointed out. "And he won't. Last night he made it perfectly clear where I stand with him."

Angel, Markie, and I will be leaving soon… The wound in my heart reopened at the memory. He wanted me to stay in Vegas—to be away from him—why would he come for me now?

"I've seen the way he looks at you," Natalia said.

She had? When? And uh… creepy. "Have you been stalking us? Wait. Are you in love with him?" I asked. If this chick was Bones's vengeful ex-girlfriend, I was screwed. After his training in the gym I might have a chance if we were one-on-one, but the guy in the passenger seat with the semi-automatic trained on me, and the wiry, over-energized driver, didn't exactly promise a fair fight.

The driver was gulping down his second energy drink in the past half hour, and he choked. The gunman chuckled and beat on his back while still keeping an eye on me.

"Puh-lease. I sure as shit wouldn't call it love," Natalia sneered. "Now shut up. You ask too many questions."

We sat in silence as minutes ticked away. Natalia rotated between looking at her cell phone and staring out the window. I had to fight to stay awake.

"There's a Jeep pulling into the lot," the driver said, startling me back to consciousness.

A Jeep. Bones. He must have come for me after all.

The idea delighted me until I came to my senses and remembered I was no princess and this wasn't a fairy tale. And I still had no idea what Natalia wanted with Bones.

"Is he alone?" she asked.

"Looks like it."

"Good." Natalia nudged me. "Your boyfriend isn't playing games. You may live through this after all."

"What are you gonna do to him?" I asked.

She didn't answer.

The driver started up the van. My heart sped up.

"What do you want from Bones?" I asked.

There was still no answer. Natalia and the gunman switched seats, bringing the semi-automatic inches from my face as he duct-taped my mouth shut.

We pulled into a parking lot behind what looked to be an abandoned warehouse. Bones stood on the loading dock, waiting. The van rolled to a stop in front of him, and the gunman opened the door a crack and redirected his aim on Bones. "Get in," he said.

"Where's Ariana?" Bones asked.

The door slid the rest of the way open and Bones leaned forward, squinting into the vehicle until his eyes locked on mine.

"You okay?" he asked.

I tried to tell him to get out of there and run for his life away from Natalia, the crazy bitch, but my words were garbled by the duct tape.

"They'll be here to pick you up in fifteen minutes," Bones said.

They secured Bones, and then threw me out of the vehicle like a sack of potatoes. I landed shoulder first on the concrete. Pain exploded down my arm and across my chest, darkening my vision. I gritted my teeth and clung to consciousness, twisting and turning to see which way the van went. It headed east. Determined to somehow go after it, I wriggled, trying to get myself to a seated position. The zip-ties dug into my wrists and my shoulder screamed in protest. Helpless and hurting, I lay there wondering if that was the last time I would ever see Bones.

No. He'll be okay. He's a badass and probably already working on a plan to escape.

Gravel crunched under tires, interrupting my thoughts, and the Hummer rolled to a stop in front of me. Doors opened and Angel and Markie jumped out.

"Ari, are you okay?" Markie asked.

I started to nod but pain made my vision swim.

Markie ripped the duct tape off my mouth.

"Ow, ow, ow! Dammit."

Angel pulled out a switchblade and cut the zip ties off my ankles and wrists. My arm sprang loose and the pain made me double over. There was nothing left in my stomach, so all I could do was dry heave. Still lying on my side, I curled up like a pill bug.

"What's wrong? What hurts?" Angel asked.

"My shoulder. I landed wrong and—" I tried to uncurl so I could sit up, but stars danced in front of my eyes, "—ohmigod it hurts."

"Let me look at it." He gently righted me to a sitting position, holding my arm tight against my body. Then he had Markie keep it still as he checked my shoulder. "You popped it out of joint and I'm going to need to put it back in."

"You? Shouldn't we get her to a hospital?" Markie asked.

"Trust me, the car ride will hurt more than what I'm about to do. I need you to relax though, Ari."

"Relax?" Just the idea of him touching it made me want to throw up again.

"Breathe, Ari," Markie added, her words contradicting the panic in her voice. "Don't watch him. Look at me."

I did as she said, forcing myself to breathe through the pain caused by the rise and fall of my chest. "You sure you know how to do this, Angel?" I asked.

"Yes. No talking, just breathe and relax," he replied.

He started at my neck, massaging in a circle around my shoulder as he slowly rotated my arm. My eyes watered from the pain, but before a single tear fell, I felt a pop and the pain eased.

"There. How's that?" He raised my arm to make small circles with my hand, widening each time it went around.

"Sore, but it doesn't hurt nearly so much anymore. Wow. Thanks. How do you know how to do that?"

"The Internet."

Of course. Angel would have to know how to treat all sorts of injuries with a friend like Bones...

"Ohmigod, Bones! What's the plan? What are we doing to get him back?"

Something passed between Angel and Markie. It looked like a combination of frustration and anger.

Fear crept up my spine. "We do have a plan, right?"

Angel stiffened. "We're going home so I can make some calls."

"Some calls? They could be killing him right now. Angel, your family is terrifying. Why aren't they doing anything to help him?"

Angel rubbed a hand down his face, and when he looked at me again, he'd aged at least ten years. "You think I don't know that?" he snapped.

"Come on, Ari," Markie said, tugging me toward the Hummer. She climbed into the back with me and we high-tailed it back to the condo while Angel pumped me for information about the trio of abductors, trying to get details about where they'd been keeping me. Thanks to whatever Piper had knocked me out with, the whole fiasco was a blur, and there wasn't much I could tell him.

Angel's frustration seemed to grow with each block he passed. He kept pulling out his phone and looking at it, but it never made a sound and he didn't contact anyone. By the time we made it back to the condo, his face was fixed in a scowl. He went straight into his bedroom and shut the door, and Markie and I went into ours. I lay on the bed and stared up at the ceiling, wishing I could get a mulligan on the past day. If we could just rewind to my birthday dinner, I'd do things completely different.

Markie sat beside me and stroked my hair out of my face like she used to do when I was little. It was comforting to have her there, but also strangely intrusive. I didn't want to be with anyone but Bones. I needed to talk to him and find out why he'd pushed me away only to rush in and rescue me.

"Talk to me, Ari," she said.

"This is all my fault. If I wouldn't have left—"

"They would have found some other way to get to him. Apparently she's been watching Bones for a while."

"Yeah, she's pretty much stalker status. But why didn't Bones do something? He just turned himself over to her. It's almost like he wanted to talk to her. Who is she?"

"Your guess is as good as mine." Markie gave my head a final tap before standing. "I'm gonna go check on Angel and see if I can do anything to help him. I'll be back." She slipped out the door.

I closed my eyes and tried to focus, wishing I could remember more about what had happened. Natalia had to have dropped a clue about where we'd been or what she planned to do with Bones.

Bones.

His absence ached way more than my shoulder did. Longing for something tangible that would remind me of him, I went into the hall closet where he kept his bedding stashed during the day. His blanket was on the shelf, but when I reached for it I felt something hard beneath it. Curious, I unwrapped the blanket to find a glass jar with ribbons tied around the neck, securing a birthday card. Inside the card, Bones had written a note.

Happy birthday, Ari. I know I don't always say the right thing, but I want you to know how important you are to me. Here are just a few of my favorite things about you. Love, Bones.

There had to be at least a hundred folded papers inside the jar. Wondering why he hadn't given this to me on my birthday, I popped off the lid and grabbed the first paper. I unfolded it.

Your smile, it read in Bones's messy handwriting. Sweet. Smiling, I reached for another.

The way you laugh.

Your sarcastic sense of humor.

The way you wrinkle your nose when you're trying a new food.

"I do not," I argued aloud, reaching for another paper.

Your neck.

The way you always know what to say to calm me down.

You hate the color pink.

I smiled, happy he remembered such a silly thing about me.

The way you raise your eyebrows when you swear.

"And I don't raise my eyebrows when I swear," I muttered, looking at myself in the hallway mirror. "Do I, bitch?" Sure enough, my eyebrows rose. Who knew? Bones apparently knew. The realization knocked the wind out of me. I'd known the guy barely a month and he knew all these things about me. He watched me that closely. My legs crumpled and I sat down hard.

Then I reached for another paper.

The way you close your eyes when you take your first sip of coffee.

How quickly you pick up on my hints. Even the ones I don't want you to get.

The way you had my back at dinner with Ma and Totino. That name! Do you think his parents wanted him to be a seventies pimp or the owner of a pizzeria?

I laughed. This was the Bones I knew and loved. Things had turned to shit between us, and I missed this Bones so much it physically hurt. A sob ripped through me. Would I ever see him again? I reached for his blanket and wrapped it around me. The smell of him enveloped me, both soothing and torturous. Tears slid down my cheeks. I brushed them away and reached for another paper, my hand trembling.

The way you squint when you're about to call me out on something.

"Ari?" Markie said, emerging from Angel's room. "What's wrong? What is that?"

"I found it in the closet," I blurted out, feeling guilty. If Bones wanted me to have this gift, he would have given it to me. Still, I couldn't make myself stop reading the papers. "It's my birthday present. But he never gave it to me."

Her face softened. She sat beside me and started reading some of the papers scattered over the floor. "Oh honey, this is… wow." She bit her lip and her eyes filled with tears.

Unable to speak, I nodded and unfolded another paper.

The way you look at me.

The way you say my name, almost like you're singing it.

Paper after paper held compliments about me. I kept reading, anticipating the giant "but" to come. Was Bones blind to all of the many bad things about me? If he noticed the way I stare at the ceiling when I think, why couldn't he see what a hot mess I was inside? Maybe he could. Maybe that's why he pushed me away. Maybe he knew all the horrible things I was capable of… all the repulsive things I'd done.

"It's like he sees you, Ari. He sees who you really are inside." Markie smiled up at me, wiping tears from her cheeks. "We'll find him. It'll all work out. You'll see."

Only it wouldn't, because Bones hadn't given me this present. He was gone now, and we had no plan for getting him back. And none of these papers told the truth about me. I suddenly needed her to know how wrong she was.

"I slept with Trent." The words bubbled out of me like carbonation from shaken soda, ruining everything in sight with the sticky truth no amount of sugar could hide.

Markie's brow furrowed. "What? Trent?"

"Trent Rodgers. Your boyfriend. I slept with him while you were away at college."

Markie shook her head, growling in frustration. "Trent? While I was in college? Ari, you were sixteen." She stiffened. "Did he—"

"He didn't drug me, if that's what you're about to ask. He didn't force me either. I was drunk, but it was all me. I slept with your boyfriend."

Her eyes flashed with pain, then anger. "You were underage. He was an adult."

The words broke some sort of dam, releasing an emotional tidal wave that crashed into me. I was worried about Bones, frustrated he hadn't given me this birthday present, confused about us, but most of all I was angry everyone refused to see me for the monster I was.

"I knew what I was doing. I was pissed at you and Trent was hot. I couldn't believe it when he kissed me. I wanted to be with him, Markie. I wanted to hurt you the way you'd hurt me by leaving."

"He was twenty, Ari. I don't care how willing you were, there are laws—"

"Laws that I broke to be with him. Because I wanted to hurt you. That's what kind of sister I am. That's the real me, Markie. Not all this shit." I gestured at the papers.

She winced. "You were a minor. He should be in jail for taking advantage of you."

I laughed and stood, tears still rolling down my cheeks. "Taking advantage of me? Get it through your head. I screwed your boyfriend and I loved every minute of it. Yeah, Trent used me, but I used him, too. He made me feel sexy and wanted. I used Matt for the same reason, and I would have used Bones if he'd have let me. But apparently he figured me out, because he never…"

My voice cracked at the lie. Bones was different. I knew he was different, because even now I couldn't get his face or his voice out of my mind. It was like they were etched in there permanently, taunting me with memories of the man I'd never be good enough to be with. The man who was probably dead by now while Angel made phone calls.

"Ari—"

"Ohmigod, Markie, get it through your brain. You know what I tried to do last night? I called Matt, because I wanted him to pick me up and get me so high I'd never come down. Does that sound like the person Bones is talking about in these?" I kicked over the glass jar. It thudded against the carpet but didn't break.

She reached for me.

"Don't touch me." I jumped back, barely avoiding her.

Angel came rushing out of his room. He froze in the doorway, taking in the scene.

"I need to get out of here." Seconds away from imploding and turning my sister into collateral damage, I grabbed my purse and headed for the door.

"Ari, please don't go," Markie said. "You're my sister and I love you. I don't care what you and Trent did. It's in the past. It doesn't define you. Stay. Please."

I couldn't. My chest hurt and I couldn't even handle myself anymore. I paused long enough to tell her good-bye, before slipping out.

"Ari, please—"

I shut the door before she could finish, escaped out the garage entrance, and hopped on the first bus that arrived. I had no clue where it was going, but I didn't care. I needed to get as far away from that jar as I could. Tears kept rolling down my face as I thought of Bones. He'd written all those things about me. Yet he didn't know me at all. Not the real me. If he did, he sure wouldn't have given himself up to save me.

There was no saving me, and I needed to get away from the people I loved before I hurt them even more than I already had. The bus merged into traffic. Bones needed me, and I was running away. That's the kind of person I was. They'd be better off without me.

Landmarks passed, blurring together through a sheen of tears which refused to stop. People were staring, but I didn't care. Memories of Bones assaulted me, each one more painful than the last. He'd written down all those things about me—like I was his freaking world—then pushed me away before giving it to me. Why?

How could I leave him? He didn't leave me.

The bus passed a park I recognized. I wiped back tears and squinted at street signs until I confirmed we were on West Lake Mead Boulevard. I suddenly knew exactly what to do. Two stops later, I got off and sprinted the block-and-a-half left, feeling hopeful for the first time since Natalia had taken Bones. By the time I reached the complex I was out of breath and overwhelmed by emotion. I dragged myself to the door and knocked.

No answer.

So close. I was so close and...

Unwilling to give up, I knocked again. Movement on the other side of the door brought another wave of tears to my eyes.

Nonna answered. She took one look at my face and ushered me into her apartment.

CHAPTER TWENTY-FOUR

Bones

I AWOKE TO darkness. My head throbbed in time to some dubstep beat in the distance while I sat on a hard surface with my arms pulled uncomfortably behind me. My own stale breath was recycled through the fibers of the dark cloth over my head. I tried to move but hard plastic restraints bit into my wrists and ankles.

The cloth was ripped from my head, creating a small static charge. Bright light blinded me, bouncing from eye to eye. I squinted, pulling against my restraints. The light clicked off, leaving me in the faint glow of overhead bulbs. I blinked to clear the glare spots from my eyes and breathed deeply through my nose. I could smell engine oil, rubber, something floral and feminine. As my vision cleared, the globs in front of me separated into two vehicles: the white van they'd brought me in and the black Camry that had been tailing me.

Before I could absorb more clues about where the hell I was, the metal barrel of a gun pressed against my temple. "Hello, Franco."

"Natalia." I recognized her voice and was willing to bet that's where the floral smell was coming from. There'd been two other people in the vehicle, though, and I wondered where they were now.

"Tell me why I shouldn't kill you," she said.

"Because you want to talk to me. Almost as much as I want to talk to you."

She laughed. "Oh yeah? What gives you that idea?"

I thought back to the times I'd seen the black Camry trailing me. She'd known how to find me, and I wasn't deluded enough to believe I could dodge a sniper's bullet. "You could have killed me, but instead you went through a lot of trouble to get me here. The question is, why?" I turned so I could see her expression.

Natalia looked to be maybe eighteen and wore a blue sweater and slim-fit jeans stuffed into black knee-high boots. Her long dark hair was loose and messy, and her high cheekbones, plump lips, and dark eyes bore a striking resemblance to a picture Pops had shown me years ago—a picture of his mom. Natalia looked a hell of a lot like family.

"Don't look at me," she said. Her eyes glistened with tears as she shoved the pistol harder into my head, forcing my gaze off her. "You'd be dead already if you didn't look so much like him."

Apparently I resembled family, too. I had a pretty good idea who she was talking about, but needed the verbal confirmation. "Like who?"

"My dad. Our dad." She sniffed. "You look just like I remember."

That shocked me. "You remember his face?" I did the math in my head. "You couldn't have been more than four or five when he disappeared."

Her shoulders dropped.

This time she let me look at her. I couldn't help but compare her to the photo of my grandmother. Same eyebrows, same dark, haunted eyes, same stubborn jaw, the resemblance was uncanny. "I had no idea you even existed until recently. And I wasn't certain who you were until I saw you. You really remember Pops?"

She nodded.

I'd been ten when the old man split and I could barely remember what he looked like. "I don't believe you."

Her jaw jutted out and anger flashed in her eyes. "I remember everything. He used to bounce me on his knee and call me *principessa*. He had the greatest smile, and he always smelled like gun oil and tobacco. He used to kiss my forehead and tuck me in." She angrily brushed a tear away.

"Sounds like a great guy, but doesn't sound like Pops at all. Well, maybe the gun oil and tobacco smell, but that's the standard wiseguy cologne."

"Gino Leone was a good father," she said.

I snorted. "I'll have to take your word for it. I rarely saw the bastard."

Her expression hardened. "Don't you dare talk about him like that!"

Natalia's tone and posture grated on my nerves. After being robbed of a childhood with my old man, I felt entitled to a little anger. "No matter what you remember, Pops wasn't some standup guy. He was a liar who cheated on his wife, abandoned his kids, and informed on the Durante family. He was almost solely responsible for your mother's family's demise. You should hate him even more than I do."

"And you should hate the asshole who killed him, but your nose is so far up Carlo Mariani's ass you can't even—"

"Carlo?" I asked. "You think Carlo killed Pops?"

"I don't think. I know he did."

I shook my head, exasperated by how stupid she had to be to believe that. Sure, I had my own questions for Carlo… questions about why he hadn't told me anything about Pops. Clearly he and my old man had been working together, and I couldn't figure out why he'd kept the details of their arrangement from me. Sure, he'd sent me to Martin, who'd pretty much filled me in, but not telling me himself was kind of a dick move. Regardless of what he'd kept from me, I still couldn't see Carlo's motivation for taking out Pops.

"I don't know where you're getting your information, but you're wrong," I said. "Pops was a spy *inside* the Durante family. He was feeding information to the Mariani family. Why would Carlo kill him?"

"Listen, bro," she said. "The Durantes were gone. Dad had outlived his usefulness. Carlo gave him one last task… ordered him to kill Joey. Joey was six at the time and my mom was taking care of him."

As she spoke, the scene played out in my mind. Pops had been a lot of things, but he wasn't a child-killer. Especially not if the woman he loved enough to leave his family for asked him to spare the kid. Carlo wouldn't take that well. Would he kill Pops over it? Possibly.

My stomach sank at the thought. Carlo was a ruthless son-of-a-bitch, but he'd taken me under his wing.

"You don't know, do you?"

Natalia's tone had softened, making her question sound a lot like pity, which just pissed me off. Carlo had trained me, taught me, hell, he'd basically raised me. I knew in my head he'd done these things to benefit the family, but somewhere deep down I thought we'd connected. He'd been more like a father to me than Pops had. All this time, was he just keeping an eye on his loose ends? Keeping me reined in and making sure I didn't find out the truth and turn on him?

Pissed, I fired back with, "I remember very little about Pops, probably because he was so damn busy with his other family. While he was sitting you on his lap and calling you princess, he was bailing on my school conferences and missing family dinners. I was ten years old when he disappeared. One day, he just didn't bother coming home anymore. He left us with nothing. If Carlo wouldn't have stepped in and offered me a job, we would have starved. I was a kid and had to provide for the family Pops bailed on. So no, I'm not ready to jump on your bandwagon yet. Hell, I don't even know for sure the old man's dead. He could be off with a third family somewhere."

I glared up at Natalia, challenging, and she glared back. After a few moments, the pressure of the gun against my head eased, and then disappeared. She walked behind me, and I wondered if she planned to shoot me in the back or just clock me over the head. Metal scraped against concrete as she dragged a chair back into my line of sight and sat in front of me, weapon still in hand and pointed in my general direction. Her scowl was gone.

She tugged something out of her pocket: a wristwatch. Unlike the platinum Rolexes worn by most mobsters, this was a black Concord with a rubber band. Its simple yet unique design was easy to recognize, especially since I'd been with Pops when he'd purchased it. It had set him back over two large, and I'd asked him why he'd spent so much on a watch with a rubber band.

"You can tell a lot about a man by his timepiece," Pops said, securing it around his wrist.

"What does this one say about you?" I asked.

He smiled down at me. "Quality and functionality; not a cheap piece of shit, but not the main man, either. I work with my hands, Son, and I don't need anything that catches the light or clanks against my wrist when I'm... working."

The rare memory of Pops spending time with me formed a lump in my throat. I swallowed past it and asked, "Where did you get that?"

"Mom. About a month ago she disappeared for a couple of days and when she came back, she had this. Said she'd met with an old friend who gave it to her and told her Carlo had killed dad."

I couldn't stop staring at the watch. If Pops was truly dead, then whoever killed him should have taken the thing and hocked it. That's what I would have done. I had an agreement with a guy off Stewart Avenue, who knew my previous owners never came looking for their shit. He'd give me at least five hundred for the watch. Wiseguys didn't give up a penny, much less five hundred bucks. No way would they just hand it over to the mistress. But if that wasn't Pops's watch, someone had gone to a lot of trouble to replicate it.

Natalia shifted, stuffing the watch back in her pocket. "By the way, Dad didn't bring down the Durantes. Mom said Great Uncle Maurizio was a monster who never should have been made into the Capo di capi. Everyone was scared of him. Half of his own family was feeding secrets to the Mariani family, and Carlo Mariani promised to protect everyone who turned on Maurizio. But Carlo's a snake." She spat. "He took out every single one of them."

My stomach sank. "What happened to your mom?"

Natalia dropped her gaze to the gun in her hands. "She was murdered right after she gave me Dad's watch."

"Which is why you're here." Everything clicked into place. "You think Carlo had her killed."

"I know he did," she growled. "Mom knew a lot of secrets about Carlo… broken promises, lies, where he buried the bodies of people he swore to protect. She should have gone to the Mariani boss years ago, but she didn't know whether Carlo was acting on his orders or flying solo."

It didn't matter. Even if the boss had no clue what Carlo was doing, Ambra Durante never would have made it in to see him. "Is that your plan? Go to the boss and tell him his uncle broke his promises to your dead family?"

She shook her head and her eyes hardened. "No."

When she didn't elaborate, I asked, "You gonna kill him?"

She shook her head. "No. Death is too good for him. I want Carlo to live while I kill the person who matters to him most."

Did anyone really matter to Carlo? He'd throw his own life away for the good of the family. Constanza, though… he'd be lost without her. He played it off like she was just a housekeeper, but I was certain there was more to them than that. I liked Constanza, and would hate to see her caught up in this mess.

"You think you can go up against Carlo?" I snorted. "You're suicidal."

"He won't even know what hit him," Natalia replied.

She was going for surprise? "Too late for that, don't you think?"

Her brow furrowed. "What do you mean?"

"Carlo knows you guys are here. Well, at least Joey."

She froze. "How does he know about Joey?"

"You can't drop dope in this city and expect Carlo not to find out about it. Because of Joey's little stunt—"

Her eyes widened and she leaned forward. "Wait, what?"

She seemed genuinely clueless, which sent a shiver up my spine. I had a bad feeling about the whole setup. "The bad dope Joey sold hit the streets and—"

"Joey didn't sell shit. Franco, Joey doesn't have any money. Look around you. We're in the garage of a rental house. What was left of our family was run out of town with little more than the clothes on our backs. How would Joey pay for dope? We don't even have the money to make it. There's just the two of us left and—" Her eyes widened. "Oh shit."

The hair on the back of my neck rose. If Carlo had killed Pops and was trying to tie up loose ends, he'd get all three of us together and take us out. "Shit. Joey's here, isn't he? He was the driver, right?"

Natalia's eyes only grew wider.

"Shit," I muttered.

"You already said that."

"I know, but there aren't enough swear words to cover what I want to say. I bet Carlo's been tracking us the whole time. He probably already has a team on the way."

"You make him sound like some sort of super-power. We're safe here, nobody knows—"

"You have no idea what he can do."

And if Natalia was telling the truth, Carlo had never planned to let me out of Vegas. I was stupid to believe he would. I knew the rules. Once you were in, the only way out of the family was in a body bag.

"You gotta let me go, Natalia. If he's coming for us..." Then what? There wasn't a single place in Vegas where we could hide. Carlo would find us. "At least give me a fighting chance."

Natalia hesitated. Her gaze went to something behind me. I turned to see the door leading to the house where Joey and their muscle were probably watching television or sleeping, not suspecting a damn thing.

"What are you waiting for?" I asked. "Cut me loose so we can warn them or we're all gonna die."

Before she could respond, I heard the faint sound of a car door shutting. The look on Natalia's face told me she heard it, too.

"Joey and Bastian," she breathed. She took a step toward the door.

The doorbell rang.

Natalia looked from the door to me, her expression torn.

"They're already dead. If you go in there, you're dead, too. We both are. You cut me loose, and we have a chance."

"For all I know, you could be with them. Why should I trust you?" she cried.

Several reasons tumbled through my mind, but I settled on the one with the most impact. "Because you don't have any other choice. We're surrounded. Cut me loose, you can drive while I shoot, and we might make it out of here."

She looked from me to the door one last time before whipping my knife out of her pocket and using it to release me. Shots rang out from inside the house. We grabbed guns on our way to the black Camry. She climbed behind the wheel, started the vehicle, and hit the garage door opener, while I got into the passenger side and rolled down my window, turning the safety off the semiautomatic.

I recognized members of Renzo's team as they filed into the garage, popping shots at the car while we waited for the garage door to roll up. I returned fire, mowing down two shooters while the rest sought cover.

A bullet shattered the windshield. I ducked, feeling it whiz by my head. Natalia fired, hitting the guy who'd shot at me. More men surged in behind him. We had to get the hell out of there before we were overrun.

"Go. Drive now!" I shouted, returning fire on the men swarming the garage.

Natalia threw the car into reverse and stepped on the gas. Tires squealed as we zipped out into the dark. She slammed on the brakes and turned the wheel. Our attackers got a few more shots off, shattering the back passenger-side window as I fired blindly at the house. Natalia punched down the gas again. We fishtailed around the corner and sped to the end of the block, turning again.

She hung a right and merged onto a bigger street.

"Where are you going?" I asked.

Natalia's hands trembled against the steering wheel. "I… I don't know." The trembling moved up her arms.

"You okay?" I asked.

"Joey," she sobbed, then clamped her mouth shut. Her body started full-on jerking.

"Pull over," I said.

She glanced behind us, clearly uncertain.

"You need a minute. Pull over. I'll drive."

She nodded and turned down a side road, rolling to a stop. Without cutting the engine, we switched seats and got back on the road.

"Wh-wh-where are we going?" she asked.

I had no goddamn clue. We were so screwed. No doubt Carlo had Tech monitoring our progress and had already dispatched additional teams to take us out. If we had any chance of surviving, I needed to pull out every resource I had access to.

"Gimme my phone," I replied.

Natalia pulled it out of her pocket and handed it to me. I called Angel.

"Bones!" The level of Angel's relief made me certain he'd already written me off for dead. "Where are you?"

"I'm with Natalia. Carlo's put a hit out on us."

"Carlo? On both of you?"

"Yep."

"Shit. What can I do? What do you need?"

Angel's uncle—the number two man in Vegas—was out to get me and Angel didn't even hesitate or ask questions before agreeing to help me. I hated the idea of possibly putting him in harm's way, but I was out of options.

"Ideas. I need ideas. You got anything for me?"

Before he could answer, my phone buzzed with an incoming call. I pulled it away from my ear long enough to see Nonna's number before returning my attention to the road.

Nonna? What the hell?

"Uh… Nonna's calling," Angel said, surprising the hell out of me. "Which gives me an idea. Let me call you back."

How could Nonna be calling him when she was calling me? Before I could ask, he hung up.

Curious, I answered her call.

"Bones?" Ariana asked.

Her voice brought instant relief, followed immediately by confusion. "Yeah. Ari? Why are you calling me from Nonna's number?"

"Why are you answering? Doesn't that psycho bitch have you tied up? I expected to be talking to her."

There was something wrong about the girl I liked calling my sister a psycho bitch, but since Natalia *had* kidnapped Ariana, I let it slide. "Yeah, we ran into some trouble and the situation changed."

"Angel's uncle, right?" Ariana asked.

Floored, I asked, "How do you know that?"

"That's why I'm calling. Nonna said you and Natalia need to get here—to Nonna's house—right now. She can help you, but only if you're here."

I glanced at Natalia, afraid of how this would play out for her. She was a Durante, after all, and Nonna was a Mariani. "Both of us? She can help both of us?"

"Yes. That's what Nonna said. But I don't get why either of you care what happens to Natalia. Who is she?"

"I'll explain later. I'm going the wrong way. I need to turn around. We'll be there in a couple of minutes."

I started to hang up, but Ariana shouted my name. Putting the phone back up to my ear, I asked, "Yeah?"

"I… I… I'm sorry. About everything."

"Me too. We'll talk when I get there."

"I… I…" She sniffled. "Just don't die, okay?"

"I won't."

Then I disconnected so I could keep the promise I'd just made.

CHAPTER TWENTY-FIVE

Ariana

IT FELT LIKE the world was on fire, but Nonna remained the queen of cool. While I paced the space between living and dining rooms, gnawing off what was left of my fingernails, she sat calmly at the table, sipping tea while she made phone calls on her home phone. Her cell phone sat on the table between us, where I'd set it after talking to Bones, and it took everything in me to not pick it up and call him back. It had been twelve minutes and forty-six seconds since I spoke to him and I needed to know he was still okay.

"Oh yes, I'm sure it's all just a big misunderstanding, which is why I'm calling you, dear. I'd hate to see anyone acting rashly and regret the decisions made in error." Nonna said into the phone.

Bones should be here by now.

I went to the window, pushed aside the curtain, and scanned the parking lot. There was still no sign of him, so I went back to pacing and listening in on Nonna's conversation.

"Angel's on his way now," Nonna said. "I'd hate for him and Markie to get caught up in this mess, so I invited them over."

Markie was coming. My stomach twisted in knots at the thought of seeing her again. I never should have told her about Trent, but I was glad I did. The secret had been eating me alive for years and I felt much better now that it was out in the open.

Now she was coming, and I needed to face her, and the horrible things I'd said to her—unless, of course, Bones got here first. Then I could reassure myself he was okay, force that bitch Natalia to give me back my phone and purse, and get out of there long before Angel and Markie made their appearance. Where would I go? I had enough money in my bank account for a few nights at a cheap motel, then…

Before I could fully contemplate my complete lack of options, someone pounded on the door. I rushed over to peer out the peephole and saw Bones and Natalia waiting.

"They're here," I said, unable to mask the relief and nervousness in my voice.

"Well, let them in," Nonna said, returning to her phone call.

I unlocked the door and ushered the two of them in. Natalia walked past me. She was gorgeous and confident and I still had no clue who she was to Bones or why she'd wanted him. Bones stopped, his eyes on me as he closed the door behind him. Then he and I stood in the entryway, staring at each other. It seemed like it had been forever since I'd seen him, and I couldn't decide whether I wanted to hug him or strangle him. Instead of either, I looked him over, inspecting him for wounds. He looked a little roughed up, but okay.

"Thank you for not dying," I said.

He cracked a smile. "You told me not to."

That smirk would be the death of me. I drank in every perfect line and curve of his face, committing them to memory. Then, it was time to get out of there while I still could. I reached for the doorknob.

"Where are you going?" Bones asked, his expression unreadable.

Since I didn't really know, I couldn't tell him, so I stuck with the facts. "I just needed to make sure you're okay. Now that I know you are, it's time for me to bounce."

"Why?" he asked, leaning against the door.

"You made it pretty clear you want me to stay in Vegas. Without you."

He winced. "So that's it, then?"

Was it? My chest hurt at the thought. "Yeah. I guess it is."

He mumbled something that sounded a lot like, "Bullshit."

Wondering if I'd heard him right, I asked, "Excuse me?"

"I call bullshit, Ari. Since when do you listen to me?"

I blinked.

His grin turned cocky.

Wanting nothing more than to wipe that ridiculous look off his face, I said the first thing I could think of. "Thanks for the birthday present."

His eyes searched mine until his smile faltered. "You found it?"

"Yeah, I did. So what's with that? You wrote all that nice shit about me and then you kicked my ass to the curb talking about my career like my decisions are yours to make. Every time you speak for me, you get it so completely wrong I want to scream."

He uncrossed his arms, grabbed my hands, and pulled me to him. He gave me a quick peck on the lips before saying, "You're right. I'm sorry. Let's start over, and you tell me what you want."

I hesitated, unsure of where to start. There were so many things I wanted, but the main one was standing in front of me. He had to know this, though. I'd done everything but throw myself at him. Okay, I had admittedly done that, too.

"You still want me?" he asked, reading my mind as he rubbed his fingers against my cheek.

I leaned into his hand and closed my eyes, welcoming his touch. I nodded.

"Good. You want to stay in Vegas and sing? I'll set it up with the talent scout and when you're not singing, I can send for you and you can—"

"I'm leaving Vegas."

"But the scout… Ari, this is a great opportunity, and—"

"I don't care how great of an opportunity it is, I…" I swallowed. I knew what I wanted to say, but it made me feel too vulnerable.

"You what?" Bones asked.

I looked away, summoning the courage I needed. I focused on the fear I'd felt when I thought I'd never see him again. It had ripped me apart, and I'd do whatever it took to make sure I never felt that way again. Even if it meant putting myself out there.

"I want to be with you," I whispered.

He cupped my face in his hands, and then ran his thumb over my bottom lip. "You will. We'll make it work. We'll rock the long-distance thing. I don't want you walking away from your dream and resenting me for the rest of your life because of it."

"Goddammit, Bones, I want out of this city! And it's my decision, not yours."

He startled at my tone.

Frustrated, and wanting him closer to me, I leaned in and gently brushed my lips against his.

Bones's entire body stiffened like it was taking everything he had in him not to jump me right then and there. Encouraged, I pulled back and let my gaze drift down his body. He wore jeans and a tight black T-shirt, both of which showed off his amazing body. My hands longed to touch every square inch of him, but not yet. First he needed to understand how this was going to work.

I pressed against him, enjoying the warmth of his rock-hard body against mine. "I know too much. This city is no longer safe for me."

He opened his mouth to object, but I laid a finger against his lips, silencing him.

"And you know what? Even if it was safe… even if I got offered an incredible gig… I'd leave. I want to be with you, Bones. Get it through your thick skull."

"So that's it, huh? That's your final answer?"

I felt my own smile widen. "Yep." I kissed him again.

This time Bones pulled me against him and deepened the kiss. My toes curled as his thick arms encompassed me, making me feel warm and protected. My fingers hooked in his back belt loops, determined to keep him close to me forever. His lips pulled away from mine, only to explore my jaw and neck. Then he whispered, "I love you, Ari."

My insides turned to goo and I couldn't stop smiling. "I love you, too."

He pulled away long enough to look me in the eyes. I don't know what he was looking for, but he must have seen it, because his grin was back.

"Oh get a room you two," Natalia said.

I nodded in her direction, unwilling to take my eyes or hands off Bones. "Who is she?"

"Uh…" He stepped back and grabbed my arm, turning us both to face Natalia. "Ari, meet Natalia, my sister."

My eyes felt like they were about to bug out of my head. "Your what?"

"His sister, dear," Nonna said. She came up behind Natalia, phone still in hand. "And now that we're all acquainted—"

Someone banged on the door. I practically jumped out of my skin. Bones picked me up and set me beside Natalia, putting himself between the door and us.

Nonna put the phone back up to her ear. "He's at the door now, just a moment, please." Then she stepped around Bones, looked through the peephole, and swung the door open. A tall man with olive skin, dark hair, and dark features, wearing a suit and bearing a strong resemblance to Angel stood in the doorway, glaring at Bones.

"Renzo, what a pleasant surprise. How are you? Please come in out of the cold."

Bones tensed, looking from the newcomer to us.

"Is this another trap?" Natalia asked, reaching for something in her pocket. "Did you bring me here just to turn me over?"

Bones lunged at her, pressing her arms to her sides in a bear hug. "I told you, we're safe here. And it would be considered disrespectful to draw that thing in here."

"Bones, I'm gonna need you and the girl to come with me," Renzo said.

"I'm afraid that's not possible," Nonna replied. "Bones and his sister are guests in my home."

"His sister?" Renzo asked.

"Yes." Nonna headed for the kitchen, phone still in hand. "I'm about to put on a pot of tea. Would you like to join us, Renzo?"

"I'm sorry, Nonna, but I can't. I'm under strict orders to take Bones and Natalia in."

Nonna spun around to face him. "Strict orders from whom?" she asked.

Renzo's face pinched into a frown. "I'm not at liberty to say. Family business."

Nonna put the phone back up to her ear and repeated Renzo's refusal. Then she handed the phone to Renzo. He blanched, and then took it.

"Hello? Yes sir. No sir, I was not aware of that. Yes sir. Twenty men, sir."

On the other side of the phone, a baritone yelled. "Twenty men?! You have twenty men at my mother's house?!"

The rest of the color drained from Renzo's face. He turned away from us. "Yes sir, way out of line. Yes, we're packing up and leaving now. I'll be sure to do that. Thank you, sir."

His hands were shaking by the time he handed the phone back to Nonna. "I'm sorry for any inconvenience I might have caused you, Nonna. I have to go, but hopefully we can get tea another time."

Nonna smiled and kissed his cheeks. "Of course we can, dear boy. Please say hello to your mother for me."

Renzo didn't even look in our direction before bolting for the door. Bones followed him, locking up behind him. Then he looked out the peephole before moving to the window.

"They're leaving," Bones said, sounding awed.

"Of course they are." Nonna headed toward the kitchen. She opened the refrigerator and started pulling out bags. "Now come help me with the food. Angel and Markie will be here soon and you all have a long drive ahead of you."

CHAPTER TWENTY-SIX

Bones

ARIANA STIRRED BESIDE me. I brushed her hair aside and leaned over to kiss her forehead. My seat belt cut into my chest, but I was so content I didn't even care. The sounds of the oldies playing on the Hummer's stereo relaxed me as we ate up the miles distancing us from Las Vegas. My mind was still reeling over the turn of last night's events.

Angel's dad and siblings had come over long enough to say good-bye. The tightness around the boss's eyes told me something big was going down, but thankfully that wasn't any of my business anymore. He did pull me aside long enough to confide in me that he was friends with my pops, and he planned to get to the bottom of Natalia's claim that Carlo had killed him. I didn't know what to say, so I thanked him and promised to watch over Angel.

Dante refused to leave the car, but the girls wept and even Georgie wiped a couple of tears from his eyes. Markie was a wreck. She bawled after they left, and then lamented about not being able to say good-bye to the kids at the orphanage, but the boss told us to leave immediately, and his tone left no room for argument.

Nonna loaded us up with enough food to stock a small third-world country and sent us on our way.

"You're not coming with us?" Ariana asked, pausing in the doorway.

"Oh heavens, no," Nonna replied, ushering her toward the Hummer. "These bones are too old for road trips. Besides, I still have a little more to do here. I've given Angel a few places to look over, and I'll fly up when you select one." Then to me, she added, "I can have your vehicle returned to the condo for the movers if you'd like?"

In all the chaos I'd completely forgotten about the Jeep, still parked behind the warehouse where Natalia picked me up.

"Please." I handed her the keys. She could have easily had it moved without them, but this would save her time and expense.

It had been after one a.m. before we left Vegas. Angel, Ariana, Markie, Natalia, and I climbed into the Hummer and headed out. We drove out of Vegas like the devil himself was on our tail, and I'm pretty sure he was. I don't think any of us took a deep breath until we crossed the California state line. We still weren't out of Carlo's reach, but at least it would cost him more time and resources to come after us. Besides, I had a feeling the boss was keeping Carlo busy.

Angel drove the first leg, while Ariana and Markie slept and Natalia alternated between staring out the window and pumping me for information about Carlo.

"But you have to know how to get to him. There's gotta be someone he cares about."

And there was, but I wasn't about to sic my sister on Carlo's sweet little housekeeper. "He's untouchable, let it go."

She growled a lot, but in the end, she dropped the subject.

It was almost five a.m. before we checked into a hotel in Bakersfield to get a few hours of sleep. Too drained to even speak, the five of us stumbled into the room, pushed the two beds together, and collapsed onto them. I woke up with Ariana in my arms, smiling at me.

"Hey," she said.

I smiled back and pushed her hair out of her face. "Hey."

Unfortunately, the moment was ruined when the alarm went off, telling us it was time to get Natalia to the bus station. After losing Joey, Natalia had informed me she wasn't up for a road trip with two nauseating sets of lovebirds, so I made a call to my brother Antonio, who invited Natalia to come and stay with him and his family for a while. Being around family would probably be the best thing for her right now, and after much debate she reluctantly agreed, admitting she had nowhere else to go. I gave my little sister a hug, we exchanged phone numbers and promised to keep in touch, and then I put her on a bus to Porterville. We got back on the road, and this time I drove, Ariana played navigator, and Angel and Markie napped in the back.

We were halfway to San Francisco when Antonio called me. The bus had arrived, but Natalia wasn't on it. I hoped my sister wasn't heading back to Vegas, but even if she was, there wasn't a damn thing I could do about it. I called her cell number and got her voice mail, but her message had been customized for me.

"Hey, Bones, I'm sure you're pissed and I'm sorry, but I couldn't get on that bus. I mean, I realize Tony is my brother, too, but I've never even met the guy and I couldn't… I just couldn't. I don't know what I'm gonna do yet, but I'll give you a call when I've got it figured out. Take care of Ari. I like the way she treats you. Be safe."

I left a message, asking her to call me.

We made it to San Francisco and checked into a hotel room. Angel was acting weird, and excused himself to make a few phone calls on the balcony. Wondering what my friend was up to, I kept one eye on him while helping the girls get situated. Angel and Markie had packed clothes for all four of us in the back of the Hummer, so it took me a few trips to bring up all the luggage. We all showered, changed, and then headed back out for an early dinner.

Since both Angel and I were sick of driving, we called a cab to take us to a popular Moroccan restaurant he had found online. Ariana, Markie, and I feasted on taster platters, trying everything the restaurant offered, while Angel tugged at his collar and downed a couple of beers. It was dark by the time we emerged from the restaurant. A limo was waiting by the curb.

"Is this for us?" Markie asked?

My friend nodded, wobbling slightly. The driver opened the door for the girls and they piled in.

I stopped beside Angel and asked, "What the hell's wrong with you?"

He patted his jacket pocket. His fingers thunked against something hollow and he grinned like an idiot. Then he climbed in beside Markie. I had no choice but to join them.

"Where are we going?" Markie asked as the limo pulled away from the curb.

"It's a surprise," Angel replied, his words running together in what appeared to be a combination of nerves and alcohol.

Ariana looked to me for more information, but I held my hands up. "Don't look at me. I know nothing."

Angel kept tugging on his collar, but the girls didn't seem to notice. They were too busy sipping champagne, chatting about the sights, and rubbernecking like tourists. The driver rolled to a stop in a deserted parking lot.

"A surprise, huh?" Markie asked, searching the area. "What are those lights? Wait, there's a sign. Ohmigosh, you brought us to The Palace of Fine Art?"

Angel grinned and he followed her out of the limo.

Ariana's brows rose as she stared me down. "Do you know what he's up to?"

"Nope. But we should probably keep an eye on them."

We emerged from the limo and Ariana shivered in her thin black dress. I took off my jacket and draped it over her shoulders. She smiled and wedged herself under my arm.

Wondering what Angel was up to, Ariana and I followed him and Markie toward the replica of the Greco-Roman ruins. A security guard opened the gate for us, and Angel slipped him some cash. We followed pillars around a lake to the rotunda in the center. Markie and Ariana marveled about the craftsmanship while Angel stayed silent.

"You okay, man?" I asked.

He nodded and grinned again. "Better than okay."

We stopped in the center of the rotunda. Markie and Ariana walked to the pillars and looked out over the lake, talking. Angel took a couple of deep breaths and handed me his phone. I looked down and saw that he'd set it up for video.

"What's going on?" I asked.

"I need you to record this for me. Focus on Markie's reaction. I promised Nonna."

"Now?" I asked, realizing what he was preparing to do.

His dopey smile answered me. "Yeah. Now."

Then he turned and walked away. I fumbled with the phone, making sure they were both in view before I hit record. As Angel approached, Ariana looked from him to me. Then she inched away from Markie and came to stand by me.

"What are you doing?" she whispered.

“Watch them,” I whispered, feeling my own dopey smile tug at my lips. My boy was about to do the craziest thing ever and I was beyond happy for him. I inched forward, making sure the camera could hear them.

“This is beautiful, Angel,” Markie said, still staring out across the water.

“I’m glad you like it,” he replied. He took her hand in his and turned her to face him. “But I need to ask you something.” He dropped to one knee and held a small, black box out to her.

“Markie Lynn Davis, will you marry me?”

Markie gasped. She looked from the box to Angel, her eyes wide.

Despite the cold, beads of sweat were forming on Angel’s forehead. We all waited in silence for what seemed like an eternity.

Then finally, Markie nodded. “Yes. Yes! Of course I will.”

Ariana squeezed me, jostling the camera. I draped my arm over her shoulders and kept filming. Angel put the ring on Markie’s finger, then stood and kissed her.

“They’re crazy, aren’t they?” Ariana whispered.

I nodded and looked at her. Her eyes were heavy with unshed tears and she was so damn beautiful. It wasn’t difficult to imagine her walking down the aisle. Maybe Angel and Markie weren’t so crazy after all. I turned off the camera and kissed Ariana. When Angel and Markie finally pulled apart, Ariana wandered over to congratulate her sister and see the ring. I patted Angel on the back and nodded. The two of us stood there, watching the girls.

“We’re free,” Angel said, clasping me on the shoulder. “I can’t believe it, but we finally got out of that shit-hole for good.”

“Yeah.” Vegas was just a spot on the map now. The families would no longer direct our lives or make us keep our loved ones secret for fear they’d be used against us. “Now we just gotta figure out where the hell we’re gonna live.”

Angel chuckled. We joined the girls. I kissed Ariana’s forehead and tucked her back under my arm. The four of us wandered around for a while longer before heading back to the hotel. We had an engagement to celebrate and a trip to plan.

I had no idea where we’d end up, but I didn’t care. We’d broken the cycle and survived, and now the world lay ahead of us.

Thank you so much for reading **Breaking Bones**. I hope you've enjoyed the journey and will watch for the Mariani Family Prequel, coming later in 2016. Please help support my work by writing a review on Amazon. Reviews only require twenty words and help me tremendously. I appreciate your support!

Also be sure to visit my website and sign up to be included on news about future releases:
http://www.amandawashington.net

Find me on Facebook, too!
https://www.facebook.com/AmandaWashington.Author

Other books by Amanda Washington

Making Angel: Mariani Crime Family Book 1
Rescuing Liberty: Perseverance Book 1
Liberty's Hope: Perseverance Book 2
Fallen: Chronicles of the Broken 1
Cut: Chronicles of the Broken 2
Forsaken: Chronicles of the Broken 3

Made in the USA
Charleston, SC
25 February 2016